CAPE TOWN'S NECKLACES OF FIRE

By:
SHADLEY FATAAR

Book 3 of the Trilogy: *In the Shadow of Table Mountain, Cape Town.*

Published by SHADLEY FATAAR, 2024.

WHO IS SHADLEY FATAAR?

SHADLEY FATAAR IS A semi-retired radiologist who grew up under the yoke of apartheid rule in Cape Town, South Africa, where the state policy of extremist racial segregation was widely regarded as social engineering gone wrong.

His politically formative teens started in 1960 when police shot and killed more than sixty peaceful anti-pass protesters in Sharpeville. His alma mater, Livingstone High School in Claremont, was a hive of anti-apartheid resistance. The school had the highest number of teachers imprisoned, banned, and exiled, including his father, Alie Fataar.

After qualifying as a doctor in 1970, Shadley worked as a medical officer in Zululand's Ceza Mission Hospital, then as a GP in a Black township in Cape Town, followed by his time as a radiologist at Groote Schuur Hospital. These professional years coincided with escalating nationwide student insurrection and police brutality, including the 1976 massacre of more than a hundred demonstrating students in Soweto, in the north of the country.

His personal and professional experiences are a rich source of material for his socio-political and historical thriller trilogy, *In the Shadow of Table Mountain, Cape Town*. The opus covers the epochal years from Sharpeville in 1960 to the collapse of apartheid in 1994.

Find out more about Shadley at his author/blog site, *Living with apartheid in the Shadow of Table Mountain, Cape Town*, at https://www.shadleyfataar.com/

ALREADY PUBLISHED IS the rest of the trilogy:
   Book 1: *Fury and Revenge in Cape Town.*
   Book 2: *Toyi-toyi, Cape Town's War Dance*

WHAT OTHERS SAY ABOUT THE BOOK.

LEONIE HENSCHKE, Writer, and former Managing Editor at Angus & Robertson Publishers.

In the third gripping novel of the trilogy, *In the Shadow of Table Mountain*, violence reaches a crescendo. Extremist, inhuman racial segregation has bred insensitivity to cruelty in all sections of South African society. Shadley Fataar, with experience as a doctor in this fractured community, gives pivotal issues and true historical events expression through strong characters. Masterful storytelling skills bring to light this unforgettable period in our modern history.

ROSALIE SKINNER, author of the eight-book series, *The Chronicles of Caleath*.

In *Cape Town's Necklaces of Fire,* we return to a city in the tumultuous months after Mandela's release from prison. A groundswell of hope grows; an end to apartheid seems possible, but Cape Town suffers a backlash of violence.

The characters display a heroism needed to cope with ever present violence. We are drawn into their lives, confronted by their fears, passion, secrets, and belief in a better future. We watch them live, love, learn, teach, grow, appreciate moments of beauty, survive moments of trauma, and hopefully survive the challenges they face.

Fataar writes with gritty realism, providing a concise and graphic insight into each character's driving passions and deepest secrets. Throughout, we are aware of historic events and their impact on these individual's lives and hopes.

ISBN: 978-0-6458246-5-0

---

1.   http://shadleyfataarwriter.com/

ACKNOWLEDGEMENTS

ZONJIA FATAAR (NEE Arnold) is still by my side with a helping hand whenever needed after 58 beautiful years together. For this, I am eternally grateful.

I remain thankful to author Margaret Penhall-Jones, for her early guidance, editing and friendship.

Initial essential information regarding prison gangs came from Louis Grammer Jr.

Leonie Henschke and Rosemary Skinner provided regular encouragement, advice, and reviews.

My editor, Laurel Cohn, added exceptional finishing touches to my opus.

IT specialist Sohrab Fataar from Pi Squared deserves special mention for setting up my stunning website, assisted by Scott Willhite.

For the cover design, my thanks go to Penny Clemens, graphics designer at Rustum Fataar's Minuteman Press (Kitchener, Ontario, Canada), and my multi-talented son, Sohrab Fataar from Pi Squared.

Last but not least, I want to thank my daughter, Natasje, for her support and quiet strength over the years.

This book is, again, the product of many individuals. I hope I will be forgiven for any omissions.

DEDICATION

I again dedicate the last of my trilogy to the thousands who lost their lives in the decades of struggle to establish democratic majority rule in South Africa.

Amandla Ngawethu! Power to the people!

1978 STEVE BIKO, South African Black Consciousness Movement leader. Letter to SRC Presidents, from *I Write What I Like*. 'Black Consciousness is an attitude of the mind and a way of life, the most positive call to emanate from the black world for a long time. Its essence is the realisation by the black man of the need to rally together with his brothers around the cause of their oppression - the blackness of their skin - and to operate as a group to rid themselves of the shackles that bind them to perpetual servitude.'

1963 **Martin Luther King** *Letter From Birmingham Jail*[1] 'We know through painful experience that freedom is never voluntarily given by the oppressor; it must be demanded by the oppressed.'

BOOK SALE PROCEEDS will go towards needy student funding in Cape Town.

---

1. *https://www.history.com/news/kings-letter-from-birmingham-jail-50-years-later*

THE COVER AND LOGO show Table Mountain, Lion's Head and Signal Hill as viewed from Milnerton Beach, Cape Town.

FROM THE AUTHOR: THE SEMANTICS OF COLOUR IN SOUTH AFRICA

(From Book1: *Fury and Revenge in Cape Town*)

THE ISSUES OF HUMAN segregation are a distorted reality of colour, race, religion, wealth, and other diverse means. Apartheid South Africa flaunted a racist disconnect in the face of near-universal condemnation.

The original lines were clear. European or non-European were simple distinctions between the conquerors and the conquered. In South Africa, as in other parts of the colonised world, colour differentiation became the prime qualifier.

Later, Whites or Non-Whites Only signs replaced the Europeans or Non-Europeans Only separatist graffiti in the country's public spaces.

The State's divide-and-rule strategy promoted Non-White subdivisions into Bantu, Coloured and Indians with a small Chinese population; the latter became 'honorary Whites' following the establishment of political ties with Taiwan.

The oppressed majority embraced the 1960s Black Consciousness. Black was a sociopolitical banner used by Africans, and many of those classified Coloured or Indian.

A few liberal Whites referred to people as Black or Non-Black. The quaint, pendular swing in terminology was not popular; likewise, the term 'Colourdians' was sometimes used in Cape Town. 'So-called Coloured', more commonly used, was more acceptable to many.

Divide and rule was the State's aim. In contrast, Black unity provided a solution, a concept promoted by Steve Biko, the Black Conscious Movement leader killed in 1977 during his police detention.

Apartheid's vilified ideology distorted our perceptions of each other in a fragmented nation. In the process, it blighted our lives with an excess proliferation of segregationist and oppressive laws and signs.

Like the author, the more politically inclined rejected all classifications; Homo sapiens is the only acceptable term for all people.

However, in writing this trilogy, one could not avoid the colour issue; it forms the basis of centuries of segregation and decades of striving towards liberation.

The author uses capitals to describe Blacks or Whites and other nationalities, e.g., British, Chinese, etc.

WHEN A JUDGE ASKED Steve Biko, "Why do you call yourself Black when you are brown?"

Biko replied, "Why do you call yourself White when you are pink?"

In a nutshell, Biko's riposte highlighted the absurdity of the South African colour issue. This brilliant leader was killed during his security police detention on 12 September 1977.

Timeline of events of the trilogy, *In the Shadow of Table Mountain, Cape Town.*

1960-1976

March 1960: The Sharpeville and Langa massacres of 60 or more people who protested the Pass Laws restricting domicile and work opportunities for the indigenous Africans.

June 1976: Soweto massacre of dozens of protesting students, followed by hundreds more in the ensuing months of student protests around the country. The nation's cemeteries become police killing fields.

Book 1, *Fury and Revenge in Cape Town*, covers the months of August and September 1976.

1985-1986

When the toyi-toyi establishes itself as a protest dance during this period, there is another peak in police-related violent deaths in South Africa.

August 1985: The Release Mandela Pollsmoor march cost over 30 lives in Cape Town, with more deaths countrywide.

October 1985: The Trojan Horse massacre in Athlone, took three protesting student's lives during an ambush in which police with shotguns hid in wooden crates on the back of a truck. (The event, filmed by the American CBS TV network, attracted international condemnation.)

March 1986: The Gugulethu 7 massacre involved a planned police ambush using disloyal ANC (African National Congress) turned fighters to set up seven youngsters.

May and June 1986: The Crossroads and KTC Fires of 1986, in which at least 30 people died, with 60,000 rendered homeless. Government-supported Witdoek [1](White cloth) forces laid waste to informal shanty housing in the two townships.

Book 2, *Toyi-toyi, Cape Town's War Dance,* includes the worst civil violent episodes in Cape Town's latter-day history.

1990-1994

Feb 1990: Nelson Mandela was released after 27 years of imprisonment.

The north of the country experienced its most violent years, with most of the fatalities attributed to heightened police activity before South Africa's first democratic elections.

There was also an increase in extremist right-wing, security police death squad activities in which hundreds around the country died from assassinations, random shootings, and targeted attacks on ANC and UDF (United Democratic Front) activists.

Cape Town went through its own trauma, including the actions of the secretive police Balaclava Gang, which created havoc in the African townships. It contributed to the existing mayhem between the ANC and Witdoeke, including the Taxi Wars, and the abhorrent practice of necklacing involving the use of fuel-driven, burning tyres placed around opposition members' necks.

26.4.1994: The day of South Africa's first-ever democratic elections.

Book 3, *Cape Town's Necklaces of Fire,* incorporates these calamitous developments from Namibia all the way to the Mother City.

CONTENTS

CHAPTER 1: POLLSMOOR PRISON

December 1977

IVAN PETTERSEN SPENT a year in prison during his indefinite pretrial detention from late 1976. Like many political detainees, the nineteen-year-old university student experienced the whole gamut of torture from sleep deprivation, waterboarding, cigarette burns, and a ruptured eardrum with electrocutions through to rib fractures from kneeing. During routine interrogation by the Special Branch (SB) of the Security Police, a naked Ivan was often suspended by the ankles from the room's barred windows.

The worst of his tormentors was the ageing local head of the Special Branch, the late Hammer van Zyl, assisted by his junior sidekick, Leeu (Lion) Kloppers. The longitudinal, black-stained ridges on Ivan's thumbnails were a constant reminder of his worst prison moments.

Ivan was six foot tall with his handsome face fringed by dark hair, its wide curls cut short during his confinement. Hazel brown eyes and prominent ears were part of his paternal lineage. He had a broad upper lip below the slightly upturned nose underlined by dark lips. He often stroked his chin cleft. His facial hair was scraggly and sparse, so he preferred the smooth skin of a daily shave. A muscular build revealed no fat on him. Proud of his deep skin colour, the

1960s popular refrain, 'Black is beautiful,' embodied his looks and his revolutionary disposition.

In 1975, Ivan passed the first year of his chemical engineering studies at the University of Cape Town (UCT) with two distinctions. His was the only double honours awarded, a rare achievement at the all-White university; his special permit from the Minister of Internal Affairs to attend UCT still stung him to the core.

The events spurring him into action were part of the 1976 nationwide insurrection after the Soweto killing of over 60 schoolchildren protesting the increased use of the Afrikaans language in African schools. Convicted of blowing up electricity substations and pylons at his brief trial in 1977, Ivan spent the next twelve years in the Pollsmoor high-security prison. Here, the dark void of jail violence replaced the terrors of his earlier security police detention.

The constricting band across his lower chest had been there since his arrest in 1976. The sensation was the norm during his time in Pollsmoor, where survival would drain him of ordinary, warm feelings; anger, hate, and even revenge filled the void, leaving no place for comfortable emotions. Despite his emotional pit, Ivan was determined to survive the high-security Pollsmoor prison no matter what it took. He had promised his parents he would one day hand over his graduation certificate to them outside UCT's Jameson Hall while wearing his graduation cap, cape, and green hood. He still intended to be the first Pettersen to graduate from a university.

By design, the State put activist students into the most formidable detention centres to share cells with the meanest common-law criminals. The only allegiance of prison gangsters was to those in their gangs - designated 26, 27 or 28. Often, fellow inmates protected the students. Ivan was fortunate as his first cellmate was from his primary school days. Sammi left school during his seventh year to follow a life of crime. The two boys shared a desk and Ivan's sandwiches during those school years. Ivan saw to an ever-hungry Sammi by bringing extra sandwiches provided by Ivan's mother.

On his first day in prison, Ivan asked Sammi. "What's with all the writing tattooed on you, pal? You look like a book."

"I am The Bible," Sammi proclaimed proudly. "All the 26 gang laws are tattooed on my body. Six other men, and I know it all by heart. They chose a lifer to be The Bible." He unbuttoned his shirt to show Ivan his cutaneous opus.

"So, you are 26's living parchment, spelling mistakes included!" Ivan chuckled. "How do the other prisoners react to you?"

Sammi looked at him, his eyes narrowed. "Ja, I must be careful. Wherever I go, there will always be at least two escorts. However, when I go to the toilet, none of them will wipe my arse for me," he laughed.

Sammi became Ivan's minder, introducing him to his new world of prison gangs; his survival required an observance of gang laws. So Sammi strove to convince Ivan that his best bet was to become a gang member.

"There are low-life scum bags in here," warned Sammi. "Some of them hate the students. They reckon youse are all la-di-da, so they will attack you, rape you or kill you. The worst places are in the showers or toilets, so you don't want to be there alone. If I cannot go with you, I will organise someone to be with you." Sammi stopped to light a self-rolled cigarette he kept behind his ear.

"On your own, you may not last long. Entry to 27 or 28 requires you to take a life; 26 accepts non-fatal stabbings to the chest or stomach. Join us; it's the best way to survive your twelve years in hell. If not, you may survive as a gang member's girlfriend."

A troubled Ivan rubbed at his lengthwise thumbnail ridges, his security police interrogation legacy. To join 26, generally required one to stab a person. *Can I do it?* The thought alone cost him many sleepless hours. Over a few weeks, while Ivan mulled over the violent price of gang membership, a couple of non-gang members were beaten up; one of them died later in hospital from his injuries. These developments contributed to Ivan's decision to join 26, the biggest group.

When Yster (Iron), the gang's general, spoke to Ivan, the man's face was a total emotional disconnect. His eyes were dark, bottomless pools of animus. Tears tattooed in a line down Yster's cheeks added to the man's overall menace, with 'XX' on the right cheek and 'V1' on the other. In the mid-neck below his Adam's apple was a dashed line with the words 'Cut on the dotted line!'. Even the toughest warders avoided him; Yster's multiple murders had earned him a life sentence. With each index finger, Ivan rubbed the full-length central ridges on the nails of his thumbs as he lay awake through a sleepless night before his morning assignment to join prison gang 26. *What task has Yster set for me? Will I be able to do it?*

CHAPTER 2: KOEVOET, POLICE DEATH SQUAD, SOUTH WEST AFRICA.

October 1979

GERRIE LEEU KLOPPERS was an infamous security police warrant officer who joined The AWB (Afrikaner Weerstandsbeweging [2] _ Afrikaner Resistance Movement) soon after its founding in 1973. The organisation's commitment to supremacist White Afrikaner nationalism appealed to Leeu so much that he tattooed the AWB insignia with a triskelion of three black sevens in a white circle on a red background on his left forearm. The symbolic perfect three sevens represented the final victory over the flawed three sixes of the anti-Christ, the satanic Beast incarnate. Somewhat reminiscent of a Nazi swastika, the tattoo had a childhood scar underlining his body art.

The AWB belief in racial purity provided much impetus to Leeu's work to stop the slide towards communist rule by Blacks in South Africa. After ten years in the force, his reputation led him to be short-listed to join the newly formed Koevoet, a counter-insurgency paramilitary police organisation. He appreciated the name Koevoet - a Crowbar - to extract the enemy from South-African-administered South West Africa as mandated by the League of Nations after World War One. South Africa, as a member of the British Commonwealth at the time, had occupied the German colony during the war, in 1915.

Koevoet had to counter the terrorist murders of Whites by PLAN (People's Liberation Army of Namibia), the military wing of the South West African Peoples Organisation. Leeu abhorred SWAPO who had to be stopped by all means possible.

Leeu prided himself as the archetypal Afrikaner with short-cropped, spiky red hair, bull neck, broad shoulders, potbelly, and size twelve veldskoen (suede) boots. Regardless of the season, he lived in long-pants safari suits in a range of shades of khaki. Cold blue eyes penetrated between his barely visible, short, pale eyelashes. The red-pink skin made a lie of the word "White". Freckles sprouted from everywhere. The well-trimmed moustache, clear of his lips, looked too thin on his face. His thick, podgy fingers looked comically stumpy on the six-foot-plus policeman, an ex-rugby union lock forward.

Leeu lived on a smallholding on the easterly edge of Cape Town in Stellenbosch Farms, close to the country's most renowned wine estates. He was not into farming, but the isolation appealed to him on his section amongst the vineyard-covered rolling hills off the M12 motorway to Stellenbosch. The front stoep (porch), where swallows nested under the eaves, gave him a partly obscured view of the Helderberg Mountains nearby. However, the scenery appealed less to him than his hidden other world in the custom-made basement where he could satisfy his dark fantasies as the Lord of the Manor.

"LEEU, HOW DID YOU COME by your nickname?" One of the two senior officers asked him during his interview to join Koevoet.

He removed a box of matches from his pocket. "My Cape Town colleagues call me Leeu because of how I use the Lion matches as an interrogation device." He tapped the red lion on the box.

After explaining his technique, his interviewers applauded. "Bloody hell. You are just what we need in Koevoet - policemen who think outside the fucking circle. It's how we work in SWA (South West Africa)."

Leeu cracked the fingers of both hands and then leaned forward. "There are too many restrictive rules. I believe in stretching the rules, better yet, making my own." Leeu smiled. He knew what they wanted to hear. He suspected his current boss wanted to move him along because his more recent excesses had caused two detainee deaths over eighteen months in Cape Town.

Leeu impressed them enough for him to be invited to visit the Koevoet headquarters in Oshakati in northern SWA. There they took him on an afternoon trip to one of their isolated bush camps in northern Ovamboland, almost on the Angolan border. Before dinner, he joined about 30 White officers for drinks as they stood around the braai (barbeque) area where slabs of meat covered a diamond-mesh metal grill on legs. An Ovambo servant tended the meat. The evening air was heavy with the smell of burning wood mixed with the roasting meat of a springbok shot in the bush nearby. Leeu could see the Black Ovambo colleagues congregating around another fire at the other end of the camp enclosure.

The White officers watched expectantly when a bloodied Ovambo prisoner was dragged over to them. The man, whose eyes were closed from his facial bruising, was forced to kneel on the base camp's loose sand close to the fire, where dinner sizzled away.

"This terr (terrorist) has told us what we want to know; shoot him," said base camp Commander van Wyk.

Leeu took the gun from van Wyk to fire a single shot to the side of the prisoner's head. The exiting bullet burrowed into the firm-packed sand, where the man's body twitched briefly. There was a round of applause from the other officers who came to congratulate him. He had passed the membership test.

Van Wyk shook Leeu's hand, "Congrats. Welcome to Koevoet."

Leeu walked away from the body, where the blood started to congeal on the sand around the prisoner's head. With smug comfort, he drank from the chilled bottle of Windhoek lager that one of the welcoming officers had pushed into his hand.

What he had seen on his visit so far appealed to him as a new member of an isolated security police death squad, though he had to return to Cape Town to sort out his affairs, especially clearing his basement. Living on base the way they did in SWA meant he had to find alternative ways to seek the extra gratification he needed. *Would things work out? Am I expecting too much from Koevoet?*

CHAPTER 3: WHEN LOVE CALLS

December 1986

THEMBANI DLAMINI LOOKED back with a certain sense of wonder over the recent events in his life. He was the sole survivor of an experience still raw after four months.

Thembani had fallen in love with the freshly widowed Nkosinati Khumalo. Thembani and his deceased friend, Curtis Fouche, had rescued her with her husband, Dumisa, from the government's Witdoek (White cloth) forces [2] when they destroyed Crossroads' informal housing in May. She had stayed with Thembani's parents in Gugulethu when Dumisa left to join protesting pondok (shanty) dwellers in another informal settlement at the Khakhaza Trading Company; a month later, KTC was aflame. Over sixty thousand people fled the two areas where burning homes became pyres, and dozens died, including Dumisa. People referred to the holocaust as The Fires of 1986, the worst of the State-inspired unrest in Cape Town's history.

For Thembani, the only good part of the tragic episode was meeting Nkosinati. Thembani's parents had insisted on the pregnant Nkosinati staying with them until after the delivery of her unborn child. Thembani visited his parents often in the spring of 1986, where he found comfort in his long chats with the attractive widow. They were the same age. She was a teacher, impressing Thembani with her general knowledge. She, too, was an avid reader and he brought her many of his books to read, enjoying their discussions afterwards. She seemed inconsolable in the way she grieved over the loss of her childhood sweetheart. By the time her son was born three weeks before Christmas, Thembani knew she was the woman for him.

On a sunny day, seated on the bench in his parents' tiny garden, Thembani held Nkosinati's hand. "May I hold your hand? I've wanted to do it since you came here. Staying at my place is difficult when I know you are at my parent's house."

Nkosinati's blush was visible through her light brown skin. She had no lipstick on her smooth pink lips, enhanced by white teeth with a slight lower dental overlap, adding to her alluring smile to send his nerves into overdrive. She dropped her eyes, responding with a squeeze of his hand.

She turned away from him. "I wondered why you came so often. It's sweet of you," she said. "Your family have been kind to me over the last few months. As you can see, I am still in black. I really miss my Dumisa. I hope he did not suffer in the end. When I think of him, I ache way inside here." Her hands went to her chest.

"How he would have loved to see his son. He believed the baby would be a boy. We chose the name Curtis-Thembani because of how the two of you saved us in Crossroads." Her eyes were downturned as she wiped at her tears.

Thembani felt his heart pound away in his throat. He felt her grief, yet he had to push on. "Curtis-Thembani is nearly a month old now. I've been patient over the months, but you'll return to the Transkei to live with your parents this weekend.

"I want to marry you, Nkosinati," he said with a tone of desperation. "Please let me go with you to seek your parents' permission. I have told my parents, who think of you as family. I already feel like a happy, proud father to Curtis-Thembani."

Nkosinati blushed deeper, her discomfort apparent, as a driven Thembani pushed on. "Your encouragement has meant I will work towards doing a few papers at uni next year. You cannot imagine how excited I am at the prospect, so let us go on this journey together. Marry me, please!" By now, his mouth was like sandpaper while his pulse continued to race away. He gripped her left hand to his chest. "This heart beats for you from the first time I saw you in Crossroads. I would be the happiest man in the world if I could be on the bus to the Transkei with you."

She turned to face him with a faint smile. Before he knew it, her lips were on his. She lingered with her lips on his before she dropped her head onto his right shoulder. Her right hand dug into his left shoulder as she pulled him towards her. She started crying.

The faint floral smell of her perfume made Thembani's head spin. *I hope she's happy! What if she's not?*

"Yes," she murmured into his chest after a few drawn-out seconds. "By all means, let us go together on the bus on Saturday."

Thembani's heart boomed away. He had never felt such elation before. He squeezed her as he held her close. "Thank you, Nkosinati, for the happiest moment of my life!"

His only concern was how troubled thoughts still plagued him. *Will the new direction in my life allow my demons to settle?*

THE LOADED BUS HAD containers filling all available spaces; the roof carrier, piled high with the passengers' possessions, included a kitchen dresser. There was a palpable excitement as many returned home to loved ones after an absence of many months or years. Most of the men were jobseekers not allowed by law to bring their families with them to the cities.

They sat on the shaded side of the bus. Open windows provided relief from the early summer heat. To have Curtis-Thembani on his lap while Nkosinati sometimes dozed with her head against his shoulder was sorely needed balm for Thembani's troubled soul of the past few months. *How will I tell Nkosinati about the events in August?*

During their trip, Curtis-Thembani slept most of the time. Thembani often held the infant, who had more fine-curled hair than any other baby he had seen. He kissed the sleeping child on the cheeks, inhaling deeply. "I enjoy the smell of his Johnson's baby powder. His hair is like yours, nearly as long, too."

"Yes. He was born with an Afro hairstyle."

Sitting so close to the first love of his life was unique to Thembani. The eight-hour bus drive to Mthatha allowed him opportunities to hold Nkosinati's hand, squeeze her shoulder or stare into her light brown eyes with their curling eyelashes. He liked her no-make-up look. Apart from a childhood scar on the chin, her skin was flawless, glowing from the face cream she used. Her radiant smile or soft laughter beguiled him further while she had an endearing way of snuggling into him whenever he held Curtis-Thembani. Their stolen kisses made him giddy with delight. By the end of the trip, he was more infatuated with Nkosinati than he had been before their journey.

"I like your name - Nkosinati," Thembani said at one stage.

Her eyes narrowed. "Yes. 'God is with us'. It's Zulu, like my mother, so beware, we are fighters. Yes, Xhosa, you take care!" Her fists were up, her impish laughter transfixed Thembani.

In Mthatha, they dismounted the bus on Victoria Street with their suitcases. Two to three-storey buildings lined the central city streets with views to the surrounding low hills, now green in the distance from the spring rains. Some of South Africa's worst agricultural land was a mocking emerald-green verdure, starkly scarred by multiple dongas where the water-eroded gullies crisscrossed the landscape with red-orange slashes from the washing away of precious topsoil by the summer rains. The chest-high maize plants in between the don-gas would soon provide locals with Africa's staple food.

When they changed buses, Nkosinati had a seat on the aisle with her baby. Alongside her sat an older woman holding onto a pair of roosters with their legs tied together with a grubby strip of floral cloth. Thembani stood proudly in the aisle alongside his family. The trip seemed to last forever as he regularly swapped his hands to hold onto the overhead rail. Finally, after thirty minutes, the bus turned off the smooth asphalt road onto a gravel road towards the west.

They felt every bump on roads now in need of their annual grad-ing. Scrawny cattle sought sustenance from the clustered clumps of scattered greenery. They looked as underfed as the occasional child-minders he saw. The boys' knees looked like knobbed protuberances on their skinny legs. With relief, they finally reached the village of Gubevu, where the Khumalos, Nkosinati's parents, ran a well-stocked store in front of their compact home.

The greying couple fussed over their first grandchild. Nkosinati was their only surviving child. Her brother, their first-born, had been killed during a university student demonstration in Durban in 1976. They were surprised at Thembani's presence, yet here was an environ-ment where no invitations were necessary; their warm greeting made him feel welcome.

They gathered in a neat lounge where a two-seat sofa, table, four chairs and a sideboard with a radio on top filled the room. There was no television reception in the area. Thembani heard the background hum of a generator. Mr Dlamini led the prayer of welcome and one for the departed Dumisa. The family members were tearful through-out the moments of blessing.

When do I approach her parents? Now? Later? Thembani had to start his new job in Cape Town with G's Builders, who wanted him to start early before the workers returned from their Christmas break in mid-January. They all settled to enjoy a cup of tea with Tennis biscuits, one of Thembani's favourites. The parents could finally hear directly from Nkosinati of her harrowing experiences in Crossroads, where Thembani and Curtis had rescued her. Her parents were thankful the Dlaminis had looked after her until Curtis-Thembani's birth.

"And now Thembani has something special to ask you two," Nkosinati said with hesitancy. Though she beamed, Thembani noticed the nervous twitching of her face as she opened the door so he could pose the question to her bemused parents.

Thembani's pulse galloped. *How do I start this?* He had a scramble of inappropriately prepared openings. He closed his eyes, reflecting briefly before facing the Khumalos.

"I know this will be unexpected, as I only asked Nkosinati a few days ago. She reminded me she is still in mourning ... whereas I was afraid I would lose her when she returned to you. In the months since Dumisa's death, I fell deeply in love with your daughter, though I did not tell her until a few days ago.

"Her imminent departure was too much, so I asked her to marry me. Now, I request your blessings so I can be with the woman who means more to me than anything else in the world." He felt the light sweat now covering his lips while his already fast pulse doubled its pace. He exhaled slowly while he waited.

Oh! That's not encouraging. Her parents looked stunned as they turned to each other, where they sat on the sofa. Mr Khumalo held his wife's hands while they spoke in hushed tones. Thembani felt Nkosinati tap his leg with her foot under the table, where they sat opposite each other. She winked at him while she gave him a thumbs-up, covered by the other hand. *Is that a healthy sign? How does she know?*

Her parents' faces, with prominent furrowed lines, were sombre. "Yes, as you said, Thembani, this is unexpected, of course," said Mrs Khumalo. "We greatly appreciate what you, Curtis and your family have already done to help Nkosinati. Our most important question as parents is what Nkosinati thinks about your proposal? How do you feel about Thembani, child?"

Her parents now had their eyes fixed on Nkosinati, who smiled when she looked at Thembani before turning to her parents. "I hardly noticed him when he came to his parent's place. After my child's birth, he was the second person after me to hold Curtis-Thembani. Imagine my shock when he said, 'Welcome to the world, my boy. I will be your father!' I had to notice him then! Why would a stranger say that to my baby? As I told him, I was still mourning; probably I will always miss Dumisa, my first love, since we were at primary school. Every time Thembani held my son, I could see how the love radiated from him to my baby. I felt comforted whenever he was around us." She turned her head to smile at Thembani.

"When he asked me to marry him, it was a beautiful shock. Yes, beautiful! I never believed I would remarry, especially so soon after Dumisa's death. Thembani is bright with much love to give. In him, I believe I would have a wonderful husband. In him, I see a natural father to my son. I enjoy feeling such a different love towards him." She blushed, looking shyly towards Thembani. "Wow! It's the first time I've said I love him," she chuckled.

With a palpitating heart, Thembani reached a hand across the table to hold hers. Nkosinati squeezed his fingers firmly. *Now, what do her parents think?*

Pangs of discomfort hit him when Mr Khumalo rose from his chair, looked at Nkosinati, and then turned to face Thembani. "Thembani, how do you feel about our grandchild?"

Thembani was a bit taken aback. He had not expected the question. After a few seconds, he said, "Like his mother, your grandson is beautiful. He has no father. I need him as a son; I need his mother as a wife. I love both dearly." He stopped to wipe sweat from his brow.

His dry mouth made talking difficult. He licked his lips, swallowing a few times.

"Some time ago, I lost my best friend Curtis, killed by the police. Last year, during the march to release Mandela, he saved my life. When I first heard your grandson's name, I was honoured he had both our names. My heart went to Curtis-Thembani when I first saw him after his birth. I felt I had to be part of his life. The best role would be as his father." By now, his breathing was fast as he wiped more sweat from his forehead with his handkerchief.

Mrs Khumalo now rose from the sofa. "Please excuse us," she said, then led the way through the kitchen to the garden. Thembani heard their earnest voices filter through to the lounge.

Nkosinati slid her hand across the table to hold his hand. "They always have these conferences on the bench in the garden. Though I feel relaxed about things, I will still keep my fingers crossed." She leaned over to kiss his hand with her eyes fixed on his. Tremulous waves spread through Thembani's body. His head reeled as he closed his eyes, in part to enjoy the sensation, in part to regain his composure. His heart continued to drum away.

The Khumalos returned, still sombre, still unsmiling. "You said you are a Dlamini, correct?" Nkosinati's father asked.

"Why, yes."

Both parents looked relaxed. "Excellent," said Mrs Khumalo. "Over many centuries, our clans have been allies."

"Do you mean it's okay?" Nkosinati interjected, half-rising from her chair.

"Yes, Thembani, you may marry Nkosinati with our blessings. Congratulations!" Mrs Khumalo grinned from ear to ear.

Nkosinati rushed around to hug her parents. A standing Thembani was nearly bowled over when she threw herself into his arms to kiss him passionately a few times. His heart felt ready to burst. They clung to each other before Thembani went over to thank the smiling Khumalos.

"We decided your family have done so much to help Nkosinati, so there is no need for lobola - the bride price is zero cattle", said Mr Khumalo, who shook Thembani's hand. "Welcome to the family, son."

"Thank you from the bottom of a heart filled with love. I will look after your daughter and grandchild with my life if need be."

As joyful as the moment was, Thembani's closeted life troubled him. *When do I tell Nkosinati about the Newlands station episode?*

CHAPTER 4: A DAY AT THE PRACTICE

August 1987

DR STANLEY GERSHON was on his way to a house call in Ninth Avenue, Elsies River, where a pregnant woman was in labour. He was in his winter gear - black jeans with a long-sleeved white tee top visible under a black sweater. While he drove east from Halt Road, he enjoyed the sun's warmth on his forearms. In his rearview mirror, the patchy cloud partly obscured the distant Table Mountain and Devil's Peak like a partly veiled, captivating woman. In all its moods, he enjoyed the view of the mountains. A mountain hike with Fay was overdue. He smiled as he recalled how he had declared his love for her on their first visit to the mountain in 1976.

IT WAS GOOD TO HAVE his new practice partner, Jayantilal Panchal, mind the rooms when he went on calls. Previously, patient numbers could double when he went on his urgent home visits. Now, the days were more manageable, with trainee hospital registrar locums handling most weekends. Stanley and JT, as he often called his colleague, had qualified together at the University of Cape Town, where both had required a special permit to attend a White university. JT, who needed a permit to live in Cape Town, away from his home province of Natal, was a knowledgeable, dedicated doctor, and both of them shared similar anti-establishment political beliefs.

Their day started with a pot of tea with biscuits. Jayantilal had returned from his home town in Pietermaritzburg, a stronghold of the IFP (Inkatha Freedom Party), the ANC's main rivals in Natal.

"People talk about the Natal Midlands War between the two groups' youth movements. I fear matters will worsen," said JT.

Stanley nodded his agreement. "Cape Town is similar with ANC (African National Congress) or UDF (United Democratic Front) supporters often in conflict with the pro-government Witdoeke (White cloths or scarves).

"Unless the government commits to majority rule, the chaos will continue," said Jayantilal.

STANLEY'S DRIVE ALONG Ninth Avenue painted a picture of change. The narrow street started with a hodge-podge of housing ranging from plastered brick structures with asbestos or corrugated iron roofs to more modern brick-and-tiled homes. Perimeter walls of face-brick, precast concrete or iron palings mixed in with occasional well-trimmed hedges to provide much-needed greenery along the street. A mishmash of corrugated iron or barbed-wire-topped diamond-mesh-wire fences separated other houses from the road.

Older buildings were often in need of fresh paint or new roofing. Converted garages had a mix of lean-to structures as add-on living areas. A narrow strip of tarred pavement ran along the northern edge where cars partly parked on the sidewalk.

Five blocks on, double-storey, older council flats stretched along both sides of the avenue with a few dated cars parked outside. Youths hung around the corners where the prominent graffiti on walls demarcated their gang affiliations. Stanley was in Achar-American territory. Two blocks down, unattractive, four-storey, asbestos-roofed breeze block barracks rose from the grey-white Cape Flats sand where loose gravel paths extended from the tarred sidewalk to the infill housing scheme. The recently built units looked like expanded stables with eight paired windows gracing each floor of the unpainted council flats. On the field opposite stood dozens of corrugated iron shanties where the most destitute lived. These homes were the battery farms of gangsterism, where diseases or the violence of poverty savaged people's lives.

Stanley drove slowly in his distinctive white Pathfinder. At each corner of the block were high, ineffectual streetlights favoured by muggers, especially on payday. A young teenage girl waved at him on the right side, where he turned in to drive towards the carpark between the last two blocks of flats. The adjacent municipal playing area was tarred, with no lawn, bark chips, gates, trees, or fences despite a moderately busy road alongside the playground. The jungle gym and slide were intact, the double swing frames had no chains or seats, and the see-saw was without seats. Why would anyone steal those items?

He felt relatively safe on all his house calls, except here, in the heart of gangland, he always had a sense of disquiet. He replaced his sunglasses with his spectacles, grabbed his emergency bag, locked the door, and then followed the chewing teenager who had greeted him with a pop of a bubble she had blown.

He returned the greetings from idle youngsters close by. "We'll look after your car, doctor. It'll be safe here." This was a standard welcome in the meanest of neighbourhoods. He gave them a thumbs up. The smell of urine assailed his nostrils at the base of the stairs. Stanley followed the youngster, who climbed the stairs two at a time to the top floor.

The galvanised iron stairs were on the outside of the drab, grey building. Each block had two sets of stairs facing the opposite block. Washing hung on lines on the ground floor level, though there were makeshift wash lines outside most front doors at the higher levels. There were no balconies, though each floor had a tiny landing area leading to the front door. Youngsters hung around the stairs, whereas the teenage girls or boys appeared later in the day in the car park with the drug pedlars.

The front door to the two-bedroom unit was ajar. Paired curtain-less lounge windows let in cool air. A snot-nosed boy pointed him to the bedroom, where he could hear a woman groaning with intermit-tent swearing. The youngster turned to join his sister in the untidy lounge with its neglected furniture scarred with age. Two stained sponge-rubber mattresses stood on their sides in one corner. There was no television.

He went to the bedroom, where the woman lay on a double bed. Her distended belly indicated her advanced pregnancy. By now, her shrieks suggested an imminent delivery. As was the case today, she was a patient he only saw when she was almost due or in labour. She always stank of alcohol.

"Good morning, Anna Hendricks. Another one? The last time I gave you a letter to organise your sterilisation at the hospital. What happened?"

"I'm sorry, doctor. The letter is still in the kitchen somewhere." A shriek followed. "I think it's coming, doctor, oh no!"

A gloved Stanley placed himself at Anna's bedside, where she lay on a folded-over towel. In her usual fashion, she gave birth to anoth-er underweight baby within minutes. He first tied, then cut the cord while the teenager brought him a plastic bag in which he placed the placenta. While he wrapped the baby in a suspect-looking towel, he realised the alcohol smell he detected came from the neonate.

"Oh no, Anna, your baby smells of alcohol! Did you drink today or last night?"

She turned her head towards the wall without replying.

"Yesterday, she had an all-night party with her friends," the fiercely chewing youngster said. "They drank their strong, home-brewed ginger beer bobbies till they dropped like they always do." At the door, the gum-blowing teenager emphasised the point with another pop of the pink bubble she had blown. Her frowning brother stood beside her, clinging to her skirt.

Stanley handed over the baby to the girl. "Here, hold him."

As he looked at the siblings, he realised they all looked similar, though not the way close relatives do. All three had tiny eyes, flattened cheeks, and a flat nose with a central flat area above a thin upper lip. There were broad skin folds on the inner aspects of the eyes. An underdeveloped jaw matched the reduced head size. They were all classic cases of foetal alcohol syndrome. The complete spectrum included physical and mental stunting; the baby was already underweight.

With a sense of despair, Stanley checked whether Anna was bleeding. Her blood pressure was acceptable.

"Why do you drink like this, Anna? You promised me you would stop. Now you have children all damaged by alcohol. Look at them. Their small heads are from the booze, woman!" Stanley's voice rose with each word. He shook his head as he struggled to contain his anger towards Anna and against the system producing too many of her ilk.

"I can't help it, doctor. I tried, yet I can't stop. I don't want to drink, though it pulls me in every day. There are days I think I'm winning until my friends pop in with their bobbies." Again, her tears flowed as strongly as they did with the previous child's delivery, although today, she seemed jittery, somewhat beside herself. What do I do with Anna?

His thoughts were interrupted by an alarmed call from the teenager. "Oh Jesus, doctor! What's going on here?"

Stanley rushed to the lounge where the baby was fitting. The jerks settled, yet the infant remained agitated. He did not know if the baby showed the effects of acute alcohol withdrawal or whether it was part of the syndrome. After a sedative injection, the restless infant soon fell asleep.

"Mummy's not looking too nice, doctor!" the youngster called as he ran from the bedroom.

Stanley rushed over to find Anna in a state of great anxiety. She swore at Stanley while she twisted on her bed. *What else did she drink or take?* At his wit's end, the experienced general practitioner opted to give her the same sedation he had given the baby. The effect was similar; Anna dozed off immediately.

He turned to the teenager. "I'm pretty certain they'll sleep for hours after the injections. However, from my rooms I'll arrange an ambulance to take them to hospital. Give the letter to the paramedics."

Once outside, Stanley felt a sense of relief. The repetitive nature of certain experiences often threatened to overwhelm him. Anna was typical of those he treated to return to the same environment where these disasters had started in the first place.

BACK AT THE ROOMS, there was a sense of apprehension in his reception staff. A burning smell assailed his nostrils.

"What's happening? What's the smell?"

Nurse Desray Daniels, a stalwart since day one in his practice, emerged from their procedure room. Desray had changed from her early overweight self to a more streamlined version. "Oh, good. You've arrived. You may want to pop in here."

Stanley entered the room where the gloved Jayantilal worked on a man's pubic area. Stanley recognised Mr Grey, who was in agony.

"What happened here?" Stanley was aghast at the burnt hair with the blistered penis and scrotal skin. The teacher's eyebrows were singed while tiny blisters covered the tip of his nose.

"It's the work of the security police," said Jayantilal. "He came here straight from detention. Mr Grey refuses to go to hospital. At least it's not a third-degree burn, only superficial blistering. A paraffin gauze dressing should do the trick."

"I'm sure that'll suffice, JT. What caused this?" Stanley asked the patient. Stanley did not look forward to hearing the expected gruesome details. Mr Grey was already under a banishment restriction order under the notorious Suppression of Communism Act now implemented more stringently under the three-year-old State of Emergency laws.

The teacher closed his eyes before he answered. "For a few days in detention, I resisted the security police pressure. They often punched me, choked me with a hood over my head, and then almost drowned me with the water they hosed onto the head covering. On my final day, they stripped me naked, tied me to a chair, then shocked me all over with their electrodes." His voice was tremulous. He stopped to compose himself with his eyes closed.

"After a while, they brought in a new guy, a fat, red-haired fellow. I shivered when I looked at him. There was something about him the others did not have, like a sense of malicious evil. His blue eyes were cold, expressionless." Mr Grey paused again, drawing a few deep breaths before he continued.

"I shivered inwardly when I looked at him. 'People call me Leeu. It's because I like Lion matches,' he said as he removed a box of matches from his pocket. 'These are amazing. Just one of these tiny sticks can burn a house down. Better yet, they can extract the truth from liars. I'm here to visit my colleagues; they tell me you're a liar.' When he looked with his face close to mine, his red-pink eyelids seemed to have no lashes." As Mr Grey paused, a visible tremor shook him.

"They passed around the brandy all the time, vowing to stick the bottleneck up my arse when they were finished drinking. I believed them capable of it. They laughed when they suggested things might go better with Coca-Cola." Mr Grey closed his eyes. "Leeu then poured brandy over my genitals. The burning sensation was intense. 'This is such a waste of brandy ... though it does the job!' said Leeu.

"I froze when, from a metre away with his thumb on the match head facing him, Leeu flicked the match against the lighting strip on the box towards my groin. He missed the first two shots at his target. They looked like flaming missiles aimed at my crotch."

Mr Grey wiped at his sweating brow with a sleeve. "He oozed with malevolence while he constantly licked at his thin lips. 'I missed deliberately. Now I go for the target if you still don't answer our questions.' He waited a few minutes. With his thick tongue covering his lower lip, his next flick hit the target. The brandy-soaked pubic hairs went up in flames, singeing my eyebrows as I threw my head back to avoid the flames. After a few seconds, they poured a bucket of water over my groin.

"I have had to deal with a few of these evil bastards, including the ultimate, Hammer van Zyl before he shot himself in the head last year. How I hope he had an agonising death, but Leeu is evil manifest like no one I ever came across before."

Stanley shook his head in disbelief. The familiar tightness across his upper abdomen had hit him when he saw Mr Grey. Stanley's constricting band was all too normal for him with the other atrocities he had had to treat over the years, including those from Hammer van Zyl. He was tempted to tell Mr Grey how Hammer had contracted TB and HIV/AIDS from the detainees the man had tortured.

"You are lucky," said Jayantilal. "I'm sure there'll be no scarring, except there may be residual skin discolouration. You'll need a check-up again after a few days."

The two doctors enjoyed a much-needed cup of tea afterwards. Stanley was introspective while he stirred away at his cup.

"Are you going to stir your tea all day?" asked Jayantilal with a grin. Both had a shared weakness of condensed milk with sugar in their tea.

"Well, JT, here's Mr Grey's shocking burn's case where he is too scared to sue the police. Then I do a call to a house full of kids with foetal alcohol syndrome. I've never before delivered a drunk baby to a drunk mother."

Local research had shown how ten per cent of Cape Flats children had FAS, the highest rate in the world. Both lapsed into silence while they sipped at their tea.

"Our government-created social quagmire sucks in all except the strongest," Jayantilal eventually responded. "It galls me how poverty-related medical deaths by far outnumber the many deaths we have from police violence."

BACK HOME OVER DINNER, Fay reminded Stanley about the fatal Newlands station attack a year ago, one day after the infamous security police officer Hammer van Zyl had committed suicide by shooting himself through the head. Over a relatively quiet dinner, Stanley reflected on the deaths of the three revolutionaries killed by plain-clothed police on the station platform. According to the news, the police had killed all of the terrorists, now regarded as martyrs by most Blacks in the Cape Flats townships. Stanley kept to himself his suspicions about a fourth member of the group whom he had seen with a gunshot wound on the same day.

CHAPTER 5: PRISON GANG 26

December 1987

IVAN CONSTANTLY FELT a grave disquiet about how he had acquired his 26 prison gang membership. He often relived the nightmare of how he became a member ten years earlier. As an adolescent who carried a knife in his jeans pocket, Ivan had always dreaded the prospect of having to stab someone; in Pollsmoor, the fear became a reality. In the narrow confines of his jail cell, where he constantly rubbed at his deformed thumbnails, flashback images of his actions in the prison yard revisited him often in his disturbed sleep.

Ivan's knotted stomach felt tighter than ever on the fateful morning of his assignment. He could only tolerate half a mug of cold water at breakfast time. Yster slipped the weapon to him under the breakfast table; the short weapon was not meant to kill his victim. The sharpened spike had been fashioned from a builder's reinforcement steel rod stolen from the site of a new prison wing extension. With a folded-over handle, old blood stained the implement, covered with a dirty piece of towel; Ivan slid the makeshift weapon up his left shirt sleeve with the grip directed towards his hand. The cold metal seemed to burn into his flesh.

Yster's message was stark. "The weapon must return with fresh blood on it. If not, your blood will join the old stuff." The cold, unblinking eyes bored through Ivan. The only other instruction was the identity of his target, whom Ivan hardly knew. There were no explanations offered. Ivan knew not to ask.

After breakfast, his associates created a diversion with a fight in the central area of the prison yard. Amidst a crowd of jeering onlookers, Ivan was close to his target, where other gang members had surrounded the prisoner. With a pulsating heart, Ivan approached the prisoner from behind, his mouth bitter with the tension.

The intended victim half-turned towards Ivan; he looked like a scared buck caught in a hunter's spotlight. Ivan held the stabbing spike in a sweaty right hand, partly concealing the weapon against his wrist with the sharpened tip directed towards the elbow. Then, at the last minute, Ivan switched his grip to a lunging style to strike at the side of the man's abdomen as instructed.

The sensation of his weapon penetrating the man's torso still sickened Ivan. Worse still was the force needed to remove the implement with the man's body tissues clinging to the diagonal ridges on the spike's shaft. When the weapon pulled free, the slurping sound as the wound sucked in air revolted Ivan even more. The prisoner collapsed; his screams mixed in with the chaos around them. During the prison yard mayhem, Ivan slipped the makeshift weapon to Yster. Both of them turned to blend in with the rioting inmates while Ivan struggled to suppress the urge to vomit with his stomach knotted tighter than ever.

IVAN'S IGNOMINIOUS entry into 26 was the low point of his prison life. The man survived the assault; knowing his victim, not a gang member, was a serial rapist of children did not ease Ivan's torment. Prison yard justice ensured these criminals often came to a sticky end; no doubt many prisoners had been abused by their ilk.

As a 26er, observance of gang etiquette was critical. Sammi explained to Ivan, "There are many strict gang laws to observe. But, first, you must learn The Book - it's different to The Bible. Every 26'er must know The Book by heart and be able to recite it when challenged to do so. You could be gone if you make a mistake." Sammi drew a finger across his neck.

"We have six basic laws: you do what 26 wants; you are prepared to die with your 26 brothers; you do not fight with your comrades; unlike in 27 or 28, sex with your 26 brothers is not allowed; respect the warders to keep the peace in prison; and you have to give two warnings before hurting a non-member." Sammi took the cigarette from behind his ear before lighting it.

"Non-fatal punishment is six stab wounds over six years without warning, like the one you inflicted on that lowlife bastard. They know it's coming, yet they never know when. We use a longer blade for the death sentence."

Sammi coughed. "It's these damned cigarettes," he said before he continued. "26 maintains the cash flow in the prison from outside drug-dealing, prostitution, car theft ...You name it, we're into it."

"How did the gangs start?"

Sammi lit a fresh, self-rolled cigarette. The smoke swirled around his head before dancing in the thin beam of sunlight filtering through the high, narrow-barred window. The cheap tobacco smell reminded Ivan of his father's early pipe-smoking days.

"Around 1890, our great leader, Nongoloza, created a country-wide prison gang which later split into three." Sammi's voice projected a hushed reverence. "He likened his gang to the Ninevites whose Old Testament city of Nineveh was destroyed by God when they turned against him. Nongoloza established his gang with a parliament, a legal system, and an army containing ranks from generals to foot soldiers. I am a captain, so watch out," Sammi teased.

"So, what happens when I leave prison?"

"Ja, like family, you always belong to 26. Blood gets you in, and blood gets you out. Now we need to organise your tattoos," said Sammi. "I've already chosen the best artist."

"I'll have the twenty as an 'XX' on the right shoulder with the six as 'VI' on the left," said Ivan. "26's trademark '$' sign above the rising sun will be on my mid-chest. On the inside of my left forearm, I want a smoking gun."

"Ah, the gun! It's become popular outside these days. A decent knife like the Okapi, my Three Star, was 'it' in my time. Any particular gun?"

'A 9mm Parabellum."

'Ja! They come in with the buttons (Mandrax sleeping tablets) shipments from India or Pakistan. Do you know you can buy the buttons right here in prison? Too many of the guys like smoking their white pipes[3]."

DURING HIS YEARS IN detention, Ivan climbed the ranks to be one of the top-ranked leaders of 26. He baulked from another stabbing, possibly fatal, to escalate further in the ranks. The political prisoners taught most gang members to read and write, while the inmates' numeracy skills improved under Ivan's tuition. Yster was barely literate when he started his lessons with Ivan. 26 gang membership now required all members to commit to learning. Ivan's Rule had pride of place tattooed on the top of Sammi's right foot.

Members of all gangs benefitted from the classes. Ivan's work gave him cross-gang currency needed to mediate gang disputes when volatile issues threatened. These functions helped him maintain a sanity of sorts in an alien other world of such strong affiliations.

FOR IVAN, THE PRISON yard attack was a dehumanising experience. The man's intense pain at the critical moment of impalement, mixed in with the initial look of suspicion, turning to fear, often swirled in Ivan's head. He used to wake sweating profusely when the images formed an ever-widening maelstrom mixed in with his earlier detention horrors involving Leeu Kloppers. The security policeman's exposed forearm tattoo, with the distinctive White supremacist triskelion underlined by a scar, capped the other visions like a rotating symbol of evil.

CHAPTER 6: LOVE'S ROCKY LEGISLATED ROAD

February 1988

LYDIAH ADAMS WALKED from the carpark towards her parents' graves in the Maitland cemetery. As was the case in legislated life, there was no mixing after death as Lydiah made her way to the 'Non-Whites-only' Cemetery Number Four.

In casual shoes, fitting blue jeans with a red tee shirt, she enjoyed the sun on her pale arms. In black shorts and singlet, her partner, Willie Germishuys, ran after their seven-year-old daughter, Suzanne, to meet the rest of Lydiah's family. They were to commemorate the anniversary of her parents' deaths four years earlier. She had missed the last three gatherings during her time in England, where she had completed her PhD on artificial intelligence in neural networks at London University. Willie had a part-time lecturer's post while there. Returning from London two months earlier, both resumed teaching at the UWC (University of the Western Cape). The purpose-built Coloureds-only university had recently opened its doors to all races.

It was a partly cloudy day, with Cape Town's mountains hazed out by smog. Traffic noise reached them from the nearby Voortrekker Road. There was no wind in a city infamous for its gale-force winds. Parts of the cemetery she walked past looked like light-grey, sandy wasteland interrupted by bent pine trees, more upright

Eucalyptus trees, with a few oleander or self-seeded wattle bushes providing much-needed colour. Skewed wooden crosses graced neglected graves, faded vases with sun-bleached plastic flowers adorned others. Lydiah ambled towards her parents' graves, marked by one of only a few headstones; a cemetery without lawns was a cheerless place.

Her father had enjoyed seven years of retirement from the CID before he succumbed to a stroke in 1984; a year later, her mother died from a heart attack. Lydiah recalled how she had caused her parents much grief during her activist student days at UWC. Her detective father used to check the prison cells at the end of the day to ensure she had evaded the security police dragnet during the 1976 State of Emergency. Her parents supported her relationship with Willie, who was classified as White. To Lydiah's surprise at the time, her conservative parents allowed Willie to live with her in the family home. Both grandparents adored their granddaughter, Suzanne.

In 1980, it was instant love when they first met in a lunchtime food queue at UWC, where they both had started lecturing. Willie had a mop of dark curly hair, now thinning. Lydiah had straight, light-brown hair, while her skin was paler than Willie's. She had green eyes like her father; Willie's eyes were brown.

Because their relationship contravened the Immorality Act, imprisonment clouded their early relationship. Lydiah dreaded how they could be raided in the dead of night by morality police keen to find only one bed with warm sheets. The Mixed Marriages Act meant they could not marry until both laws were scrapped in 1985, just after they left to live in London. Lydiah inherited the family home where the young family lived when they returned. Still, under the Group Areas Act, Willie was not legally entitled to live in Elsies River.

Often, Willie teased how Suzanne was the product of broken laws. 'Suzanne may have been born illegitimate, but hybrids are the best. Look at her,' he often declared proudly. They had been married by the rebellious Father Laughton - though the marriage could not be registered. He also baptised Suzanne, whose scrambled genes gave her blonde streaks in her darker-hued mop of soft curls tumbling around her pale face. Her eyes were sky blue, while a gap tooth with a faint lisp enhanced her endearing smile.

Lydiah's family and friends all embraced their romance. Not so the Germishuys family, who made Willie an outcast once they knew of his affair with someone who was classified as other than White. The family members were all pro-Afrikaner National Party support-ers. They saw Willie as a reprobate who had let the side down. They rejected Lydiah even though she had lighter skin and smoother hair than most of them.

"Your family must have dark DNA in their past," Lydiah some-times made fun of Willie.

"Too bloody right, my love. The Germishuys' were a wild bunch. They slept with anyone in those early days, whereas I'm all about love for you."

Deep in thought, Lydiah shivered when she came to a set of fa-miliar intersecting gravel pathways. The gravel crunching underfoot reminded her of her close call with death in 1976 at the funeral of a primary school student shot in the head by troops. Lydiah was shot in the leg as the police dispersed the mourners, seven of whom, lost their lives that day.

She could still see the face of the White policeman behind the gun when he tried to kill her where she now stood. Her belly muscles went taut as she relived the nightmarish, painful crawl along the gravel paths to escape. Scarred knees bore testimony to her funeral experience. 1976 was the year when Black cemeteries became police killing fields[4].

Lydiah stopped to cross herself after briefly praying to Jim Davids, her saviour on the day. Jim had recommended she go to his GP friend, Stanley Gershon, with her injury rather than run the gauntlet of arrest while attending the local hospital. Her gut-wrenching trauma worsened with her rescuer's untimely death in Stanley's arms after her detective father shot Jim during a confrontation over his serial knife assaults on township paedophiles and the death of a teacher.

LYDIAH GREETED HER two sisters with their spouses at the graves. The rowdy bunch, all in shorts, soon lifted her spirits. Suzanne had already run off to join her cousins, who scrambled over or around the headstones nearby.

At the end of the formalities to pay respect to the dead, the family seated themselves on the low wall around the family plot to chat. On a blanket lay bottles of soft drinks, fruit with a few packets of Romany cream biscuits surrounding two buckets of Kentucky fried chicken; all were family favourites. The children flitted about from food or drinks to their play.

"I enjoy watching these cousins muck about here the way they do," said Willie with a broad smile. Willie whooped as he fell in behind the ribbon of headstone-hopping cousins. Lydiah watched with a smile. Like their parents, the children ranged in colour from rich chocolate to Suzanne, the fairest. During their family gatherings, Lydiah saw the South Africa of a future she hoped to see one day.

"We missed you two during the last three gatherings," said Liz, the eldest of the sisters. "Now that you are back, will we finally have formal wedding bells or not?"

Lydiah sipped at her ginger beer. She looked at Willie, who nodded his head slowly without speaking. Lydiah stiffened and raised her head, directing her gaze towards the distant mountains before speaking.

"Yeah. We have often discussed the issue. Thanks to Father Laughton at the time, we are married in the eyes of the Lord. We can now sleep together legally, even be married, but the Group Areas Act is still in place, so, technically, we'd have to live apart!" She glanced at her lap, where her hands were in tight balls.

"Until we live in a more normal society, we'll remain as we are," said Willie. "If we wish, we can stay at a five-star hotel because that's legal. We only need discounted rates to afford them."

Soft laughter rippled through the group who were familiar with Willy's mischievous sense of humour. Lydiah's family all regarded him as their adopted brother.

"I knew it," said Liz. "Now we'll have no normal marriage in an abnormal society!"

"Well put, Liz," said Willie. "But the way things are going, we may be married sooner than we think."

"I'm not sure I share your enthusiasm about any quick changes," said Lydiah.

The conversation drifted from the serious to the trivial, often interrupted by hungry or thirsty children searching for food or drink.

"We worry about the school kids," said Chris, Liz's husband, a school teacher. "Sadly, students have taken on the 'no education before liberation' stance. What kind of liberation will we have with illiterates as an end-product? Even their inferior education is better than none."

"We campaigned against the same issue during my student days at UWC," said Lydiah. She pulled a face. "It's tragic how it's still attractive to so many students."

"At least our evening adult literacy classes in Crossroads are still popular," said Willie. As volunteer teachers, they taught in two modified shipping containers split into two classes each. They had resumed their Wednesday sessions, allowing them to reconnect with Stanley Gershon and Fay Ismail at the new SACLA[5] clinic opposite their night school. Before leaving the country, the four of them had become close friends. The former clinic had been destroyed by government forces during the Crossroads Fires of 1986.

"As much as we enjoy our teaching in Crossroads, the tension there is much higher than when we left in 1985."

"Yes," said Liz. "Since the Fires of 1986, there are more frequent clashes between the State-supported Contra forces against ANC or UDF members in Crossroads. With the escalation in deaths in the townships, you two must take care." Liz's face was a mask of furrowed lines as she looked at Willie and Lydiah.

The afternoon wind blew a sandy haze around the graves. Their discourse continued as they expressed their concerns intermingled with their hopes for a better future in a democratic country. Despite the heavy subject matter, Lydiah relished her family time despite her nagging doubts. *Have we done the right thing by returning to live in South Africa with Suzanne?*

CHAPTER 7: TRUTH EXTRACTION, KOEVOET-STYLE

March 1988

LEEU'S NINE YEARS IN Koevoet saw the growth of their successful strike force from a band of one hundred to a thousand-strong unit with three hundred White officers; most of the seven hundred local Ovambos were turned ex-PLAN terrorists.

For those they captured, the only hope of survival was to become a member of Koevoet. Once in front of a trench, captured PLAN fighters were told, 'Join us or die, shoot or be shot!' White officers stood well behind a prisoner with their drawn guns pointed at the fighter who had to kill a fellow detainee before him with a gun containing a single bullet. In a form of Russian roulette, the prisoner had to pull the trigger until the gun went off. Most joined rather than land in the trench where they burned the corpses; a bulldozer covered the burial pit the following day.

Leeu felt animated on his trips with Koevoet, who operated without the restrictions of standard police or military ethical conventions. Today they were off to one of their peripheral bush camps to interrogate a terrorist who had refused to tell them the truth so far.

"The men tell me he's resisted their best efforts to talk, so it's time to let him embrace nature," said a grinning Commander van Wyk to Leeu.

When they arrived at the West Kavango camp after a dusty, bouncing Land Rover ride on the pot-holed tracks, they bound the prisoner to the front bumper of the mine-proof Casspir[6] vehicle. His feet dangled from the bumper to which they had tied his widely spread knees. His clothes were already splattered with blood. Commander van Wyk opened the scored visor of a heavily scratched crash helmet on the man's head. His puffy, bruised eyes were from his earlier interrogation. After a couple of minutes of talking to the prisoner who swore at van Wyk, the officer spat into the helmet before he slammed close the visor.

"He still won't talk. We'll show him. These fucking terrs (terrorists) think they are tough. We'll see while we drive."

The ever-present acacia bushes had won a healthy respect from Leeu during his time with Koevoet. Their tiny yellow pom-pom flowers were visible around the camp; their faint, honeyed scent filled the air. Leeu's pulse always quickened at the start of these interrogation trips. There was a unique pleasure in obtaining the truth using such a simple technique. When they drove the vehicle through the first of the acacia bushes outside the base campsite, the screams from their prisoner were nerve-wracking. Every bush they went through caused the most hysterical wailing. As accustomed as Leeu was to inflicting agony, these truth drives always had him shaking by the time they stopped. He felt chilled to the core by the man's constant shrieking, accentuated whenever they drove through another thorny growth. During the drive, they kept all the sliding windows closed.

They scrambled from the vehicle after driving over the fourth bush. The ten-foot-high growths were equally broad; slim, paired thorns as long as six centimetres covered the branches almost to their tips. The sweet-thorn acacia thorns had the longest and sharpest spikes. He recalled how one of these thorns had penetrated the thick rubber sole of his sandal when he was a teenager visiting an uncle's farm in the semi-desert Karroo. From the indigenous locals, he learned to chew the sweet, firm gum of the bush as a treat. Now he saw the plant as the quintessential truth device.

Leeu remained awestruck by the way the thorns made a blood-spattered mess of the man who blubbered incoherently after the troop carrier halted. The thorns had slashed him everywhere. His clothing was in shreds, his groin a grisly mess. The helmet enabled the person to speak after his ordeal.

Van Wyk seemed satisfied with the answers he directed at the bound man after he had removed the helmet. With his gun, he shot the prisoner through the head. The body slumped forward on the bumper, where the limbs twitched a few times. No more shots were necessary.

Van Wyk turned to Leeu. "I always tell them we will go twice as long the next time. I never knew anyone who did not talk immediately." They preferred the lower bushes as the tall growths could tear the prisoners apart. Van Wyk lit two cigarettes facing into a stiff breeze, then handed one to Leeu.

"He told me where there's a stash of arms with a few fighters," said van Wyk. We'll go after them tonight to strike them hard at sunrise."

Relying on speed, they would follow a group of terrorists, guided by their Ovambo trackers, who were the best in the world. These men could see things Leeu could not recognise even when they pointed the signs to him. Once they returned to bush camp, they placed their kill in a trench they called the Vulture Restaurant. Over a few days, the circling birds of prey sent a message visible to all from great distances away. At night, the cackling laugh of hungry hyenas outside the fence reinforced the message. They finally burnt the remains using wood soaked with diesel fuel.

On Leeu's first trip, van Wyk had pointed to the bush around them. "Out there, people know what's happening. They must fear they could be in the next smoke column or become vulture turds."

Leeu thrived on these Koevoet moments as they defined him and White Power. *White is right! White is might!*

CHAPTER 8: NECKLACING

November 1988

A FEW BLOCKS AWAY FROM his home in Crossroads, close to Klipfontein Road, Thembani Dlamini watched as a bloodied victim stumbled along the narrow street; his hands were bound behind him with a twisted double strand of insulated white electric wire. The crowd had attacked their man when he exited the station after returning from work. Two policemen at the station did not intervene. Instead, they had backed off into the shadows.

The victim's shirt had been ripped off him; blood gelled on his body from his face where a brick had smashed in his left eye socket. Blood ran from the unseeing eye to a still-bleeding mouth where the same blow had removed teeth. The victim's injuries nauseated Thembani, who instead looked at the exposed fibrous casing of the worn tyre he was wheeling. Shadowy figures ran around the injured man. Have they not had enough sport with him tonight? Yet Thembani stayed on his course; there was more to come in which he had a role to play.

Knives flashed. Many wanted blood; the mob's call was the dreaded 'Mazif isinja' (The 'dogs must die'). They dragged the victim between the pondoks along the muddy track leading towards an informal soccer ground - a mix of sand with scattered patches of weeds flattened by daily groups of players. Here, an ecstatic crowd in need of distractions from the shanty dwellers' daily lot usually applauded the weekend dribbling skills of their local team. Tonight, though, the same spectators wanted blood, not goals.

The victim slid again, a result of the recent rains. Knives prodded him towards the field where he would be the evening's sport.

Thembani hated the practice of necklacing, yet he found its seductive allure hard to resist. In the African township conflicts, the use of petrol-fired, flaming tyres over victims' necks had become an increasingly fashionable punishment against political opposition groups. Starting in 1985 in the Eastern Cape, the practice soon blighted the struggle against the government throughout the country. The call 'Mazif isinja' became a popular Comrades' refrain when angry mobs necklaced State-appointed councillors or other collaborators, especially the Witdoek traitors. In turn, the Witdoeke retaliated against Comrades or UDF members in an escalating number of attacks. Everyone seemed to be doing it; Thembani heard of victims set alight by the Balaclava Gang, believed to be part of a security police death squad.

Still torn between leaving or staying, Thembani, with his balding tyre, followed along the narrow track partly obscured by the surrounding pondoks in the gloom of early evening.

Agitated people shouted aloud, "Traitor! Death to the informer."

"We know how to deal with these snakes in the grass."

"Viva Comrades, viva!"

Cries of "Amandla, ngawethu! (Power, to the people!)" followed as Black Power salutes passed through the rabble in a Mexican wave of fists.

Thembani knew nothing about the man. Most likely, he was one of the Witdoeke. In the victim's absence, an informal court would have found him guilty before sentencing him. Collaboration was a difficult charge to deny. Someone with a grudge against a person could start a whispering campaign; simply talking to a policeman could be interpreted as collusion. The main necklacing targets were informers or police collaborators. Black soldiers or policemen were more difficult to access; likewise, the councillors with their armed Witdoeke or kitskonstabel (instant constables) bodyguards. The nobodies of the township were more accessible.

Way above the mob's cacophony, Thembani heard a female ululate with a couple of answering calls. The voice pierced through his brain. The evocation of ancestral spirits was a signal to spur men on to battle. Thembani was more inclined to flee, though his entrancement propelled him on, rolling before him the victim's necklace-to-be.

The raucous crowd force-marched the stranger to the centre of the field, where there were three patches of blackened grass. Thembani shuddered at the thought the man would become the fourth blemish by sunrise. *Will the man be thinking of his fate? His family?*

Chants of 'Amandla ngawethu' continued to resonate around the field. The scrambled shacks formed a rough ring around the amphitheatre of destitution. Finally, they stopped at a spot close to where flour marked the centre circle of a soccer match. The man dropped his head. *Is he crying?* No one would have seen his blood-stained tears; no one would have cared.

A yellow plastic container of fuel was placed alongside him, with the cap already removed.

'Where's the necklace?' called his chief tormentor.

A tremulous Thembani moved forward, rolling the tyre alongside him before he placed the deadly ring over the man's shoulders. In the evening gloom, the victim lifted his bloodied head.

Then, with horror, Thembani heard the man call out: "Thembani Dlamini, it is I, Zuko. We work at G's Builders. Help me, please!" Thembani stared at him with wide eyes before he hastily withdrew himself from the area with his head held low as they lifted the can to pour the petrol into the tilted tyre and over Zuko's bowed head. A spluttering Zuko coughed with his eyes closed tight as the smell of the fuel permeated the air.

There was raucous laughter around the field as the clamour increased. From his position now at the fringe of the crowd, Thembani heard the unmistakable chanting of people toyi-toying. "Ay, ay, ay! Viva, viva, viva!" The popular dance of protest was now Zuko's dance of death.

The call "Mazif izinja" passed like a ripple through the expectant horde.

Thembani knew Zuko, a labourer from the Ciskei. He was a migrant worker with a young family whom Zuko had not seen in two years, though he had plans to bring them to Cape Town soon to join him. Zuko's name meant glory, which would not be his destiny. Thembani turned to flee from what would soon be a gruesome scene.

A Bic lighter would probably be used. Thembani did not relish the idea the labourer would soon be transformed into the crazed, screaming, fuel-driven flames stumbling around for several drawn-out minutes. The next day, the kids would again play soccer on the field. Dribbling prowess with the messages of vengeance, violence or death were learnt from an early age. On their way home, Thembani had once seen children munch at their lollies while they kicked at a few charred remnants left behind after the body had been removed. Dear Lord, spare Zuko such a fate!

His macabre interest in necklacing did not extend to watching the whole process; dying was not his attraction. The burning always smelt like a barbeque gone wrong. He had not expected the quiet Zuko to be the night's benefactor of the tyre he had sourced from a local car wrecker's yard. He did not want to see Zuko become a human fireball from his necklace of spluttering conflagration feeding a thick column of spiralling black smoke while flames would sprout from his darkened head like a red-orange halo. He closed his ears to block out Zuko's final screams; no doubt the fire-silhouetted mouth, opened wide, would soon be silent before Zuko tumbled to the ground, first onto his knees, then into a prone position on the ground. Thembani's body shook, and his head spun as he dry-retched on the sand past the group of shanties.

Thembani had to leave immediately; he promised himself his third episode would be his last. He worried how Nkosinati was in the dark about his past experience and present magnetism with necklacing. *Is this my penance following my actions on Newlands' station platform two years ago?*

CHAPTER 9: THE PEACE MARCH

13 September 1989

FAY SNUGGLED INTO STANLEY on the seaside bench, seeking more than a bit of warmth. They had finished their regular Sunday run along the paved promenade from Green Point to Sea Point, then back again. Behind them, the distinctive square, red-and-white-banded Green Point lighthouse starkly contrasted with the clustered low-rise apartment buildings. Joggers or walkers were already enjoying the sunny break from the recent rains. The winter snow caps still clung to the distant easterly Helderberg Mountains as Fay breathed in the early morning sea smell. The sun reflected off Table Bay, where the flat grey hump of Robben Island projected from a waveless blue sea.

"Even though he's no longer there, I can never look at the Island without thinking about our leader," said Fay. Now in Paarl, Nelson Mandela had spent eighteen years on the Island before his transfer to Pollsmoor prison. Since President de Klerk replaced Botha a month earlier, Mandela's release was in the offing.

"Maybe I'm a pessimist, Stanley, but nothing de Klerk says sounds promising." Fay grimaced. "So, what about the UDF's Peace march on Wednesday?"

Over the past six weeks, the UDF's MDM (Mass Democratic Movement) had mobilised Blacks to flood Whites-only hospitals, beaches, buses, trains, park benches, swimming pools, toilets, waiting rooms, post offices ... Due to their work commitments, the two had not attended the other major protests at Whites-only beaches.

"I can take off from work. What about you?" asked Fay.

"Jayantilal can mind the rooms while I'm away in the afternoon."

"I hope it's more peaceful than last week's parliamentary elections," said Fay. The police had killed more than twenty protesters in Cape Town during recent general elections. In a historical first-time vote with Whites, those classified as Coloureds and Indians voted to establish the new tricameral government; Africans could not. Most Blacks boycotted the ballot.

"With those elections, they give us crumbs while holding onto the loaf of bread," snorted Stanley.

ON WEDNESDAY, FAY AND Stanley collected Lydiah Adams and Willie Germishuys on their way to the march. All of them were in jeans with long-sleeved tops rolled down against the cool of the kilometre-long walk from St George's Cathedral to the Grand Parade.

"Well," said Stanley, "It's wonderful you could come. Where's Suzanne?"

"Because of the violence after last week's election shenanigans, we left Suzanne with her aunt Liz," said Willie.

"How do you two feel about today?" asked Lydiah.

"My stomach is filled with jittery butterflies," said Fay.

Recent peaceful demonstrations with a sit-down in the central city streets had not ended well when police fired rubber bullets and tear gas, followed by water cannons with a purple dye, after which they arrested anyone with a purple stain.

Willie sniggered. "I was surprised when the TV news showed how one protester jumped on top of the truck to turn the water cannon onto the surrounding buildings. We can see the dye as high as four storeys over there," he pointed. "Look at the graffiti. 'The purple shall govern.' says so much about the character of Capetonians, which I missed while overseas."

"I had my fill of drama at a schoolgirl's funeral in '76," said Lydiah, who shuddered visibly. "I can do without any today." Willie put his arm over her shoulder to hold her close.

Stanley chose a car park close to St George's Cathedral. When they walked along Adderley Street towards the Cathedral on the corner, Fay looked at the oak-tree-lined Government Avenue walkway between Parliament House on the left and Cape Town Gardens on the right. "It's such a peaceful walk in the Avenue with the oak trees in their spring plumage," said Fay. "And there is so much violence in the country, so we, the majority, can have a say in the big building over here," she pointed towards Parliament House.

"I was about here during the '76 demonstrations when I saw a tourist photographing squirrels at this bench here," said Fay. "At the same time, I could hear police shooting at students a few blocks away. Talk about surreal!"

"Too true. As a UWC student in 1976, our protest marches often ended in clouds of tear gas, police violence or death," said Lydiah. "But look, thousands are outside the church; we'll never get in."

The sizeable crowd filled the Cathedral and the surrounding pavements.

"At least there are no police to be seen," said Willie.

"Ahh, look!" said Fay. "Tutu is leading the group leaving the Church. He's my hero. Amandla, ngawethu!" She fisted the air as her friends responded to her call.

The purple-cloaked Archbishop Tutu was arm-in-arm with Mayor Gordon Oliver, alongside Reverend Frank Chikane, Moulana Farid Esack, Nazeem Mohammed and Allan Boesak."

"This epochal moment must be the biggest gathering Cape Town has ever seen," said Stanley.

Fay could see Stanley's excitement; his whole demeanour was ecstatic, as was hers. "There are ANC flags all over the place." Banned
photos of Oliver Tambo and Nelson Mandela were everywhere.
"Ohh! I love it all!" Fay felt like her chest would burst with joy.

"People of all colours are here," said Willie. "Ah! Here they
come." Part of the fist-waving crowd came past, with their toyi-toyi
steps all in unison. "Viva, viva. Ay, Ay. Ay!" Willie joined the chant
with his eyes aglow as his feet stomped in tune with theirs.

"Oh, Willie," said Lydiah. "You're so funny. Even in our UK flat,
he would toyi-toyi whenever he saw the news clips. Now he can toyi-
toyi in the flesh with the rest of them," she applauded softly.

A panting Willie returned to their group. "Toyi-toyi is so em-
powering! You can feel the collective energy in the harmonious foot-
stomping."

Already ahead of them, the seven-lane Adderley Street was
packed with people making their slow way towards the City Hall.
Home-made UDF banners were everywhere; many wanted a halt to
police killings. When they entered Darling Street three blocks down,
Fay felt sardined in with the tall central city buildings on each side.

The daily street photographers outside the central Post Office
building were not around to take snapshots of people. The ancient
Ackermans clothing retail store on Plein Street's corner had closed,
as had metal-shuttered shops nearby. Fay had a sense of relief as they
inched their way along to where the lower buildings now picture-
framed the Grand Parade's single row of palm trees on the left, with
the lower reaches of Devil's Peak in the distance and the ornate City
Hall building to the right.

Fay's heart raced as she squeezed Stanley's hand. Lydiah and
Willie also held hands. The crowd jostled them as freedom songs
erupted all around. Along with thousands, Fay joined in the singing
of the banned *We Shall Overcome*. Finally, the four friends stopped
in the middle of Darling Street, virtually in front of the City Hall en-

trance, where they stood in the welcome shade of one of the tall palm trees. The Hall's limestone building had distinctive Italian Renaissance-style Edwardian architecture. At half the size, the clock tower was modelled on London's Big Ben.

"Wow!" said Lydiah. "Walking less than a kilometre has taken us over an hour." The Grand Parade behind them was packed with people.

"Look at that!" Willie pointed to where a White youth, with his face covered by his jacket, tied an ANC flag to the wrought-iron balustrade between the imposing red-brown marble pillars at the Hall's entrance. The crowd applauded his action. "Besides the flag, we must be breaking every law covered by the State of Emergency regulations today."

In her life, Fay had never experienced such joy. "This is history in the making," she said with gleaming eyes.

"Our time is nigh," Stanley responded.

A buzz went through the fervently cheering crowd when the distinctive purple cloak of Archbishop Tutu appeared alongside his entourage on the balcony above the City Hall's main entrance. The speakers' voices boomed forth from a bullhorn.

The popular dimple-cheeked Reverend Alan Boesak proclaimed to much applause how de Klerk would be the last White President of South Africa.

Tutu declared the march as a victory towards peace. "We are the rainbow people of God! We are unstoppable! Nobody can stop us on our march to victory! No one, no guns, nothing! Nothing will stop us, for we are marching to freedom! Mr de Klerk, if you know what is good for you, then join us in the struggle for a new South Africa. We are unstoppable!"

While the rapturous crowd applauded Tutu, Fay, and many people around her burst into tears. "The man is so amazing," she managed to utter while she clung to Stanley, who held her close.

"It's the first time he called us a rainbow people." Stanley turned to hug Fay.

Willie and Lydiah were in a huddle beside them, as were many other couples around them. The tumultuous crowd waved and clapped while many toyi-toyed as one; their freedom songs heralded change. Cape Town had never before seen anything like it. The area where they had military parades during colonial days had been transformed into a victory display by tens of thousands of people.

IT WAS LATE AFTERNOON when the foursome eventually returned to collect Stanley's vehicle. Outside the parking garage, Willie bumped into a stout man with a woman by his side.

"Thembani Dlamini!" exclaimed Willie.

"How lovely to see you," Lydiah almost shrieked as she hugged the couple.

"It's nice to see you too, Willie and Lydiah," said Thembani. "How are you, Dr Gershon?" he smiled, his eyes lowered; he seemed guarded in Stanley's presence.

"It's been a while, Thembani. I hope you'll call me Stanley one day. You remember Fay?"

"Yes. By the way, meet Nkosinati, my wife," said Thembani.

They exchanged firm handshakes with broad smiles. Fay recognised Thembani from the time of his hip injury on the same day she showed Stanley The Herald report of security police chief Hammer van Zyl's suicide by shooting in 1986.

"Was the march something else or what!" exclaimed Willie.

"It was certainly uplifting," Nkosinati beamed from ear to ear. "I loved every minute. We arrived in time to hear the brief service in the packed Cathedral, where we had to stand close to the doors."

"I enjoyed Tutu's speech. My only concern is if we mix all those rainbow-coloured people, then we'll all end up White." Thembani guffawed aloud, with the others joining his infectious laughter.

"With your sense of humour, I need to keep you away from Willie," said Lydiah.

"There's nothing wrong with us!" said Willie with his arm around a grinning Thembani's shoulder.

Fay looked at her watch. "I hate to spoil the party, but work calls. Thembani and Nkosinati, keep well."

Back in the car Stanley started the vehicle as Willie began singing through the open car window. "We are the Rainbow Nation!"

"I'm not too sure about the singing, Caruso, though I hope they can hear you over there in Parliament House," said Lydiah.

"It was nice to see Thembani and Nkosinati," said Lydiah. "He must be the brightest student I ever came across."

"I've never met a person with such a photographic memory," said Willie. "He had been wasting away as a caddy until he joined UWC. As a part-time student, he achieved honours in English last year and will probably do it again this year."

After they dropped off Willie and Lydiah, Stanley and Fay sat briefly in the car outside Fay's pharmacy on Halt Road.

"Thembani looks happy," said Fay.

"At least he was not a patient today," said Stanley. "It must be Nkosinati. But, like me, every happy man needs a wonderful woman in his life." Stanley leaned over to kiss Fay goodbye.

When Stanley departed, a lingering Fay glanced past the empty lot across from her pharmacy on Halt Road, Elsies River, two blocks away from Stanley's rooms. Table Mountain and Devil's Peak had never looked better; the clear mountains looked like a bright portent for the future.

CHAPTER 10: PRISON RELEASE - DINGANE'S DAY

16 December 1989

IVAN WAS RELEASED ON Dingane's Day[7]. In the 1838 Battle of Blood River, shields and spears were no match against guns and cannons. More than thirty thousand warriors, led by their King Dingane, lost their lives in a battle in which not a single Afrikaner died. The attack, led by Andries Pretorius, avenged the February deaths of 100 Voortrekkers (Afrikaner settlers), including their leader Piet Retief. The victory marked a significant turning point in South Africa's history by crushing the militant Zulus, who had refused to have any settlers or missionaries live amongst them.

During Ivan's twelve years in prison, the political detainees always celebrated Dingane's day, coinciding with the 1961 formation of the ANC's militant wing, MK (Umkhonto we Sizwe). In the 1960 Sharpeville[8] carnage, police killed over one hundred demonstrators, followed by a draconian State of Emergency allowing them to detain tens of thousands of Blacks during peaceful anti-pass-law protests around the country.

The sun was pleasantly warm on Ivan's skin on a cloudless day without a breeze in the usually windy city. Ivan felt suppressed relief when he passed through the Pollsmoor prison gates. After his time inside, he had forgotten what the outside roads looked like. Pine and eucalyptus trees lined Steenberg Road, partly concealing the prison's precast, concrete-slabbed fence topped with rolls of razor wire. He inhaled deeply at the aroma of freedom from the trees. Across the road, one of Cape Town's oldest vineyards sported green grapes needing more summer sun to ripen.

To the left, the road curved southwards to where the Muizenberg Mountains angled towards False Bay's Whites-only Muizenberg beach, undeniably Cape Town's finest. To the north were glimpses of the Constantiaberg range directed towards Devil's Peak and Table Mountain, often obscured by tall trees shielding the opulent homes of leafy White suburbs.

Ivan felt comfortable in his faded Levi's blue jeans with white teeshirt, both not worn since his arrest another lifetime ago. He intended to let his curly hair grow till his scalp itched. Grey streaks flecked the previously dark hair. He wanted the longer strand of hair to grow again down the middle of his forehead.

Ivan's elongated face was more lined than when he entered Pollsmoor. He still had no fat on him. His hazel brown eyes were intense, though the prison years had given them a hardness, a look of existing, of endurance, of pulling through to the end. They easily smouldered, especially when he thought of the wasted time suspended in survival mode with the most hardened criminals from a marginalised Cape Flats environment where they bred like rabbits.

Ivan looked forward to seeing his father, who was to collect him. His cellmate Sammi had trimmed Ivan's beard. He knew his mother would prefer him clean-shaven; removing his beard would come later, after his task to annul his gang membership, usually meant to be permanent. Ivan had a message to deliver to Yster's partner Ses (Six), the Elsies River Achar-American chapter leader.

Once outside, he looked at his ageing father; his mother had chosen to stay home. Prison had a way to suppress and destroy warm emotions. Ivan was not surprised at his lack of feeling. Prison time had made him into a block of hard, cold granite with haunting memories troubling him most days. He had to be rid of this part of himself to return to normal. He gripped his father around the shoulders, consoled by a stirring of sorts as the frail man's tears flowed freely when he rested his head on Ivan's chest.

Ivan sat in the back of the Austin 1100 alongside his father with Mr Bailey, their next-door neighbour, driving. Along De Waal Drive, they passed the leafy, White suburbs of Constantia, Wynberg, Claremont and Newlands, some of Cape Town's most expensive real estate, from which thousands of Blacks had been evicted under the axe of the Group Areas Act. Ivan looked with a sense of nostalgia when they slipped past the University of Cape Town on the left.

"I hope you'll continue your studies there," said his father, pointing towards the university buildings.

"I hope so too, Dad. We'll see."

They turned off onto Settler's Way to exit at the Athlone Power station, whose smoke columns rose straight into a brilliant blue sky. Along Jan Smuts Drive, the luxurious White homes in Pinelands on the left contrasted starkly with the rows of African men's barracks opposite them in Langa township. A rail track with a barbed-wire-topped, diamond-mesh fence on each side provided the inevitable barrier between the races. To Ivan, the fence was more than a physical barrier; it went to the heart of separatist apartheid. Ivan clenched his teeth, an old, involuntary reflex. Prison could not destroy emotions like anger, outrage, or hatred. Hostility, part of his survival, had provided the original impetus of his revolutionary zeal. His response to seeing Langa township did not surprise him, though he now needed to channel his energy in a more positive direction than before.

He asked his father questions about family and friends. When they turned into Halt Road from Viking Way, he saw how four-storied, sub-economic housing complexes had replaced many of the original informal shanties as they drove home towards Eleventh Avenue. He could not suppress his anger at the stark contrast to the suburbs at the start of his trip. Nothing had changed; if anything, the recently built unpainted breeze-block flats looked worse than the shanties they had replaced. Similar scenes were the reason he had become an activist in the first place. He noticed how tightly balled his hands were.

"It looks like a council-built slum has replaced the original shanty slum," said Ivan.

"Too true, Ivan. The council built their so-called in-fill housing with those four-storey barracks over there. The local population has almost doubled while crime is much worse than before, so you must be extra careful on the streets these days." His father shook his head. "Your mother and I never go out at night like before. We even stopped our weekly visit to the movies."

The overall tiredness of one of the most impoverished areas on the Cape Flats remained, though there seemed to be more listless, unemployed youth hanging around and interfering with the passing girls. Graffiti-covered walls signalled the streets' gang affiliations, as did the dress code of the youngsters - ordinarily red, white, and blue, often with the American flag on shirts, tight headscarves, or bandanas of the dominant Achar-American gang members.

"We are in the middle of a gang war." His father lifted both hands. "The HighLifers are trying to muscle in on the Achar-Americans' territory. They have been at each other over the years now, driven by the need to control the Mandrax-*dagga* (cannabis) market," his father said with a sigh.

"Guns are much more common than when you went to prison. The police are useless; the gangsters are the only authority here."

Ivan was aware of how they collected taxes from all businesses while the police, who were not interested in everyday crime, either worked with the gangs or were there only to suppress anti-state activity.

"In prison, I heard inmates say the police supply the gangs with guns, or they drop off drug supplies to them," said Ivan.

"The drugs keep the kids in la-la-land - they fight each other's gangs, not the State the way you or others tried. We suspect the gangs act as State hitmen with a few top UDF members assassinated recently."

"Hey! The government has a lot to answer for."

"So true, my boy."

IVAN LOOKED AT A RELATIVELY quiet street when they approached the family home in the failing light of late afternoon. A few new, modest family homes added to minor changes in their road. His mother came to the car to greet him. Like his father had done, she clung to him, shedding tears in his arms. He felt her pain as he always had. Prison life had not destroyed the warmth of his mother, how he needed it. He kissed her on each cheek. With an aching heart, Ivan shed no tears while he held her close.

"I'm okay, Ma. I'm okay." The stirrings of a smothered inner self struggled to emerge. He felt comforted knowing his mother could arouse those more hidden emotions. At least they were still there, somewhere; he wanted more; he needed it. Ivan wished he could cry, yet he knew he could not.

With a loud shriek from the front door, Colleen, his only sibling, rushed to greet him. She was all over him with her kisses, her sobbing, and her shouting. Again, he sensed a pleasant inner stirring. She had gained a bit of weight over the years. A two-year-old child followed her, holding onto Colleen's skirt. Like Ivan, the boy and Colleen shared the curly hair with a cleft in the chin.

Ivan went onto his knees to hold his arms to Lance. Without any hesitation, the nephew he did not know threw himself into his uncle's arms. An overwhelmed Ivan held onto the bundle of giggly laughter who called Ivan's name many times over. The boy's curly-haired head snuggled deep into Ivan's chest. Ivan laughed along with Lance. He started to revel in the warmth spreading outwards from his icy core. Here was a bundle of love full of giggles with two deep dimples. His heart went out to Lance, who clung to Ivan's chest with shrieks of delight as Ivan wondered who the father was.

"Where's Fluffy, Mom?"

His mother raised her hand heavenward. "He's gone, Ivan. He died three years ago."

"When? How? He would only be thirteen years old now. Maltese poodles live more than fifteen."

No one replied. All looked uncomfortable. *Am I missing something here?*

His father interjected. "Let's go in, son. We all have so much to catch up. Your mother has made your favourite dish."

"Oh! *Bobotie* (Cape Malay minced meatloaf), I hope. With yellow rice, pumpkin, and sweet potato? Tell me it's so!"

"It's so, my boy. Followed by trifle, of course."

All of them laughed. The dishes were family favourites done to perfection by his mother. These were the moments he needed to return to normal, yet the whole family seemed troubled. A somewhat distracted, Ivan rubbed at his ridged thumbnails. The stark physical reminder of his prison time with his worst tormentor now tumbled around his brain with the unknown family drama. *What are they hiding from me?*

CHAPTER 11: SEARCH AND DESTROY - DAY OF THE COVENANT

16 December 1989

LEEU KLOPPERS WAS READY to go on his last outing with Koevoet. The ten years since he had joined them had passed so fast. When the Commander addressed his White colleagues, an already saddened Leeu had never before seen van Wyk look so animated.

"On our mission today, let us remember our Day of the Covenant," said a solemn van Wyk. "I will read the vow our people made after the Battle of Blood River. Many of us are on our last mission today as our beloved Koevoet will soon be disbanded thanks to those damned government lackeys in Pretoria bowing to the whims of the fucking United Nations."

He cleared his throat, his eyes tearing. "We stand here before the Holy God of heaven and earth to make a vow to Him that, if He will protect us and give our enemy into our hand, we shall keep this day and date every year as a day of thanksgiving, like a sabbath. Amen."

All the officers crossed themselves.

"Sabbath it is. May it be successful." Many of the officers applauded, waving their submachine guns in the air.

For Leeu's last search-and-destroy mission, they were after an armed group close to the Angolan border. The forty Ovambo, with eight White officers, took off in four mine proof Casspirs with two Blesbok logistics vehicles carrying enough supplies to last a week in the bush. The hunt was on once the trackers detected any spoor. They could call in helicopter gunships from a base nearby to assist in attacks on groups or strafe a village.

"That's how we control these murderous terrs!" Van Wyk had explained on one of Leeu's earliest trips. Over the years, he had learned to admire van Wyk, whose fervour matched his own.

PLAN (People's Liberation Army of Namibia) fighters had a formidable reputation. They knew torture or death awaited them if caught alive. "This is a no-mercy fight to the end," said van Wyk one day. "They know it. We know it! We have to stop these communists. They don't believe in God the way we do. They're not educated like us; they just do as they are told. We built the bloody country; now they want our land, our mines, our women. Our philosophy is simple - he who shoots first survives." Here was a significant part of why Leeu enjoyed his years with Koevoet.

Their trip was a standard gung-ho ride. At high speed, they passed through villages where children, adults and dogs kept out of sight as the throaty diesel engines could be heard before the Casspirs entered the village. They overtook a convoy of South African Defence Force vehicles while hooting or waving at them. With Koevoet's higher kill rates than the army boys, the two groups disliked each other.

Their open vehicle rooftops allowed many to stand on the seats to survey their surroundings. Leeu had learned to recognise the fauna of the arid semidesert. The thorny acacias had proved their worth as a truth extraction tool. Most of the grass was still dry, awaiting the overdue summer rainfall. The land was relatively flat, with scattered hills or rocks to break the featureless terrain.

Once they were close to their target area, the trackers dismounted, then walked as they crisscrossed each other ahead of the four

Casspirs driving about fifty metres apart. They were now in hunting mode. The trackers often pointed at virtually invisible telltale marks in the undergrowth using their metre-long sticks cut from tree branches. They soon concluded they were following seven men trying to cover their tracks by sweeping the ground with leafy twigs.

When they were close enough, two armed Ovambo groups broke away to head off their quarry on each side before the leading Koevoet group attacked them from behind with rocket-propelled grenade launchers or automatic rifles. At full speed in a more central position, the noisy Casspirs then advanced to add heavy machine-gun fire to the action.

Leeu likened the attack formation to a bull's head, with the Ovambo infantrymen lined on the sides like horns. The famed Zulu King Shaka, Africa's Napoleon, devised a similar deployment of his troops' assegai-based attacks in the early 1800s. His superior fighting troops used long shields with short stabbing spears to improve their close combat killing rates.

Leeu, seated behind the Casspir's roof-top-mounted machine gun, thrilled to the power of his weapon. His spirits soared with the way the weapon cut a lethal swathe through the terrorist campsite. He felt like the soloist in an orchestral concerto of death with the surrounding bursts of automatic gunfire or rocket-propelled grenade explosions. The sour, ammonia-like smell of cordite in the air with a sharp, pungent taste on his tongue added to the moment's exhilaration. He was as hot as his gun when the short-lived attack was over. *This is when I feel truly alive!*

The troops went around to put a final bullet through the head of each body. One of the Ovambo trackers had been killed by a landmine blast. There were no other troop casualties of a fitting tribute to their sacred day.

The men regrouped at the destroyed campsite. The seven terrorist's bodies in their PLAN camouflage gear lay on the sand alongside one of the Casspirs. An assortment of weapons was in a pile, mainly Kalashnikov rifles, pistols, hand grenades and a few anti-tank mines.

Van Wyk surveyed their handiwork before addressing his men. "I must thank all of you today as we stuck to the Vow while honouring our Day of the Covenant." Many of the White officers fired their automatic rifles into the air. The rest of them high-fived each other. "Now, men, we need to make our routine statement to the villagers on the way back."

While troops loaded the captured weapons, others lashed the bodies onto the vehicles to display them as drive-by viewing when they passed through villages on their return to base camp. There, the bodies would be left in the Vulture Restaurant for a week before they burned any remains before burial. The leading Casspir had two bodies strapped face-up across the front hood with another over each of the front wheels' high expanded bumpers.

The final three bodies, tied to the rear bumper with a rope around the shoulders, were dragged back all the way. Van Wyk had boasted long ago that those bodies were the ultimate reminder to people to behave or face a similar fate. After many kilometres on the rough routes, the three corpses were not a pretty sight.

At a slower speed than before, they again drove through the villages, often stopping to ask about any terrorists people may have seen in the area. This gave the villagers a chance to have a close-up look at the kill of the day. On longer trips of two to three days, any smell sent an equally powerful message to the locals.

On an earlier trip, van Wyk had explained to Leeu: "Minds and hearts? We prefer bodies. Captured terrs all become KIA (killed in action). We never issue reports about 'civilians killed in crossfire' or 'civilians killed while running with terrorists' the way they used to report in South Africa in the early days."

Leeu felt the Germans had not gone far enough in 1904 when General van Trotha decreed every Herero had to be shot regardless of age. After killing seventy-five thousand, they dispossessed the remaining twenty-five thousand Hereros of all their lands and cattle. The Namas suffered the same fate. There was no explanation of why the Germans spared the Ovambos, who later became the main enemy.

On his first trip, Leeu had asked, "Why display the bodies, yet you bury them later? Why not leave them here at the villages?"

"We cannot have bodies all over the show as proof of the claims the churches have made against us. It's why we sometimes burn their churches. Brute force matters. It's all these animals understand. Sometimes, a terr runs into a hut to hide. We run the Casspir right over the house. We kill the terr, maybe a wife or children too. Every kill adds to the headcount! This is what all-out war is about."

LEEU'S SMOKE-FILLED, brandy-fuelled days in the SWA veld kept him going. Alcohol was an essential part of the officers' survival kits. Many were drunk much of the time. *Dagga* (cannabis) was another excellent way to relax after a demanding day when death was always possible. His only regret in SWA was his inability to replace the secret moments he had in his basement in Cape Town.

It was no surprise that his Koevoet Ovambo colleagues adopted his match-under-the-nail technique. He had never done ten fingers the way they did, often including all the toes. Leeu's genital flaming strategy was popular. Those who participated paid ten rands towards a kitty. Numbers were drawn to determine the 'fire squad' order before they were blindfolded, then spun around a few times before they were allowed to flick their solitary match from two metres away. When successful, the winner claimed the kitty. They did not bother to extinguish the flames, preferring to use petrol rather than waste their brandy on a fiery, non-necklacing, terminal strategy.

Penny excelled at the game. "Peneyambeko means 'there is a blessing' in the Oshiwambo language." Those were the first words Penny spoke to him when they met in Oshakati. Leeu never remembered his surname or his first name. Leeu presumed Penny judged the position of the genital target by the breeze on his face. Penny kept the secret of his success to himself. The game's winner would eventually shoot the burned prisoner to add to his monthly bounty payments. A kill was worth one to two thousand rands. Captured weapons were worth less.

Penny, built like an ox, had the most bounty strikes to his name; he was their best tracker. His killer premiums undoubtedly subsidised his gold front teeth caps, which flashed with his broad smile whenever he greeted Leeu.

IN THE BEGINNING, THE troops' behaviour had stunned a hardened Leeu already accustomed to the excesses of urban police brutality, but Koevoet's savagery soon became the norm for Leeu too. He lost track of how many terrorists he had killed. There was a time when he could recall how many there were, the circumstances of their deaths or their faces; they soon became a blurred scramble during his time in SWA. Those killed took on a mindless dimension with the suppression of communism as a primary goal while protecting White lives from terrorist butchery. The Leeus of the world had to deal with these Ovambo murderers of women and children.

Leeu pulled at his ear. At least he still had his piece of paradise in Kuils River. The place needed a few repairs, while he looked forward to restocking his basement again. He firmed up at the mere thought of the place; he had not been able to have a similar facility in SWA. The passenger seat of his Toyota Hilux bakkie (pick-up) could not compete with the basement setup he planned to re-establish once he was home. *What else awaits me on my return to Cape Town?*

CHAPTER 12: FAMILY TIME

17 December 1989

IVAN LOOKED AROUND the family home, where not much had changed during his absence; a fresh coat of paint was overdue. The inner lace curtains had developed a few more holes. The two mismatched lounge chairs remained on the opposite sides of the front room, with no space for a dining table or chairs. The same pictures with a few family photos adorned the walls; the lounge's only addition was a twelve-inch black and white television on top of the sideboard. The dark blue material of their three-seater couch was more threadbare. Alongside the TV, a recent colour photograph of Lance held pride of place beside a black-and-white shot of Ivan at about the same age. Both of them had the same tumbled mop of wide curls. He smiled at the sight.

Ivan looked through to the tidy kitchen, where the four-seater table stood to the side with two solid chairs against the wall and the bench under the table where he used to sit with Colleen during meals. He walked through to his bedroom past the room Colleen shared with Lance, who ducked behind his mother in his own game of peekaboo with his newfound uncle.

"Those are impressive dimples," said Ivan. "They must be the deepest I've ever seen." Ivan rubbed the youngster's hair. While he sat on one of the easy chairs, he placed Lance on his shoulders before tipping him from side to side. Ivan smiled from ear to ear as he thrilled to the shrieks of unadulterated joy from Lance.

"Who's the father?" Ivan asked when he let Lance slip off his shoulders to slide the length of Ivan's body onto the floor.

"A guy. We've moved on." Colleen said after a while. She looked at her feet, scuffing her shoes. She hadn't changed; she always showed her discomfort whenever she lied.

"Why's that?"

"It was better. He was a piece of rubbish."

"Are those the father's dimples?"

"Yes." Colleen turned away to walk to her room.

Saddened, Ivan turned to focus on Lance, who charged him at full speed to crash into his legs. "I suspect you must tire the whole household, kid." He flung Lance high, then caught the squealing, giggling bundle on the way down. The youngster's merriment was infectious, reaching to Ivan's core.

The special lunch was the standard noisy affair when the family shared a meal. They had decided to avoid prison talk. Ivan wanted to know about family members and neighbours, including all the gossip.

"While you were away, the main concern has been the increase in crime in the townships," said his mother after a while. "Drugs are everywhere. It's as if the youngsters only want to sit around to smoke their white pipes, play dice or get into trouble. Unemployment is high, so they have to steal to buy their drugs."

"The police are too busy keeping us oppressed to worry about crime," said his father. "In two years, there've been more than 20 deaths from gang shoot-outs. We've lost track of the numbers. It's terrible."

"You're probably aware of major political developments in the country," said his mother. "You can marry or sleep with a White person, though I reckon the best law change is how Africans no longer have to carry their *dompasses*. They've already removed many of their racist signs from around the city."

"You can swim at the city's beaches, but not beyond Cape Town," said Colleen. "Elsewhere, most of their apartheid rubbish still exists."

"They say they want to change, yet their sops are all too little, and too late!" said his father with his hands raised. Ivan enjoyed seeing his father so animated, as he did not usually espouse the cause of freedom.

"Yes, I managed to follow those developments. We had a few senior political prisoners there too. Many of us participated in adult classes. Unfortunately, we did not see much of Mandela, who came there from Robben Island, from 1982 till last year."

"You met him?" asked an incredulous Colleen. "I so admire the man. He is our leader. He has already refused to be released because they wanted him to renounce violence first. In South Africa, the State's barbarity causes more deaths than the bloody criminals do."

Ivan was impressed; another family member was again speaking forcefully about the changes needed. "How I love being here with all of you," said a smiling Ivan. "I've missed you guys so much. I just need a few days to settle down. Now, where's my Morrie?"

"Your car's parked at the back, son. It's covered with a new tarpaulin I bought last year. The canvas cover was kaput. I managed to start Morrie every month while I polished her every year."

"Maybe I should finally teach you to drive, Pappa."

"No. I'm happy on my bicycle, which takes me everywhere I want in the township. You sound like your Mamma, who won't ride on the bike with me anymore. She's gone all sturvy (haughty) on me, like so!"

They all laughed as his father tipped his elevated nose with a finger.

In the garden, his father half-lifted the tarpaulin to show Ivan his vehicle. "It still looks and sounds okay. Do you want to drive today?"

"All in good time, Pappa. I didn't see any Morris Minors on the road on our way home from Pollsmoor. I always loved the deep British racing-green colour. Mr G will be pleased when he sees his car on the road again."

"He hopes to see you soon. You are too bright not to go on with your studies. That's his words, not mine." They both laughed. Ivan's father ran the supplies shed for years at G's construction company. Mr G had assisted Ivan with his university fees.

"I must visit him soon."

The compact garden was filled with fence-to-fence neat rows of vegetables with a few fruit trees. Ivan's favourite was the loquat tree. From a pip he had planted, the tree was now much higher than before.

"You should've been freed last month when the last loquats were on the tree," said his father. "We had a bumper crop."

The two men sat on the rickety bench outside the kitchen door.

"It will take me a while to settle down, Pappa, though there are a few things I need to do first."

"Take your time, son. We are pleased you're back, but can you stay clear of trouble in future?"

Ivan looked at his father. He put his hand around his father's shoulder, squeezing him firmly. Until he completed Yster's mission, he could not promise his father anything.

"You have a lovely grandson, though all of you looked so uncomfortable when I asked about the father. Colleen was evasive with her reply. What's up, Dad?"

His father looked toward the partly cloud-covered mountains in the west. His face was a mask of lines. His Dad remained silent, clearly ill at ease.

"Is there something you are trying to spare me? I've been through a hell of a lot. I can handle any truth. Tell me, please."

Ivan watched his father inhale deeply with his eyes closed. A couple of tears rolled down his father's lined cheeks. *Now I really must know!*

"Pappa, answer me. After what I've been through in prison, I can handle anything." He dug his fingers into his father's arm.

His frail father's eyes were distant. "Your sister was raped," he whispered.

His father had confirmed Ivan's worst fear. *Who? When? How?* Struggling to control himself, he eased the pressure on his father's forearm. "Now, you must tell me *everything.*"

Again, his father's eyes closed. "Some gangsters pushed her into a car late one afternoon while she took her daily walk with Fluffy around the block. A car full of Achar-American gang members shot Fluffy, then drove off with your sister to the gang leader's place. He wanted her after seeing her somewhere. We were so frantic when she did not come home. They dropped her off late that night outside our place. The police are still 'looking into things'. Most of them are probably on the gang's payroll, so what can we expect from them?"

With clenched hands, Ivan noticed his father's slumped shoulders with his face deeply lined.

"We have not heard anything yet from them. When we realised she was pregnant, we sought guidance from the Church."

His father's body stiffened with the stressful memory. "Continue with the pregnancy or obtain an illegal abortion were our only options. Lance is the result. He's a wonderful grandchild surrounded by love. I noticed how well you related to him, too."

His father, still tearful, nodded his head before wiping at his eyes.

A choked-up Ivan realised he had again dug his fingers into his father's arm. He let go of the arm, looking at his disconsolate father. "Did Ses do it?"

"Yes."

Ses (Six) was a brutal man, as testified by his nickname from the six deaths to his credit when he became the leader of the Achar-Americans. Ivan knew of the man's reputation with girls who caught his eye. Ses lived a few suburbs away in the more upmarket area of Belhar.

"Thanks, Pappa. I needed to hear the full story." The painful news was the electrical jolt needed to bring him close to a more normal emotional state. The pit of prison life quickly aroused fiery stirrings. The feelings were raw, like burned skin. They made him feel more alive, like shedding the dark emotional cloak of his internment.

While Ivan hugged his father, Ses filled his thoughts. He now had two reasons to kill Ses - freedom from the gang and revenge. Yster wanted the job done by Christmas. The mere thought of killing made Ivan's stomach turn.

CHAPTER 13: BACK AT G'S BUILDERS

18 December 1989

IVAN HAD ANOTHER ROUGH night. The images of the stabbed prisoner had become bloodier over the years, the facial distortions more exaggerated with the anguished scream ever louder. The words 'Please don't' were still audible to him above the noise of the melee around them at the time of the man's near-death episode. Typically, his victim's scream woke Ivan in the middle of the night.

The non-fatal stabbing of the prison inmate still haunted him ten years later. Adding to Ivan's sense of panic was Ses. A gnawing ate away at his insides. *How will I react to killing Ses?*

Despite his disturbed sleep, Ivan was awake early to visit Mr Grant, widely known as Mr G. It felt strange to be awake without the familiar prison noises or the hum of voices from swearing prisoners or warders barking orders while cell doors slammed close. He lay in bed, enjoying the relative silence. Ivan could hear his parents moving around somewhere inside. He smiled as he heard Colleen scrambling, seemingly late to catch her bus, a habit of hers since her school days.

At G's Builders, Ivan had worked as a labourer on most weekends or school holidays throughout his senior schooling and university years. Mr G, recognising his potential, had encouraged him to go to university. Three other scholarships helped, as did the Morris Minor

1000 given to him by Mr G a week before he started his chemical engineering degree at the University of Cape Town, fifteen kilometres away on the base of Devil's Peak.

The noisy banter over the breakfast table was as he remembered it, except he now had a serious-faced nephew who squeezed in on the bench to sit close to his uncle.

"This will be my seat next to you, Uncle Ivan."

"Tell you what, Lance, that's fine by me, as long as you only call me Ivan."

"But you are my uncle!" Lance protested with his face all frowns, his thick brows knotted, his dimples deep.

"That's true. It's just I'm not old enough to be called Uncle. Understand?"

"Okay. I'll try, Ivan." He high-fived Ivan, who then rubbed Lance's curly mop-top.

After breakfast, Ivan farewelled his father when he left on his bicycle. Colleen rushed to catch a bus and a train to her central city clerical job while Ivan helped his mother clear the breakfast table.

"That's a nasty tattoo on your arm, my boy. Why a gun?" His mother shivered.

"Oh, prison boredom. I used the gun to scare off the bad guys. They all had one," he chuckled, despite the vivid evocation of his wasted years represented by his coarse tattoos.

"Have you any plans, son?" Her deep facial lines were more prominent than he remembered from the past. Her grey streaks had more than doubled during his time inside.

"Yes, Mamma. I had enough time to plan my future. Years ago, I promised to be the first Pettersen to obtain a university degree. I will let nothing stand in my way to achieve it; nothing." His compressed lips and narrowed eyes emphasised his sentiments, similar to his thoughts when he first entered Pollsmoor. The drive towards his goal had intensified with time.

His mother's tears were no surprise. He could only imagine her pain through the years. Again, she brought out those inner lost stirrings. He gave her a long hug. Both needed it.

"Thank you, my boy." He felt her relief in the way she held on to him.

"Are you alright, Granny? Why are you crying?" A bewildered Lance looked at her while he pulled at his grandmother's skirt.

"They are joyful tears, my boy. Ivan made Granny very happy." She bent down, lifting Lance to kiss each cheek. In turn, Lance embraced her with his cheeks now all dimpled.

"The first thing I will do today, Mamma, is visit Mr G. I'll walk there to see the changes. Afterwards, Mr Bailey will check the Morrie before I put her on the road again."

"Yes. When Mr Bailey heard you were coming home, he offered to service the car when you are here because he wants to hear the prison stories about his hero, Nelson Mandela."

From his mother's laugh, he sensed her joy and relief; he intended to eventually maintain these feelings.

THE WIDOWED MR G WAS greyer and a bit fatter, yet there was no mistaking the broad smile with twinkling blue eyes of Ivan's mentor of many years. They hugged each other before he held Ivan at arm's length.

"You've aged a bit; so have I, especially my belly." He slapped his stomach to emphasise the point. "Please sit down. As you can see the office is still cramped, though it should be bigger as the business has expanded and we are busier than before. Today is our final day before the Christmas break, although most workers finished off yesterday." Mr G drummed his fingers on the desk.

"Your Dad told me you would be released yesterday. I'm honoured you're seeing me so soon after your release. I hope your time inside was not too rough, as Pollsmoor prison is said to be one of the toughest."

"Correct. My prison time was no picnic. Now, here I am, ready to bounce back."

Mr G looked at him fondly with a smile across his face. "Bouncing back can mean many things. Will you try to study again at UCT? You would still be credited with your earlier work. Not many engineering students achieve two distinctions in their first year, you know."

"It's my intention to continue where I left off. My 1976 stuff was all about youthful anger."

"But are you now over the anger, over the hatred? Maybe it's worse after your prison time?"

"I believe the bitterness cannot be easily removed from my system. Apartheid deformed me; now I will be a committed student while the goal to remove our government remains intense." Ivan flexed his fingers without fisting them. Mr G's familiar eyes never left Ivan's.

Mr G seemed pensive. "My part-time studies through UNISA paid off when I obtained my law degree last year."

"Wow, congratulations, Mr G. That's wonderful."

"I do not intend to practice as a lawyer, though I now understand the business world more as I included commerce papers in my studies. I will soon have a double degree." his eyes again fixed on Ivan's as Mr G raised a finger.

"A new world awaits us, Ivan. Change is coming. The kind of pressures created by your activities and the actions of others have made apartheid economically unsustainable." Mr G paused again, looking fervently at Ivan. Rampant unemployment with ANC military incursions undermined investor confidence while the rand slid in value. "With a secret defence budget probably over 20 per cent, the country is effectively bankrupt." Mr G slammed a hand on his desk.

"My studies have been directed towards the inevitable change towards majority rule. I have my ducks in a row. What about yours?"

The familiar blue eyes focussed on Ivan, who scratched at his chin cleft through his beard. The sun through the window was warm on his forearms, the tattoo covered by a long-sleeved shirt. Mr G's eyes radiated a familiar warmth.

"I applied to UCT in September, so I will soon know if it's possible. I've written to the scholarship trustees to see if they will again support me. I suspect the two church-based scholarships will come through, though I have my doubts about the City Council bursary."

"Ahh!" said Mr G, lifting a finger before he rummaged in a drawer of his desk to retrieve a stapled set of forms. "I'm glad to hear about your plans. I'm on the NUSAS (National Union of South African Students) local committee as a community member. You can use these forms. Their annual scholarship application closes soon. It's worth quite a bit. Don't hesitate to mention your imprisonment. The committee members may favour you as they are a bit left-wing."

"Thanks. I'll post the forms tomorrow."

Mr G looked at his watch. "I'm sorry, I have to leave soon. How's the Morris?"

"Dad says she still starts. He has kept Morrie spotless over the years. I was hoping I can again do some holiday work on-site as before."

"There's always work around here, my boy. Let me know when you are ready."

"I may start the new year with a few Saturdays too."

"You can start anytime, Ivan. There's always something to do around the yard or on a site. If you're at a loose end over the festive season, the work yard needs tidying, so there's a few days there you can pick up, preferably not on Christmas Day, please."

Their laughter was interrupted by a dark-skinned, stout man of about Ivan's age. "Excuse me, Mr G, I need you to sign a form, please." The stranger's frown exaggerated a prominent scar across his forehead.

Mr G signed with a flourish and then introduced the two men. "Thembani Dlamini meet Ivan Pettersen. You two will bump into each other over the next few months. Thembani works as the company quantity surveyor. His computer skills have been invaluable with our expansion in the past year." He left the two men to shake hands.

"Pleased to meet you," both said simultaneously. They smiled at each other as Ivan pulled at his beard.

"That's a nasty scar on your forehead," said Ivan.

"Yes. It's a memento from my childhood traditional stick-fighting days. Your father told me you were coming. Because I am in charge of building estimates, I work with your Dad, who knows where every nail or screw is located in the supplies shed." Thembani stopped to rub at his nose with his fingers.

Ivan nodded his head. "So, how did you come to be working here?"

"About eighteen months ago, Mr G took me on as a labourer. On day one here in the office, I mentioned he needed to computerise his office. After a brief chat, he promoted me immediately. He said it was an overdue project. With the help of my two lecturers, Lydiah Adams, and Willie Germishuys, I did well in the computer papers at UWC, where I go twice a week. Like Mr G, they both encouraged me to apply to UCT."

"We may be on campus at the same time," said Ivan. "I've reapplied, so I may be a full-timer again. I had two distinctions in my first year of chemical engineering."

Thembani nodded his head approvingly. "At UWC, I obtained a distinction in each of my two years as a part-time student. Mr G thinks it should help my application to study at UCT. So far, UCT is still a 'White university,' of course," He fingered the speech marks in the air. "But recently, a trickle of African students has enrolled there. Already a few of us are at UWC, a 'Coloured university.'" He again fingered the air.

"That's so like Mr G. Always able to spot and promote talent. He steered me towards chemical engineering before my detention."

"Yes, your Dad told me a bit about your imprisonment. The State has so much to answer for, though I see positive signs telling me South Africa is in serious trouble," said Thembani.

"I'm positive, too," said Ivan.

"I see you were released on Dingane's Day," said Thembani, smiling broadly.

"Yes," said Ivan. "There's no way I'd call it the Day of the Covenant."

"I hate the Vow which binds the Boers to celebrate the victory of good over evil, of Christian over heathen, of White over Black."

"Know what? I reckon you would have done well in Pollsmoor. There are so many brilliant thinkers locked away there." Both of them laughed while high fiving each other. "By the way, where do you live?"

"I'm in the Crossroads new township. The State forced many people to move there or to Khayelitsha after the destructive Fires of '86. I live in a council-built home with my wife Nkosinati and a three-year-old son who thinks he is much older."

"Many political prisoners worried about their families after those shameful events in Crossroads," said Ivan. "I heard from fellow inmates how difficult it is to acquire a council house."

Thembani laughed. "I coached a UDF member's son in English and history. I'm embarrassed to admit his father's connections helped me. While they are not the best-constructed houses, they are better than my pondok, and I moved in a few days before I brought my new wife here in '87 when she returned from her parent's place in the Transkei. Nkosinati teaches close to home at a primary school where she is the only qualified teacher in a school of three hundred children."

"That's shocking!" said Ivan. "Most White teachers are qualified."

Thembani explained how he had fallen in love with Nkosinati after her husband died in the Fires of 1986. Curtis-Thembani, their son, was born six months after his father's death. "Curtis-Thembani is named after a close friend and me ..." With his eyes closed, he stopped to regain his composure. "No doubt you have a few stories to tell, too."

"Yes. Prison time is full of stories." Ivan chuckled. "It's a long, boring drive, so if we are both at UCT, we could travel together with only a short detour to collect you."

"Why, thank you." Thembani smiled. "I've been scratching my head about various unattractive transport options. The State uses their divide and rule strategy to stir unrest in the townships through the Taxi Wars."

"The taxi dispute was topical when I left Pollsmoor." Ivan knew how the UDF and ANC supported the Lagunya Taxi Association (LTA), which opposed the pro-government Western Cape Black Taxi Association (WEBTA).

"Gullible Whites believe the State's lies about the Taxi Wars. Much of the township violence is generated by the Balaclava Gang." Thembani punched one hand into the other.

"The Gang was another hot topic before my release, said Ivan. "I look forward to our future chats. Now I need to be home when a neighbour will service my Morrie. I need to feel grease on my hands again."

The pair shook hands before Ivan went on his way, hoping they would be able to commute together. Thembani had seemed troubled when he spoke about Curtis-Thembani. *I wonder what skeletons he has?*

IVAN MEANDERED VIA a different route through the back streets towards home. Much had changed, much had not. There were new business premises, yet informal shanty complexes remained, interspersed with more recently built, drab council-built flats, four storeys high. Outside many of these complexes, Ivan could see drug deals transacted in the open. The changes he saw alarmed him, with gang visibility much more prevalent than before, though these were distractions from the task he needed to undertake before anything else. He absent-mindedly rubbed at his deformed thumbnails, the constant reminder of his time inside. With his deadline a week away, Ivan shivered at the prospect of his mission. He had never had to kill anyone before. *Will killing Ses lay to rest the haunting images still as painfully fresh as the day they occurred?*

CHAPTER 14: A DAY AT THE CLINIC

20 December 1989

STANLEY AND FAY STILL attended the rebuilt Empelisweni SACLA Clinic in Crossroads on a Wednesday as volunteers at the free clinic. The State-supported Witdoeke (White cloths) had destroyed the original clinic during the destructive Fires of 1986.

The 1986 pogrom was an orchestrated holocaust against Black shanty-dwellers, Cape Town's most destitute. A rusted pile of iron sheets marked the site close to the clinic where the couple had heard the final fateful cries of a baby consumed in the flames of a burning pondok. Stanley still shuddered at the memory of those agonising minutes as the infant's crying diminished into death while the mother's wailing crescendoed. He and Fay rarely spoke about the tragic event.

THERE WAS HARDLY SUCH a thing as a routine day when a dispirited Stanley sat at his desk looking at the first two cases of the day opposite him. A miserable two-year-old child sat on her mother's knee with her belly distended; the skin on all limbs had peeled away to expose the glistening-moist, pink subcutaneous tissue. Stanley turned to Peter, a wide-eyed medical student.

"The child is a classic case of Kwashiorkor, Peter. Now look at the mother's arms," Ivan pointed towards her peeling skin. "That's pellagra."

Ivan asked the nurse to take his patients to the waiting room before he turned to Peter.

"Those two represent the by-product of apartheid and abject poverty." Stanley closed his eyes. Sighing, he said, "I call the mother-child complex the Malnutrition Syndrome. It's not a name you'll find in your textbooks. Kwashiorkor results from a severe lack of protein in the child's diet. These kids have pseudo-blonde hair because they can't even produce melanin. His apathetic face is what potentially imminent death looks like."

Stanley sighed again. "The mother completes my syndrome. The raw oozing skin on the backs of her hands and forearms is from pellagra due to a thiamine deficiency - one of the vitamin Bs."

"These are the first cases I'm seeing. How'd they come about?" asked a concerned Peter.

"Starvation! There is muscle wasting in the mentally stunted child. The mother will have three or four "D's" - dermatitis - her classic skin changes; diarrhoea; dementia, a late manifestation, while death could follow later. It's criminal to have such cases in Africa's wealthiest country - no wonder we are regarded as the world's most iniquitous society."

Stanley closed his eyes briefly. "Do you mind arranging the ambulance to take these two to the hospital, Peter?"

He needed to be outside, feel the wind on his face, to try to feel normal. With hands fisted, Stanley stood outside, where he inhaled deeply. The distant setting sun outlined the dark silhouette of his beloved Cape Town Mountains with their partial cloud-covered tops. Despite his feelings, Ivan felt a sense of obscenity to have such beauty overlook the social depravity on the Cape Flats. At moments like this, the Flats lived up to its moniker as the Mother City's refuse tip of apartheid.

STANLEY JOINED FAY during a brief tea break. Lydiah Adams and Willie Germishuys had popped in, accompanied by Thembani. He had joined his two UWC lecturers as part of a volunteer group of teachers in classes held in two converted shipping containers across the street from the clinic.

"I'm glad to see all of you today," said Stanley. "It's been a while, Thembani." Stanley was probably the only person who knew of Thembani's 1986 dramas.

"You may see more of me, Dr Gershon," said a guarded Thembani. "I have joined Willie and Lydiah's teaching group. The two of them have also encouraged me to apply to UCT."

"That's amazing. I wish you the best of luck with your studies," said Stanley, who sensed Thembani's discomfort, which had also manifested when they met after September's Peace march for Mandela.

"He's so bright he needs to be at the best university in the country," said Lydiah. "UWC had never before had a part-time student with distinctions two years in a row."

"Wow!" whooped Fay. "That's impressive. I never had one; Stanley did."

"Look who's here!" said the nurse manager, Thulani, who was after a cup of coffee. She traded kisses with the couple and then introduced herself to Thembani.

"How have things been around here recently?" asked Lydiah.

"Our main concern is the Balaclava Gang," said Thulani. They have almost replaced the Witdoeke as the primary agents of state terror in the townships. People all suspect they are linked to the police."

"They terrorise the township with arson attacks, assassinations or drive-by shootings," added Thembani.

"We can spend hours discussing how they target anyone who is against the State, but work calls," said Thulani. "I look forward to seeing you three again."

"I need to check on my student. All of you keep well." Stanley rose from his chair to return to Peter.

STANLEY JOINED PETER in the consultation area, where his junior colleague called him to look at a man's legs.

"I have another patient with rather shiny skin on his lower legs, though these limbs do not look like the pellagra lady's limbs," he said. "He's in much pain from the intensely hard calves, almost like wood. Are the legs infected?"

Stanley looked at the man's limbs, not believing his eyes. "That's scurvy! I've never seen a case in Cape Town. His diet must seriously lack vitamin C. See how rough his skin is with those swollen, bleeding gums. The last time I saw scurvy like this was a batch of cases from a coal mine close to the mission hospital I worked at in Kwazulu in the early 70s. Our social worker will have to look into the case."

"The patient comes from the local building sand works where the company feeds the migrant workers. He says there are a few other workers with the same condition."

"This is shocking! One Outspan orange a day would have prevented the scurvy; they grow the fruit just a few kilometres away from here." Stanley shook his head.

FAY'S BUBBLY PRESENCE did not relieve him on the drive home. He told her about the malnutrition cases he had seen. "In one day, no doctor should have to see three patients with the worst examples of malnutrition known to humanity. Will these things never end?"

Fay placed a hand on his forearm. "To survive, we tramp, dive, or travel, yet the horrors we experience break through occasionally."

Stanley reached over to rub Fay's shoulder, which she raised to her cheek while she drove on with care. Seeing her was therapeutic; speaking to her helped ease his tensions, though he knew she needed his care too with their shared socioeconomic and political-based pressures. *Why had we not emigrated in 1986 the way Fay wanted? I had thought of leaving in '76. Maybe we need to rethink the issue again.*

CHAPTER 15: IN THE HEART OF THE WHORE

21 December 1989

THEMBANI DRUMMED HIS fingers on the desk, satisfied at the spreadsheet costing of their new job done on the software he had drafted with Lydiah and Willie's help.

Ivan appeared late in the day after returning with the rest of the work crew from an urgent pre-Christmas concreting of a driveway.

"That's a nice tan you have. Hard work suits you," said Thembani.

"I've enjoyed working these muscles again. It'll be better when the brain gets into gear as well. Now I have a bit of news ..."

Thembani interrupted him. "You're in! Tell me UCT accepted you. They accepted me."

"Yes, we're both in!"

Thembani rushed around his desk to hug Ivan. "Nkosinati is beside herself with joy as she pushed me to apply. I'll attend UCT three days a week. My UWC credits mean I could be done in three years. I can still work three days a week here at Mr G's. Except when I married Nkosinati, I've never been happier."

"I must say, my confirmation letter yesterday felt much better than before. My two church scholarships came through. What about you?"

"Have you not seen the morning's Cape Times?"

"No," said Ivan, looking quizzically at him. "I was on the road well before sunrise."

Thembani went around the desk. "Here, look on page three." Thembani pointed at the photos of the two of them below the heading, 'Two top Cape Town students share 1990 NUSAS scholarship.'

Ivan whooped as he rushed around the desk to lift Thembani off his feet in a bear hug. "I can't believe it. Both of us are in *and* sharing the NUSAS scholarship."

"That's such a relief to my family," said Thembani. "This will help me across the line with the informal scholarship I receive from Mr Goldberg. I used to be his caddy at the King David Country Club. He's been supporting me since I started at UWC. He's pretty left-wing."

"Awesome is the word! Well done, you two!" Mr G had entered the office and firmly shook their hands. "As a NUSAS committee member over the past five years, it's the first unanimous decision I've seen. I'm sure you two will do us proud."

Thembani shared in the fervour suffusing the cramped office. A staff member brought in a tray with biscuits and tea.

Ivan dipped a ginger nut into his tea. "This is the only way to eat these," he said.

"I prefer the crunchiness when I bite into them," said Thembani, munching away with vigour to emphasise the point.

"I'm pleased to see you two looking so delighted. However, on a more sombre note, you may be interested in the latest Vrye Weekblad (Free Weekly) magazine." He opened his briefcase.

"I've never heard of it," said Ivan.

"It's a left-wing Transvaal newspaper started last year," said Thembani. "It gets under the government's skin by publishing news the mainstream media won't. It's a surprise the State has not banned them yet."

Mr G removed the newspaper from his briefcase. "I subscribe to them. Their latest copy is the most shocking revelation of South African police brutality I've ever seen. While you two read the article, I must pop into the supplies shed to speak to your father, Ivan."

The article lifted the cover on the government's much-denied security police death squads. One of the 1979 founders, Colonel Dirk Coetsee, had recently blown the whistle on them. The operations centre was on a farm called Vlakplaas near Pretoria. Dozens of people deemed a threat to the State were killed there, or they planned kidnappings or assassinations from Vlakplaas, as they eventually named the group.

When Mr G returned, the two men were in a heated discussion.

"We always knew they ran a death squad; now Colonel Coetsee has spilled all the beans," said Thembani, throwing his hands in the air.

"It exposes the unbridled police power in the country," said a steamed-up Ivan, slamming his hand on the desk.

"Yes," said Mr G. "Colonel Eugene de Kock [9] took over in 1985. So now they'll probably try to kill the whistleblower." Coetsee had gone into hiding with ANC assistance.

Thembani pointed at the front page. "Coetsee says here he was in the heart of the whore as commander of Vlakplaas."

Coetsee described how they often destroyed bodies with explosives before they burned the remains. Askaris (turned guerilla fighters) did much of the dirty work, including the death in Durban of the ANC lawyer Griffiths Mxenge, whom they stabbed forty-five times, and slit his throat before they cut off his ears.

"Barbarism is too mild a word to describe their evil," said Thembani. "These revelations make my stomach turn."

"Individual operatives have each killed dozens of people," said Ivan.

"There must be links with Koevoet in SWA," said Thembani. "There are enough stories about their atrocities."

"Where does the Balaclava Gang fit in with the Vlakplaas and Koevoet death squads?" asked Ivan.

"Or are they a third force seeking to undermine any attempts at change in South Africa?" asked Mr G.

"The Balaclava Gang seems to be a smorgasbord of killers comprised of White supremacist security policemen with Black askaris, Witdoek forces and kitskonstabels (instant constables)," said an overwrought Thembani.

"They always proclaim how Christian they are while they sup with the devil." Mr G wiped the sweat from his brow with a handkerchief. "This article has hit the headlines overseas, though not here in South Africa. No one else has dared to run with the story." Mr G walked around to Thembani's side of the desk.

"Is this the work on our new project, Thembani? Excuse us, Ivan. As interesting as the Weekblad article is, I need to review the spreadsheet with Thembani."

"Well, I have to be off too," said Ivan. "I may not see you before Christmas, so have an enjoyable day. I know I will."

IVAN'S THOUGHTS TURNED to his mission as he shook hands with Mr G and Thembani. Besides the constant tension in his belly, his mouth was like sandpaper, knowing he had to deal with Ses in two days. Ivan had confirmed how Ses still did his rounds of the neighbouring areas on a Saturday. Ivan had a vague plan of action. *Would things work?* As repulsive as the prospect of killing Ses was, Ivan shuddered at what he had to do. *Would the bastard be there two days before Christmas?*

CHAPTER 16: PAY-BACK TIME

23 December 1989

IVAN REVISITED HIS prison horrors most nights. Disturbing images flicked between the tattoo on the security policeman's forearm while Leeu worked on Ivan's nails. There was also the image of the stabbing spike penetrating the prisoner's abdomen, followed by the final slurping sound when he withdrew the weapon from the man's belly. Those last seconds typically marked the end of his nightmare, with a sweating Ivan sitting bolt upright in bed with the victim's screams in his ears.

BEFORE HIS IMPRISONMENT, Ivan had heard much about how Yster and Ses built the Achar-Americans to be the most powerful gang in the northern townships. The Cape Flats gangs thrived on the social detritus of poverty with the dislocations of enforced group area's evictions of over two hundred thousand people of colour from their established communities around the Cape Peninsula.

Every street corner he walked past was part of a domain where gang members trafficked drugs in the open. Distinctive clothing and their tattoos gave them status in an area with few alternative role models. The gold teeth, jewellery, provocative walk, and their violence enticed many to join. The higher ranks often had their molls in skimpy clothing as accessories to their fancy cars. Ordinary gang members sported tattoos like 'Die young to make a handsome corpse' or 'Join us so you can live to die'. They inked these messages on visible body parts; facial tattoos, popular on those with prison time, represented a farther alienation from society's norms.

These were the youthful temptations resisted by a younger, more driven Ivan as his alternative mentors steered him towards university instead. He hoped to put his derailed life on track again if he was successful with the day's task.

In prison, Sammi told him about Ses, Yster's original gang partner. Yster was still the acknowledged President of the Achar-Americans. "Ses became the defacto boss in the township," said Sammi. "His reputation thrives on violence."

Ses could not stay away from girls, with junior gang members forced into letting him have his way with their attractive sisters or partners.

In the late afternoon sun, Ivan walked many blocks away from home. His pulse skyrocketed when he saw Ses' bright-red 1959 Chevrolet Impala crawl along the one-lane concrete strip between the barracks of cement-breeze-block flats. The car's rear end always looked like an opened seagull's wings, while the soft top made it a scarce classic. The knife in Ivan's back pocket was part of an uncertain plan to deal with the gang leader. Ivan's mouth was dry; his stomach knotted to the point of vomiting.

Ses drove with a thick cigar poking from his pouting lips. The radio music was loud. A gang member sat behind the front passenger seat with a briefcase by his side. Children ran behind the car, with the teenagers pushing the youngsters aside. Before the car stopped, the bodyguard threw a few handfuls of cash from the briefcase through each of the rear windows. There was a mad scramble behind the vehicle. When the Chevrolet stopped, the kids crowded around, though none dared to touch the Chev; they knew better than to leave marks on the shiny car.

Ses went to the front of the car to wave away anyone too close to his treasured Impala. A tailored dark suit covered his burly frame while a black-banded beige Panama hat obscured the tattoos on his shaved head. Open top buttons of his white shirt exposed a couple of thick gold chains around his neck with tightly curled dark hair on his chest. He pointed a stubby finger at those he wanted to address while high fiving a few others. Expensive rings on each finger flashed whenever he gesticulated to emphasise a point or two. Obsequious minions drugged or not, laughed aloud at all his utterances.

Seeing how Ses adored the adulation, Ivan ground his teeth at the obscene spectacle. *How many of them are already destroyed by the drugs he provides?* He threw cash to youngsters, who immediately turned to the vendors to buy more drugs. Uhh! The more Ivan looked, the more he bristled; with his abdominal muscles contracted, he flexed his fingers a few times to keep his emotions under control. Finally, after a few deep breaths, Ivan's pulse slowed down.

The still bearded Ivan, baseball cap down low with sunglasses on, approached the car from the driver's side. He rubbed his sweaty palms on his jeans while he tried hard to look relaxed, even self-effacing. Ivan saw Ses' hand move to the inside of his jacket when Ses saw Ivan approaching him. His backseat passenger, a brute of a man, watched Ivan through narrowed eyes with his hand in the briefcase on the seat beside him. *Is he holding his gun? First, I need to be on board with them. Then what?* He had a vague plan.

"I'm Ivan. Yster says hi."

The man's handshake was soft, limp like a rag doll. In stark contrast with Ivan's sandpaper-coarse prison hands, Ses' manicured soft hands felt like they had been creamed. Ivan deliberately held firmly onto Ses' hand; his aftershave lotion smelled expensive. His lifeless eyes were like Yster's, though he had no facial tattoos to enhance his menace.

"And how's the boss?" Ses' lips curled as he sucked hard on his cigar, seemingly stuck in his mouth.

"He's okay. I suppose it's another day in paradise where he is." Ivan's mouth pulled into a crooked smile, contradicting his inner revulsion.

"I was told you were coming with a message."

"Who told you?"

"No matter. Yster wants you in our gang. We'll see. What's the message?"

"Not here; too many of these around." He waved his hand around him. Ses looked suspicious as his right hand still hovered around his open jacket. His gun in a black shoulder holster was visible to Ivan. His bodyguard looked twitchy, his hand still in the briefcase. Ivan's knife hardly seemed like an appropriate weapon. *Do I have a go at him while he's driving? I need to be on board with him.* He licked at his dry lips with an equally dry tongue.

Ivan was not surprised at the intensity of his feelings right then. What affected him most were the deep dimples on Ses' cheeks. To look at those characteristic features left him in no doubt that he was in the presence of Lance's father. The child also shared Ses' prominent eyebrows. Ivan struggled to maintain his self-control. *He's so fucking full of himself!*

"Can you drive? I need a driver. The last one died last week, sort of." He slapped his thighs, laughing aloud with his bodyguard. *Had Ses shot him the way he had done to a few of his own gang members?*

Ivan nodded his head. "Yes, I can drive. I learned to drive on my uncle's hard-top Chevvy." He kept to himself how clapped-out the model was.

"That's excellent. You drive, just be careful, as the brakes are deadly. It's a souped-up V-8, so the thing can fly!" His left hand simulated a plane in flight. "If you damage my Chevvy, I will blow you away," he patted his gun, smirking broadly. "I like speed the way I like women, though I love my car more."

Ses settled into the passenger seat after turning off the radio while Ivan slipped into the driver's seat.

"Your car used to be white."

"I was bored with the colour. Red gets me more girls, and I can have them here in my car like take-aways." He grabbed his crotch with his left hand, laughing as the gold teeth flashed. His right hand remained close to his gun.

Ivan's fingers wrapped tightly around the steering wheel. *Colleen as a takeaway?* It was an effort not to turn towards his sister's rapist to punch him before throttling him. His fingers tingled with the prospect of action. He could not use the knife. *Can I use the car as a weapon?*

"So. Where to?" Ivan turned the key in the car's ignition. He clipped on his seat belt, satisfied when neither Ses nor his bodyguard attached theirs. It suited his vague plan based on a recent news story following a carjacking which had become all too common during his imprisonment. He exhaled deeply. The car's engine purred; there was no mistaking the power when he drove towards the main street.

"Go left on Halt Road, then left again onto Modderdam Road to return via Fransie van Zyl Drive. By doing a spin around the township, I can see how you handle my car."

Despite his revulsion towards Ses, Ivan smiled inwardly. Ses had chosen his death bed somewhere on the dual-laned Modderdam Road. They soon turned into the busy motorway, where Ivan accelerated. Although the speed limit was a hundred kilometres an hour, the non-metricated speedometer needle was quickly over one hundred miles an hour. His plan did not need much more speed.

"You drive okay," said Ses. "The driving job's yours if you want it. What do you think?"

"It's a decent machine. I always liked the power of my uncle's car," said Ivan.

His pulse raced faster than when he had stabbed the prisoner. The dryness of his mouth almost prevented him from speaking. Ivan struggled to keep his inner fire under control; he felt ready to explode.

"So, what's the message?" Ses stared hard at Ivan, his hand still close to his jacket front.

"Yster is worried."

"Yster worried? Why? Hey, watch it, man. You're going too fast!"

"I thought you said you enjoyed speed. Relax. I can handle it. 'Why?' you asked. He thinks you are stealing from him. From the business."

"What? How can he say or think that? I'm loyal to my bro."

"He does not think so. Someone's been talking. He reckons more than twenty per cent is going missing. He says no one else would do it except you. Anyone else would be too afraid."

"Bullshit." Ses drew his gun. "I think I should blow you away right now!" He held the gun close to Ivan's chest.

"Relax, man. I'm only the messenger. He wants you to stop." In his rearview mirror, he saw the minder now had his gun in hand, pointing at Ivan, whose heart banged away in his chest cage.

"How the fuck can I stop what I'm not doing?" Ses banged the gun on the dashboard. "Damn. What swine is spreading lies about me?" Sweat beaded his lip. His prominent lips were tight. He chewed on his cigar.

"I don't know about any lies. That's Yster's message to you. You should speak to him."

"Fuck you! I don't need your bloody advice." He snarled as he again directed the gun at Ivan.

"Calm down. People say you should not shoot the messenger."

"People? What people? What the fuck do they know?"

"Well, they say you rape girls."

"What the hell? Yster wants to know this?"

"No. Me!" Ses jammed the gun into Ivan's ribs. Ivan gasped with the pain as they flashed past the slower vehicles.

"Before I shoot you, tell me why you want to know?" Ses' left-hand fingers opened repeatedly. "And don't fucking drive so fast. You want to kill us?"

"Do you know Colleen?"

"No. Should I know the bitch?"

"You should. You raped her!"

"Maybe she wanted it like they all do. I don't care. I thought I told you to slow down, you bastard." Sweat now beaded his tattooed forehead below the brim of his hat.

"Colleen is my sister. Her son has your dimples."

"Fuck you! There are many dimpled bastards around the township. You think they're all mine?"

Ivan winced as Ses' gun jammed even harder against his rib cage. "Bitch? Bastard? You're talking about my family, Ses."

Fifty metres ahead, Ivan saw his target: a flatbed truck with a metal tray about shoulder high to him in the car. Ivan put his accelerator foot down onto the floorboards. The car lurched forward as Ses, and the bodyguard rocked backwards. The speedometer needle swung well past a hundred miles an hour. Ses was right. The V-8 engine had oodles of power. In seconds he closed the gap to the truck's tray.

Ses tried to regain his composure as Ivan swung the Impala's right-side wheels across the midline of the two lanes. The car's bonnet passed clear under the back of the truck before ripping into the Chev at the height of the windscreen base. The point of impact allowed the side corner of the truck's tray to strike the middle of the windscreen, missing Ivan by inches.

Immediately before the impact, Ivan dropped his capped head while he lifted his fully sleeved left arm to shield his face from the shattered windscreen glass fragments. The loud din of solid steel on collapsing iron or fragmenting glass was all he heard. Through his narrowed eyes, Ivan saw how the truck's metal tray struck Ses at mid-neck level as Ivan slammed on the brakes.

The truck driver must have braked, too. The Impala's wheels screeched with their better brakes while the truck rolled forward to detach itself from the car wreck. The Chevrolet bonnet was intact, with the engine still running, though the convertible's left front roof was a mess. The driver's side was relatively untouched, apart from the buckled bit of the remaining windscreen frame with the crumpled soft top angled upwards.

Ivan could steer the Chev towards the side of the road, where the car bumped onto the pavement to run down a steep embankment towards a thick cluster of tall wattle bushes amongst the low dunes at the side of the road.

The car disappeared into the greenery as Ivan ducked under the overhead branches rushing by the now open roof. The vehicle came to an abrupt halt against a group of wattles with trunks as thick as his thighs. Ivan's seatbelt cut painfully into his right shoulder. He could smell fuel. When he released his seat belt, he leaned forward to drag Ses' legs over to the driver's side of the car. Flames rose from under the bonnet as Ivan retrieved the gun from the floor. With the heat increasing, he swung his feet over the jammed front door to clamber through the window.

Somewhat in awe, Ivan looked at Ses' headless body on the front seat. A few final arterial spurts of blood from the neck stump streaked the cream leather of the seat. The detached head lay on the car's rear seat with the Panama hat still in place. Muscular death spasm kept the crushed cigar in Ses' mouth. The eyes were wide open with a look of terror frozen on the face. A grim satisfaction spread through Ivan's body at the spectacle.

Beside the head on the cream leather back seat was another gory mess. The bodyguard was dead with a gaping, bloody hole where his upper chest should have been. Not having a seatbelt on had caused him to rocket forward into the right-angled corner of the truck's metal tail bed at the time of impact. Ivan's sharp braking had added impetus to the body slamming into the vehicle. Despite feeling sick to the core, he grunted with sombre smugness.

The flames soon spread to the rest of the car. Ivan threw the baseball cap into the fire, then made his way north with the dense wattle bushes concealing him all the way. He heard the Impala explode when he crested the low dune still under cover. He had no injuries apart from a couple of puncture wounds to his right hand with hardly any bleeding. His cap had protected his scalp. Behind him, he could hear people calling as they approached Ses' car. He was confident no one had seen him. The fire would make a mess of the Chev with the bodies; his fingerprints would disappear.

Ivan made his way through the thinning bush. Navigation on the Cape Flats was not difficult as long as one could see Table Mountain and Devil's Peak, both still visible in the dwindling light at the day's end. Ivan was surprised there was no blood on himself or his clothing. He looked at a pink-streaked sunset from the top of the last low dune. The view gave him a sense of hope regarding a future free of prison gang ties. Yster had guaranteed it. Those dark pits for eyes still retained an invisible decency in their fathomless depths.

Now Ivan had to work his way through the Parow industrial area ahead of him to be close to home. A complete shave beckoned, his first in many months. His mother would see his chin cleft again as she wished.

The day's success left Ivan with a reassuring stirring of his frozen inner core. He now tingled at the prospect of spending time with his adorable nephew, with whom he had a Christmas tree to decorate. His healing was underway. *Maybe now my night terrors will end.*

CHAPTER 17: PARADISE LOST, PARADISE REGAINED

15 January 1990

LEEU FELT A DEVASTATING sense of loss of self at the imminent closure of Koevoet. "SWA should never become independent," he told his commander. There was no way Leeu would ever call SWA by the designated new name, Namibia. It was a galling disappointment that SWA would follow as the next Communist State after Angola and Mozambique. He felt his time in the SWA bush had all come to nought.

"I'm still in shock," said van Wyk. "During a decade of bush raids against PLAN, we became the world's best counterintelligence, anti-terrorist organisation."

Koevoet had established a fearsome reputation with a 25:1 kill ratio, more than double the SADF (South African Defence Force) average. Koevoet's thousand men were a more cost-effective killing unit than the sixty-thousand-strong army whose non-disclosable SADF budget probably consumed more than twenty per cent of South Africa's budget.

"And now they are closing us down. Damn them!" said van Wyk, smashing his fist into the other hand. "I blame the fucking churches who blew the whistle on our work to the UN. So now our government regard Koevoet as an embarrassment. Imagine that?" With his neck veins distended, his face was redder than usual.

"We fought a no-holds-barred war out there. Did they want us to give lollipops or Bibles to stop those bloody murderous terrs?" van Wyk lifted his hands in despair. "We kept people safe in their homes; now we are called terrorists, murderers, assassins. The damned traitor Dirk Coetsee did not help our cause. I would happily twist my knife in his guts."

CAPE TOWN IN 1990 WAS a different place politically from what Leeu had left behind in 1979. Apartheid was under more significant threats from within and without. Trusted laws had been lifted. Mandela, the ultimate terrorist, was likely to be released soon. *So why did he not fucken swing long ago like other terrorists?*

With the Pass laws lifted, *they* would soon overwhelm the cities. The Russian-armed bastards had infiltrated the whole country; even the beautiful Cape Town, so far from the country's borders, was a rat's nest of mainly ANC or UDF activists who needed to be eradicated. This was his goal.

He sat in his vehicle while the air-conditioner cooled his Toyota bakkie before the two-thousand-kilometre trip to the Mother City. He rubbed at the itching scar below the AWB tattoo on his left forearm before driving towards an uncertain future in Cape Town. Leeu was to join the shadowy security police force group referred to in the townships as the Balaclava Gang. From what he had heard of their activities, Leeu felt optimistic about his new job, where his Koevoet experience was sure to come in handy. Whites had to prevail in South Africa. *White is right! White is might!*

THE BALACLAVA GANG met in a warehouse on the outskirts of the industrial complex of Epping, where the nearest factories to them were two blocks away. Tall wattle bushes surrounded the building with a wide concrete driveway leading to roller doors where they could drive into the building with their vehicles. There were dingy toilet facilities and a kitchen unit with a beer-filled fridge. Impromptu meals could be prepared on a sizeable gas barbeque, especially after work on Fridays.

Running parallel with an extended workbench along the wall was an overhead thick wooden beam where they suspended suspects during interrogations. Leeu appreciated the beam's proximity to the workbench's garden hose, black hoods, and electrocution hardware. Stains on the concrete floor followed the line of the overhead beam. Thorough hosing of spilt blood was not a significant preoccupation with this mob.

The gang called the unassuming building their Truth Factory, where they met before any planned township missions. There were no surprises when Leeu found a few familiar faces on his first visit to the warehouse. Ex-Koevoet Black members with reputations as ruthless operators were already members of the group.

The first person to greet Leeu was Penny, his Ovambo Koevoet colleague.

"It's wonderful to see you here, Leeu. I heard you were coming. Welcome." They never socialised together in SWA, though their camaraderie was built on the backveldt's shared battlefield, where their style of warfare built up Koevoet's reputation in Ovamboland. Now, they had to do the same as the Balaclava Gang.

Commander du Plessis was another familiar ex-Koevoet colleague. "Know what I miss the most about SWA, Leeu? The isolation. Near the border with Angola, we were about as far from civilisation as possible, allowing us to excel at our work. Those nosey Ovambo churches with United Nations assistance really messed us up." Dupi's well-trimmed moustache bristled when he spoke.

They walked over towards a group of four cream Kombis parked along one side of the warehouse close to the sliding door. "These are our ops vehicles," said du Plessis. "They're a far cry from Koevoet's Casspirs. Two White officers sit in front, while six askaris sit behind them when we go on a mission. As needed, we provide them with AK 47s." Du Plessis flicked away the stub after a final draw on his cigarette.

"Now, Leeu, I need you to be involved with our kitskonstabels," said the commander as he exhaled the smoke in a thin, forceful stream. "These men are given a week of basic training as policemen; we cannot keep their training going much longer. No money, you know; it all goes to those pansies in the army." He paused to light another cigarette, as did Leeu.

"We try to put them in areas away from their homes so Cape Town will have many Zulus here. Xhosas, Cape Town's dominant group, are sent to Zululand. - those two tribes are centuries old enemies. Locally, we use the Witdoeke to tackle the Comrades, though the ex-Koevoet Ovambos probably have the highest number of bounty kills in most months." Du Plessis nodded his head with satisfaction.

"Our mixed bag of men includes the askaris who can't return home - they are traitors to their people." Van Wyk smiled. "They probably hate us too, yet we pay them well for their loyalty; you will be in charge of them.

Du Plessis offered him another cigarette while both men stood away from the rest of the men who chatted with a beer or brandy in hand the way they did in SWA. Already, he felt at home.

"I look forward to my new responsibilities," said Leeu, pulling on his ear. "By the way, Dupi, what do you do with the bodies?"

"Yes. Unlike SWA, we cannot leave them to the vultures or burn them. It's easier here. We dump the corpses from a moving vehicle in a dark street somewhere in the African townships. There's so much shit going on there, so no one notices another black body. They are like roadkill, often blamed on the Taxi Wars in our police releases to the media."

Leeu felt a lightness in his chest as he drew deep on his cigarette. In his first week after returning, he had cleaned his house, where a heavy dresser now obscured the door leading to the stairs of the cleaned-up basement. Now, he had to find two compliant occupants to provide the final touch to his home. He had not expected to feel at home so soon in the Mother City.

CHAPTER 18: NIGHT SCHOOL

Mid-January 1990

IVAN HAD BEEN WRONG to think Ses' death would ease his night terrors; instead, they were more terrifying, more bloody. The scramble of images now included the hole in the bodyguard's chest, Ses' body with arterial jets of blood pumping away, and the severed head grinning at him from the back seat. The head intermittently uttered, 'I can have them here as takeaways,' while the headless Ses grabbed at his crotch. He sweated at the thought of the accident. *How long will my new nightmares last?*

IVAN PARKED OUTSIDE the two shipping container classrooms housing the adult classes run by a handful of volunteers five days a week in Crossroads township.

Thembani approached him as Ivan locked the car door. "Welcome, Ivan. I'm so glad you made it. We have three classes on the go, so you can sit in on each to see how we function here."

They eased themselves through the first container's partly open metal swing doors. A couple of fluorescent tube lights provided ample lighting inside. The seating faced sideways in two sets, with each group facing a whiteboard.

Ivan returned the greeting of the adult pupils. He sat on an empty chair near the back. The desks, tables and seats were a mishmash of donated items. He was impressed to see so many students of such diverse ages, from the late teens to the sixties.

A balding man who seemed to be in his thirties waved briefly at Ivan before continuing his lesson. *He must be Willie.* When he looked over to the other group, his heart skipped a beat at the sight of the attractive teacher in red who waved to him enthusiastically before she continued her maths lesson. Ivan acknowledged Lydiah's wave as he caught his breath. He could not take his eyes off her despite knowing she was Willie's partner. Ivan focused on Willie with difficulty, though his eyes often darted in Lydiah's direction while he sat there. Ivan had never reacted this way towards any woman.

Thembani had excused himself to teach in the other classroom. Ivan looked around at the attentive students to distract himself. All he could hear were their teachers' voices, with an occasional scraping of a chair.

After half an hour, Ivan excused himself to join Thembani's class. Thembani had a relaxed style, though his earnestness held his students' attention. Ivan tried not to let his thoughts drift to Lydiah, whose earnest voice seemed to caress him when he sat there spellbound. *Don't do this, Ivan; you're tormenting yourself.*

His thoughts were interrupted when automatic rifle shots shattered the peace with the staccato rhythm of the bullets on impact with the metal container walls. People threw themselves onto the floor. Thembani switched off the lights before rushing to close the partly open door and bolting it shut on the inside. The attack was over in a minute. Ivan's ears still rang with the sound of the bullets impacting the container.

People whispered to each other. Thembani's voice called out. "Listen!"

Ivan heard raucous laughter in the distance. A vehicle then pulled off. In the dark, his heart still palpitated. He listened to the bolt sliding back. The door opened slightly as Thembani slipped outside, returning after a few minutes.

"They've left," he told his students after he switched the lights on again. "Those in the other class are all fine - just as well the containers are bulletproof, but we probably should all go home now. It's their second such attack in six months. We will resume classes tomorrow; take care on your way home. By the way, I still expect all of you to do your homework." A nervous smile crossed the faces several students.

Thembani opened one door to allow people through. The two other teachers joined Thembani after they had locked their classroom. Willie and Lydiah hugged each other when they came into the container.

"I must say we can do without these interruptions to our classes," said Thembani. "My main concern is they will try to toss a hand grenade through the door one night." He slammed his hand on the desk in front of him.

"But excuse me. Introductions are needed. Ivan Pettersen, meet Lydiah Adams with her husband Willie Germishuys. These two have been here much longer than me - from a time in the late '70s when there was only one container."

Ivan shook hands with the couple. He was embarrassed at the stirrings he still had when he looked at Lydiah. He felt envious of Willie when he saw how close the couple was.

"Well, after such a fine introduction to our adult classes, what do you think, Ivan?" asked Willie.

"But what was the shooting all about?'" asked Ivan.

Thembani flicked at his nose. "We think they are the Balaclava Gang who do these drive-by shootings around the townships. They dress in black, wear balaclavas, and only strike at night when they travel in VW Kombis." Thembani cleared his throat.

"Others have seen about eight of them to a van with two Whites in front who use black camouflage paint to obscure themselves. After a shooting, people who played dead heard the Whites speak only Afrikaans - they're bloody *amaboona!* (Afrikaner Boers)," Thembani snapped angrily.

"It's a bit of a mess here in Crossroads," said Lydiah. "Many regard the area as an MK (Umkhonto we Sizwe) liberation hotspot."

"Will you still want to join us, Ivan?" asked Willie.

"My answer should be no," Ivan laughed. He stopped, aware he was again rubbing his thumbnails. "But I was touched by the intensity I saw on every face here tonight. You people must be so gratified with pupils like this. I know I was when we conducted our prison classes. You can count me in." Ivan offered to attend one night a week to teach Maths and English.

"It will be best to have you join us on a Wednesday. Then, we can have a full house with four of us here. That's if a Wednesday suits you," said Lydiah.

"Before we go, I'd like to ask you a question, Ivan," said Willie.

"By all means, go ahead."

"You do not have to answer, though I'm curious. You often rub these ridges on your thumbnails. What are they due to?"

Ivan was taken aback. As he contemplated his reply, he found himself rubbing at the scarred nails reflexly. Ivan could still feel the pain while seeing his torturer's white forearm with the AWB tattoo on it. He trembled within himself.

"Where do I start? You may know I did twelve years in Pollsmoor after bombing electricity distribution systems as I did not want any civilian casualties. The worst of my interrogators were the ageing local head of the Special Branch, the late Hammer van Zyl, with his junior sidekick Leeu (Lion) Kloppers." Ivan paused, reflecting on those moments of torment still fresh in his mind. "Leeu damaged my nails during interrogation."

"Excuse my asking," said Willie. "I had a friend with similar nails inflicted on him by Leeu who boasted about Lionising liars with his Lion matches."

"Those were his very words," said Ivan. "In front of me, the sadistic bastard sharpened the back ends of two matches. With my fingers duct-taped to the arms of my chair, the swine then pushed the sharpened ends under my thumbnails. When I still refused to talk, he set them alight, one at a time." Ivan closed his eyes, his mind numb, as he could still smell the flaming matches in his burning flesh. A visible tremor went through his body. "That's how you end up with thumbnails like this."

"How bloody awful," said Lydiah, her face distorted with the intensity of her lined face.

"Awful indeed," said Willie. "Leeu Kloppers and I went to the same school. He was the class bully, while scrawny me was one of his favourite targets. How I hated the boy. I heard he joined the police in SWA years ago, so he dropped off the radar."

"I'm sure we'll have more stories to share in the future," said Lydiah. "But now we have a nine-year-old daughter to collect from her aunt's place. Both of you keep well."

"They look like an interesting couple," said Ivan, still preoccupied with his earlier feelings about Lydiah.

"Yes," said Thembani. "Willie is classified White, Lydiah Coloured and Willie, a chronic tease, says their daughter is an illegal alien. Those two are crazy about each other, real love birds."

"I noticed," said Ivan. "Now, shall I drop you off close by? I will get lost in the dark if I try to take you home."

"Thanks. I can take a taxi from the nearby station. Those minibus taxis are cheap, though they are Cape Town's worst drivers with their overloaded, poorly maintained vehicles driven at high speed. I mainly use the UDF-affiliated LTA guys."

Once alone, Ivan recalled Lydiah's every word or facial nuances when she spoke. *Forget her man; she's off limits!* He berated himself.

CHAPTER 19: FIRST DAY BACK

29 January 1990

THEMBANI HOPPED ABOARD a minibus taxi before the vehicle stopped altogether. The driver's assistant, who had hailed him through the open sliding door, helped him aboard, then pushed him into the van where hardly any room was left. This was a standard peak hour load from Crossroads to Heideveldt station.

As arranged, Ivan collected Thembani from the front of the cramped supermarket opposite the station.

"How are you?" Ivan asked.

"Yeah. I'm good. You?"

"Excited, I suppose."

"Maybe we should be at the beach instead," Thembani muttered.

"You okay. You sound … different. What's up?"

Thembani looked away, wincing. "It's the station where the police shot my Dad in '76." He struggled to contain the tears as he recalled seeing his injured father go down. He managed to carry his dad to the Heideveld Day Clinic with the help of his pals. "After weeks in the hospital, he still limps from his hip injury. A few days later, my Mom lost an eye to a police rubber bullet outside our home."

'Yes. '76 was a tough year." Ivan's arrest at home in the dead of night was a traumatic family affair with a houseful of armed police with sniffer dogs.

"Also, '85 to '86. Now look at us - on our way to our first day at UCT, a White university."

A pensive Thembani paused. "I suspect another life was lost to necklacing last night," said Thembani. I could smell the burning outside on my way home from the shop. It was probably a few blocks away, on an open field. The characteristic smell is of burnt meat with petrol. Uhh! It's nauseating. At least I was too far away to hear any screams."

"I would hate to see one of those," said Ivan. "It must be gruesome."

"'What's worse?" asked Thembani. "Death by fire or death from shooting or stabbing? All are awful means to an awful end. There have been about seventy cases of necklacing over the past four years. On the other hand, the police kill hundreds, maybe even thousands each year, yet necklacing gets front-page media headlines every time."

Thembani lapsed into silence, recalling pictures like a rerun of awful necklacing images made worse by the inexplicable, macabre hold it had over him. He had a momentary glimpse of his blood-spattered workmate Zuko from over a year ago. Thembani still heard his plaintiff call. 'It is I, Zuko. We work at G's Builders. Help me. Please!'

There were times when Zuko's images mixed in with those of other dark moments of 1986. Was necklacing the escape he sought from those painful experiences? He had only once seen the body after the flames had settled. Besides the charred remnants, the victim's exposed, blackened ribs made him vomit. He had Nkosinati, Curtis-Thembani and his studies to consider. *I have to stop!*

Thembani shook himself to clear his head. "Do you think Morrie will get us all the way to the campus, Ivan?"

"Don't worry, slow she may be, though steady wins the race." Ivan patted the steering wheel as he changed lanes on Settler's Way to head left towards UCT.

After parking the car, they walked downhill to Jameson Hall, where Ivan pointed to the main highlights from the top of the university's famous steps.

"It's a great view from here with Devil's Peak behind us with the Helderberg Mountains way over there on the other side of the Cape Flats," Thembani said.

"I love the view from here, but listen, Thembani, I left a form in the car. Morrie is parked near the chemical engineering block where I need to be. The Arts block is across the road over there where you have to go. We can meet at the students' union behind us at lunchtime."

"I'm sure I'll manage. I'll see you then."

THEMBANI WAS DONE BY midday. With a sense of wonder, he sat on the steps before Jameson Hall, where many other students had gathered. A few sat alone while many clustered together, poring over their forms. He had to pinch himself. Then, he heard Curtis Fouche's voice. 'In you, I see a professor in a liberated country one day, brother.' Thembani smiled, as he always did with pleasant memories of Curtis. Thembani pictured himself on graduation day with his family standing right where he sat, maybe three years from now. *How special the moment will be?*

"Thembani!" The high-pitched squeal came from Lydiah, who sat beside Thembani and hugged him. "I was hoping to see you. I thought the best place would be near food here at the student's union," she laughed.

"Lydiah! How wonderful to see you. Are you here as a student or a lecturer?"

"I have my appointment as a senior lecturer. I'm still so excited."

"Congratulations. I'm not surprised." He squeezed her around her shoulder.

"So, where's Ivan? I have the newspaper cutting of the two of you. The NUSAS scholarship is prestigious. Well done."

"It's thanks to my wonderful reference written by you, Willie, and Mr G. I'm supposed to meet Ivan in the union. We better go over there now."

She slipped her arm through his as they strolled off. Lydiah hardly stopped talking; she was like explosive bubbles of effervescence.

Ivan saw Lydiah and Thembani head towards the union. Despite his keenness to see Lydiah again, he did not rush after them. Instead, he sat on the steps to take in the atmosphere as he had done before prison. Ivan munched through his traditional fare of cheddar cheese sandwiches the way he had dreamed on many occasions. Nothing could have tasted better right then. His other vision was of him standing there with his parents on each arm when he graduated. These images had sustained him through his worst lows; they had kept him sane.

By the time he found Thembani, Lydiah had already left.

"I'm sorry I'm a bit late. I was delayed."

"I had lunch with Lydiah. She sends her best wishes. She has a senior lecturer post here."

"She was humble. She's an associate professor, one short of a full professor."

"I thought so," said Thembani. "Lydia would downplay her position. I suppose a PhD helps one in these places."

"That's what you should be aiming for, you know."

"Nkosinati thinks I should major in English or History, maybe both. My Master's may involve the 19th-century Hut Tax introduced to force Africans to work. With people building fewer huts, the subsequent overcrowding allowed TB to flourish. Afterwards, I would research African writers towards a PhD. What about you?"

Ivan laughed. "I love your ambition, though I've not looked so far ahead yet. All I want is to revel in being home again. I saw you heading here with Lydiah. As keen as I was to join you two, I wanted to sit on the steps, cheese sandwich in hand, to absorb the atmosphere again."

"Well, I'll be nagging you later about your PhD. As Mr G said, a new South Africa will need us." He flicked open a knife from his pocket to peel the apple he had brought to finish off his lunch.

"An Okapi Three Star. That's a serious knife."

"No man should be without one," said Thembani as he closed the knife with one hand. "It used to belong to Curtis."

"Curtis meant a lot to you, didn't he?"

Thembani was silent. He slipped the knife into his pocket. "Yes. He saved my life more than once. He was my brother, my Comrade, my friend, the only one." He looked away, though the emotion in his voice was unmistakable. "Can we leave now as I need to do some work with Mr G?"

"Yes. I also need to talk to him about the work he wants me to do."

On their way to the car, Ivan felt a rare comfort - dating back to a time before his detention. All he had to do now was to qualify, though his nightmares had now mutated into an amalgam of brief movie clips of the wrecked Impala, prison torture, and the final stabbing of the prisoner.

CHAPTER 20: LIONISED NECKLACE

February 1990

LEEU, ALONG WITH HIS White colleagues, faced a stern-faced Commander du Plessis.

"Who wants to deal with the bastard?" du Plessis pointed to the blood-spattered man suspended from the beam. "The main thing we have from his treatment so far is he is MK (military wing of the ANC). He seems to be more of a foot soldier than a leader; he dared to spit at me when I suggested he become an askari to work with us."

Seven hands responded.

"A seven-man firing squad would be one way. Or we can draw lots."

Seven hands favoured the latter option.

"I thought so, so I have seven matches ready to be drawn. One is shorter than the rest." Du Plessis held out his closed hand with the match heads showing. Leeu was the first to draw a stick.

"Yes! He's mine." Leeu showed all of them the shortened match-stick. The faces of the others reflected their disappointment.

"Anything special you want to do to him?" asked du Plessis.

"I'd like to Lionise him with a tyre. I've never done one," said Leeu.

The other officers applauded, slapping Leeu on the back.

Du Plessis nodded his head. "We've already done one in the bush along the Kuils River, so you'll have to go there. There's an old tyre in the store room."

Leeu and his partner, Koos van de Merwe, applied their black makeup paste. "This is the only part of the job I hate," said Koos.

"Me too," said Leeu. "I would prefer to show them how White is Might! Hiding under black paste is bloody bullshit."

"Those damned know-alls at HQ insist we camouflage ourselves."

A knock on the door heralded the arrival of the first of their Black colleagues. The lubricating brandy was soon doing the rounds. Leeu savoured a generous mouthful of his Klipdrift, whose burn radiated throughout his body. The prospect of flicking a flaming match at the petrol-filled tyre for the first time thrilled him.

Leeu did not join in the rowdy exuberance of his men on their way to the Kuils River. While he drove, he was self-absorbed at the prospect of his first necklacing.

"You okay?" Koos asked, handing him the bottle, now already half empty.

Leeu swallowed another couple of mouthfuls of drink before handing the bottle to Koos. "I'm excited about Lionising him." He jerked his head toward where the MK man lay bound on the floor at the rear of the van. The rest of Leeu's team sat with their feet on the man whom they occasionally kicked as their alcohol did the rounds. He hated their Richelieu brandy. *The pretentious black shits must fancy the French name.*

Leeu's heartbeat accelerated when they turned off the N2 motorway onto a sandy track towards a dense clump of wattle bushes with a central clearing close to the river. The van's lights showed no other tracks converging on the area.

The spirited tormentors pushed their prisoner towards the centre of the clearing. One of them placed the tyre around the man's neck as Penny brought along the jerry can with petrol. The men cheered when he poured the fuel into the tyre and over the man's head. Throughout the process, their victim remained silent.

With a palpitating heartbeat, Leeu licked at his dry lips when he stood in front of the man who stood tall, almost defiant in his stance.

Leeu cracked the fingers of both hands before withdrawing the Lion matchbox from his pocket. "It's time to meet your maker, MK man. These tiny sticks are the ultimate cure for lying terrs like you. What do you think?" Leeu held a match in front of the man's face.

The man squinted at him. "When I look at you, all I think of is One settler, One bullet![10] Mayibuye, iAfrika!"

"And fuck you too, terrorist." With his thumb holding the head of the reversed match against the lighting strip on the box, Leeu flicked the match away from himself towards his target. As if in slow motion, he watched the flaming match arc its way towards the man. He stepped backwards when the petrol-filled tyre went up in a roar of flames, engulfing the man who kneeled in his fiery halo. Not a sound erupted from him. Long scorching tongues smothered the head, still held upright. There was no sound from the burning bundle when the man fell forward where the flames from the spilt petrol on the ground burned the rest of the body.

Within minutes, the initial raging intensity slowed down to an angry flickering, seeking sustenance from the charring body. The right hand, now free from the rope, extended upwards into a clenched fist above the carbonised head where a few flares rose skyward as they did from other body parts down to his feet. Leeu screwed his nose at the combined smell of petrol with burnt flesh. He stepped away from the intense heat.

"Bloody hell," said Koos, pointing. "He's giving the Black Power salute!"

"Yes. A fuckwit to the end."

The rest of the crew all slapped Leeu on the back. Penny shook his hand with his gold tooth prominent in his broad smile. "That was something else, Leeu. May I do the next one? I'll practice the match-flicking till then." The rest joined in his laughter.

"Alright, you men. The show is over. Let's go."

"I admired the guy - not a peep from him. Nothing!" said Koos.

"Admire? No, loathe! His fucken type is here to kill us Whites, to steal our country. He got what he deserved. We sent him on his way to the fires of his fucken afterlife!" Leeu spat through the Kombi's open window.

"Know what," said Leeu as they passed by the containerised classes. "We've shot at those things a few times now. It's become boring. Those teachers are still preparing more terrorists. We need to deal with them one day. What do you think, Koos?"

"Ja. Shooting at those steel containers makes a nice noise, but we need more than noise."

"We must think about it," said Leeu.

"What I really liked in their police records last month was the photo of the bitch, Lydiah Adams," said Koos. "She's so hot - I'd love to spend a few minutes with her."

"The guy always with her is Willie Germishuys," said Leeu. "At school, we called him Miggie (Little insect)."

Leeu told Koos how the liberal shit had dared to express his opposition to apartheid. With his school gang mates, Leeu had pushed Willie's head into the toilet bowl after Leeu had used it. On another occasion, Leeu held him against the wall by the neck while the other boys pulled off his shorts before throwing them onto the toilet roof. They were especially amused as Willie wore no underpants. Leeu smirked at the memory.

The security police records revealed how Lydiah and Willie had lectured at UWC before they went to the UK. There were no further data entries against their names. Lydiah Adams was the daughter of a deceased CID detective. The folder contained 1976 photographs of Lydiah as a student with a burning UWC building behind her.

How did Miggie manage to land himself such a good-looking woman? Leeu knew Lydiah was classified as Coloured, even though she was whiter than Willie. So not only did he have a Coloured girlfriend, but he dared to teach *Kaffirs* to read and think in Crossroads.

"I loved tormenting him at school; now he's a *Kaffirboetie* (nigger-lover, lit.) with a *Hotnot* (derogatory term directed at people classified Coloured) girlfriend. I think we should teach both a lesson one day," said Leeu, whose thoughts now turned to the end of the day. The prospect of his first night of licentious action with his two new basement inmates had him drive faster to drop Koos off at the Factory. Cape Town certainly had attractions well beyond being the fairest Cape in the world from Sir Francis Drake's time in the 16th century.

CHAPTER 21: MANDELA'S GRAND PARADE

11 February 1990

FAY AND STANLEY ARRIVED at Mr G's home, where one of his grandsons took them to the rear verandah to join the rest of the people at long trestle tables arranged in a U-shape with a large television at the open end.

Mr G, a close friend, came over to greet them. "Welcome. I'm glad you could make it. Mandela is about to be released, so your timing is perfect."

The couple thanked their host before heading to a table where Lydiah waved wildly at them. Suzanne sat beside her while Willie stood behind Lydiah in a huddle with Thembani, Nkosinati and a stranger. In her typical fashion, Lydiah was all over Fay and Stanley.

They greeted the group while Lydiah introduced the couple to Ivan.

"Are you Ivan Pettersen?" asked Stanley.

Ivan paused before he answered. "Yes."

"I'm pleased to meet you. You look so like your sister, Colleen."

"Yes. Colleen said you are the family GP these days. She says you're good."

"Oh enough, please. He'll have a swollen head," said Fay.

"Mandela should have appeared an hour ago," said Willie. "The Black Pimpernel lives on; now you see him, now you don't," he laughed.

Fay smiled. Only Willie would look on the funny side of things this way.

"We heard shooting last night in our area," said Nkosinati. "It seems the Balaclava Gang drove through our streets last night, targeting any gathering of people."

"Were they trying to stop people celebrating Mandela's release today?" asked Fay.

"Well, they failed - there he is. It's on!" said Willie. He pointed at the television.

The hushed group soon erupted into joyous applause when a grey-suited Nelson Mandela strode hand in hand with Winnie Mandela by his side outside Victor Verster Prison in Paarl. His hair was greyer, befitting a man of seventy-one years old. He was tall, upright, and elegant, with a pointed white handkerchief in the breast pocket of his jacket. He oozed a graceful dignity in his bearing; prison time had not stooped him.

By his side, Winnie smiled broadly and looked immaculate in her black and white outfit. Dignitaries or bodyguards kept the area around the Mandelas clear as they walked, their faces somewhat shaded in the late afternoon sun of a typical Cape summer's day. There was an abundance of ANC flags held above the mass of cheering people, many of whom wore ANC khaki outfits or yellow teeshirts. Fay's memory of her lost twin brother Fah tempered her moment of joy. He had died as an MK guerrilla fighter somewhere on the South African border in 1972. How he would have thrilled to see their hero freed at last.

The surrounding applause broke her melancholy. Winnie had her fisted left hand in the air in the style so typical of her; she was the ultimate symbol of defiance over the years despite her isolation under house arrest. Fay responded in like fashion with her own fist pump. Thousands outside the prison responded with Black Power salutes. To see her beside Mandela brought tears to Fay's eyes.

Within a few paces, Mandela's single, then double-fisted salute followed. His face remained intense. He smiled broadly when he shook the hands of a White man who approached him. To Fay, there was an irony in having a White stranger as the first person to shake his hand outside prison.[11]

A bare-chested supporter ran close to the Mandelas, waving an ANC flag. Alongside him, another bare-topped man had the ANC flag painted on his torso. Close to their waiting car, the Mandelas walked past a hand-painted sign saying, 'Welcome home.' Once seated in the back of the vehicle, they continued with their fisted salutes. Fay was ecstatic to see Winnie's radiant smile with a more sombre-faced Mandela beside her.

With a convoy of police motorcycles leading the way, the motorcade slowly passed through the crowd outside the prison. People ran alongside, slapping on the roof of the passing car, which looked like an older model silver-grey Toyota Camry. A sticker on the vehicle had an ANC flag with a shield and an assegaai on each side. 'ANC LIVES!' ran across the top, with 'ANC LEADS!' along the bottom of the vehicle.

Fay's tears now flowed freely. An overwhelmed Stanley kissed her a few times. Many of the other couples around them were in each other's arms.

"Amandla!" Fay called as all responded, "Ngawethu!" as all fists pumped the air.

After the Mandelas drove off, Stanley held Fay by the hand and led her to the garden, where they helped themselves to a drink at an informal bar.

"I wanted a few minutes with you. It's such a wonderful day." He put his free arm around Fay's shoulders to draw her closer. She snuggled into his side.

"It's been an amazing day. Ivan looks interesting with the gun tattoo on his forearm. Is he a gangster?"

"I doubt it. He spent twelve years in Pollsmoor Prison after he blew up a few electricity pylons in '76. He was a bright chemical engineering student at the time."

"Wow!" exclaimed Fay. "Ivan would have a few stories to tell. He must have met Mandela during his time there. I could not help noticing how he looked at Lydia. I think he has an eye on her."

"Only a woman would have noticed something like that within a few seconds." Stanley chuckled.

Once their drinks were done, Fay went inside while Stanley ambled over to Thembani, where he sat alone on a garden bench.

"It's been a while since we saw each other, Thembani."

"It has, Dr Gershon," said Thembani with eyes downcast, clearly discomfited.

"You must be pleased about Mandela's release. I'm ecstatic."

"Me too, Doctor. I was reflecting on the events of the past few years."

"Yes. We've had a few rough periods. How is life at UCT?"

"It's good. My attention is fully focused on my studies and my new family these days."

"I noticed your family. They look lovely. I see your son's name is Curtis-Thembani."

"With her late husband, Dumisa, Nkosinati chose the name after Curtis Fouche, and I saved them from Witdoeke in Crossroads. Dumisa died in the Fires of '86."

"It must be such an honour to have your son named after one of our township's martyrs with the way Curtis, Pat de Bruin and

Ebrahim Khan died during their Newlands station attack in 1986," said Stanley.

"Yes," said Thembani with a heavily furrowed brow as he fought back the tears. "The three of them saved my life when they brought me to you with my arm injury in '85. They would have loved to be here today - Mandela was their hero."

"The three of them will always be remembered for dying to right the wrongs of our country, Thembani. Now I better join Fay inside. I will watch your progress at UCT with interest. Now, when will you address me as Stanley?"

"Maybe, one day. Thanks, Dr Gershon." Thembani offered him a weak smile of acknowledgement; he still looked unsettled when Stanley turned to find Fay. Stanley realised he would never know the whole story regarding the tragic deaths of Thembani's three friends in 1986.

Everyone at the table seemed to be talking at the same time.

"Now we wait till he reaches Cape Town City Hall," said Ivan. "The trip would normally take an hour. I'll not miss his speech."

"I suspect it'll take at least two hours before he arrives," said Fay.

"Even more," added Lydiah, still grinning broadly along with the others.

The conversations ranged from the trivial to the more profound while they waited, though hilarity was preferred to more serious debates. Eventually, people became restive, though they became livelier when they saw another overhead helicopter shot of the Grand Parade in Cape Town. The announcer seemed optimistic the Mandelas would soon appear on the Town Hall's first floor balcony to address an estimated quarter of a million people squeezed into the Grand Parade opposite the Hall. All eyes focused on the screen. Stanley felt an excitement different to anything else he had experienced previously as Mandela's release was tinged with sadness at a life wasted in prison.

With the stalwart ANC veteran Walter Sisulu alongside them, the Mandelas finally appeared on the balcony. The thunderous roar greeting him from the assembled mass of people on the Grand Parade would have gone round the country, including the applause from the gathering at Mr G's. A communist red and gold flag hung over the balcony railing where enthusiastic supporters had attached it.

With a lump in his throat, Stanley hugged a tearful Fay. Lydiah, Willie, and Suzanne were in a family huddle while Thembani, with Curtis-Thembani on his arm, had Nkosinati wrapped around his neck. Ivan had a fist on high while he hand-slapped his way around the tables, whooping as he went along. In his easy chair, Mr G wiped away at his eyes with his sleeves, his cherubic face creased into a broad grin.

All settled again as the grey-haired Sisulu presented Mandela to the crowd. The long-awaited leader raised his right fist and called out, "Amandla!" Never was there such a mass of people to respond "Ngawethu!". Black power salutes rippled like a tsunami Mexican wave through the largest crowd South Africa had ever seen. Mandela repeated the call, as did the rest of the crowd. The chant never sounded more right or more powerful than then. Stanley's sobbing was like an opening of the tap after a lifetime of pent-up agony.

Mandela followed with "Mayibuye," as the tens of thousands replied, "iAfrika." They had waited ages to welcome a leader hidden too long from the country's people. Stanley jumped high with his fist leading the way. No doubt, millions in the whole country would have responded in a similar fashion, releasing all their years of pent-up frustrations mixed with their hopes of a better future in a democratic country.

Mandela put on his spectacles to read his prepared speech. Stanley was impressed at his firm voice and eloquence, with such clear enunciation through the speaker system. He spoke with authority, without bombast. Like the rest of their group, Stanley could not contain himself at Mandela's opening words when he greeted everyone in the name of peace, democracy, and freedom.

Mandela's steadfastness was breathtaking in the way he indicated there was still a long way to go. With no deals struck yet, he wanted negotiations between the ANC and the governing National Party to start as soon as possible. Mandela appealed to foreign powers not to stop the international sanctions against the racist state.

"The man is unbelievable, awesome," whispered Fay. "Listen to how defiant he still is after all these years."

When Mandela was done, the gathered group at Mr G's applauded as people spoke in hushed voices. Maybe the enormity of what lay ahead tempered their fervour.

"I'm so glad I have lived to experience today. Now I can die in peace," said Willie, who dramatically clutched at his chest.

"No, you won't," said an unsmiling Lydiah. "I want you here by my side, always!" She gave him a kiss on the cheek.

Thembani stood on a bench while he tapped a dessert spoon on an empty bottle to draw people's attention. "I'm sure you'll all agree Mandela made a fine speech. I loved the way he opened - 'I stand here before you not as a prophet, but as a humble servant of you, the people. We have waited too long for our freedom.'" Thembani rubbed at his nose.

"His final words were how he concluded his address to the court at the end of his 1964 Rivonia trial. I would love to recite the final lines, which have always been a favourite of mine."

"I would love to hear that part of the speech again," said Mr G.

"Count me in, too," said Lydiah, who sat on the bench with her arm hooked into Willie's. Fay, likewise, linked into Stanley with her head against his shoulder.

Everyone was silent, keen to hear Thembani, who stepped onto the floor. After clearing his throat, he looked around. "Here it is.

'I have fought against white domination, and I have fought against black domination. I have cherished the idea of a democratic and free society in which all persons live together in harmony and with equal opportunities. It is an ideal which I hope to live for and to achieve. But, if need be, it is an ideal for which I am prepared to die.'

"Thank you all for listening to me. I get the chills every time I read or recite those words, never more so than today. Amandla, Ngawethu!"

Everyone rose, as did the fists accompanying the calls to start people's power. Stanley had been transfixed by Thembani's rendition of Mandela's speech. Maybe with Mandela at the helm, they would have a much-needed peace after all. Yet Stanley remained cautious; there was so much in the country in need of redressing. *Are we expecting too much from change?*

MANDELA'S RELEASE WAS not without violence. The police shot dead an alleged looter a block away from the City Hall, where hundreds had to run from police gunfire. There were other episodes of conflict around the country, including three killed and 20 wounded by police in the Ciskei. Such was the inauspicious start towards a more democratic country.

CHAPTER 22: GENERAL PRACTICE ISSUES

Mid-April 1990

STANLEY'S MORNING CASES were routine until nurse Desray Daniels asked him to join Jayantilal with a patient. One of the advantages of having an on-site partner was consulting together with interesting or challenging cases.

"What do you think of the baby, Stanley? Granny says the kid is losing weight and has a poor appetite, fever, and irritability. I think there's more to the baby than gastroenteritis."

Jayantilal was one of the best clinicians he knew, so Stanley was always cautious when JT wanted his opinion.

"Two things cause me concern," Stanley said after examining the underweight infant. There is a fine body rash with oral thrush. Do we know anything about the mother?"

"Granny says she is unwell at home. What are you thinking?"

"I've not had a paediatric case yet, but HIV AIDS comes to mind."

Jayantilal nodded his head. "Great minds think alike! It's my first case, too. Can you take Gran with the baby to the waiting room, Desiree? I'll write the hospital referral." He faced Stanley. "I'm anxious about South Africa's alarming increase in HIV case numbers over the past few years." Jayantilal frowned, his eyes more intense through his black-rimmed spectacles with its thick lenses.

"I had my first practice case in a White adult four years ago," said Stanley. "Now a disinterested State ignores HIV even though Black lives will be decimated by the disease."

DURING THEIR AFTERNOON lunch break, deep lines marked his concerned partner's face while they chatted about his recent trip to his hometown.

"While I enjoyed the family time at home in Pietermaritzburg, Natal is imploding since Mandela's release. "Gatsha Buthelezi with his IFP (Inkatha Freedom Party) have a lot to answer for; the media called the last week of March the 'Seven Day War.'"

Like the Crossroads' Fires of '86, there were sixty thousand homeless, with more than sixty dead in a month of fighting in Pietermaritzburg.

"During your absence, Cape Town's Taxi War attacks have increased in frequency, though I suspect most of them are due to the Balaclava Gang," said Stanley.

FOR THE REST OF THE day, a constant unease gnawed away at Stanley as it did most days when the complex issues of life in South Africa clashed with his professional life in the township. He gave Fay a prolonged hug when he arrived home.

"Tough day?" Fay asked.

"Yes. Maybe no."

Fay held him by the hand to lead the way to their kitchen nook, where she had organised a few nibbles with the red wine already poured. Stanley sat where the setting sun's rays warmed their seating in the kitchen nook. The orange-red sunset glow highlighted Table Mountain and Devil's Peak in the distance.

"Thanks. I needed this." He waved his hand at the table.

"I ordered the sunset, too," said Fay with a broad smile. "So, yes, maybe, no?"

"The yes part is because JT is back. He sends his regards. He spent a fair bit of his holiday helping the wounded in what sounds like a civil war in Pietermaritzburg."

"Gatsha Buthelezi is playing a dangerous game in wanting Zulu-land's independence from a future South Africa," said Fay.

"True. The no bit is how HIV AIDS is now entrenched in the community, yet we have a government doing nothing to control it."

"The main people affected to date are gay White men," said Fay. "This government thinks they'll have fewer problems with less Blacks, maybe fewer gays too."

"I only hope they come to their senses sooner rather than later."

Fay snuggled into Stanley, who wrapped his arms around her. He noticed how relaxed her body felt.

CHAPTER 23: TAXI WARS

June 1990

THEMBANI WAS ACCUSTOMED to the peak hour crush in the minibus taxis. On his way home today, he managed a rare aisle seat. The driver's assistant had wedged four people into the three-seater bench seats. "Don't worry about the space," he said. "Your next trip will be free!" Thembani never saw anyone have a free ride unless the passenger was an attractive woman.

There was banter of all sorts during the trips. Mandela was the star feature since his release. Already, people looked ahead to their days of freedom.

"Me, I want to live in Constantia[12] one day, away from our hell hole in Crossroads," said a gap-toothed man. "I'm interested in the house on the corner where I work at my boss' house."

"You can't even afford the rent there, let alone buy the place," said another youngster.

"True, though it's actually the maid's quarters I'm interested in."

"Ahh. Now you're talking. Tell us more."

"Miriam is her name. You should see her." With his toothless grin, his hands air-carved a shapely contour.

Other laughing passengers added to the story.

Thembani loved these moments when he was hemmed in by humanity like this. Despite the travails of slum life with so much police brutality, a touch of humour was the balm many needed. As usual, though, reality intervened, with all voices chipping in.

"Did you hear about last night's shootings?"

"Do you mean the one at the taxi rank?"

"No. People were coming from a prayer meeting near the rank."

"Were any people killed?"

"I don't know."

"Who was shooting?"

"Don't know. It's probably the Balaclava Gang. They target any gathering."

"Somebody must sort them out. The police are useless."

"But they are the police!"

There was a general hum of consensus as others contributed additional stories about the all-too-common drive-by shootings from Kombis.

Along with a few other passengers, Thembani exited the taxi on Klipfontein Road outside Boy's Town, a decades-old, charitable children's home. He lived close by in Imbumba Street. Thembani crossed the road to the Africa Cash Store to buy a loaf of bread brought in fresh every afternoon. Thembani suspected they were reject loaves from the bakery, but they were cheap, while Nkosinati enjoyed the fresh bread.

The store was an add-on to the rear of a house. With no door, Thembani joined three others outside at the double-grilled metal serving hatches. The outer breeze block walls were recently painted tomato red and adorned with a six-foot-high Bull Brand corned beef advert. The words' Strong like a bull' emphasised the popular product's qualities.

Another taxi stopped opposite on the low pavement, where a few people stood around the popular informal drop-off point. From the western end, he saw a white Kombi approach at speed along the poorly lit Klipfontein Road. An inexplicable sense of dread hit

Thembani as he moved a few paces closer to the tall Eucalyptus tree in front of the store.

The Kombi screeched to a halt next to the taxi as automatic gunfire shots shattered the relative quiet of the night. Men in balaclavas fired at the parked taxi through the Kombi's open windows. There was mayhem, with terrified screams cutting through the night air above the staccato bursts of gunfire.

Thembani's heart drummed away in his throat. The familiar dryness hit his mouth while his throat constricted. His stomach tightened as he hugged the tree while still able to look towards the awful scene across the road where a couple of bodies lay sprawled on the ground. The balaclava-clad kombi driver turned to face the shop. Thembani could not see his features, though he saw the gun directed at the store.

As he pulled his head behind the tree, a burst of semi-automatic rifle bullets struck the freshly painted wall behind him as well as his tree. His ears rang with the noise of the gunshots as the Kombi roared off with a few shots let off while driving away. The attack, lasting seconds, felt like endless minutes. From one end of the storefront to the other ran a chest-high line of bullet holes broken only where the bullets had struck the tree instead.

No one at the store was hit. Two people had pushed in behind Thembani; another had thrown herself onto the ground. At least four bodies were on the sandy strip in front of the Boys Town property. The taxi was riddled with bullet holes while the engine still ran with the vehicle's lights on. All the windows were shattered. The blood-spattered driver's body lay slumped over the steering wheel. Many of the wounded hobbled around or sat on the pavement. The taxi had had the average jam-packed peak-hour load.

A woman screamed aloud. "Why? Why?"

"It was the Balaclava Gang!"

"Those varke (pigs) must pay one day."

Thembani crossed the road. There was a ripple of palpable anger among the survivors. Deep inside, he felt cold with rage, impotence, and a sense of wanting revenge. *Oh no, not that feeling again!* It had driven him to extremist action in 1986.

The people not injured were already scurrying home. A police van rounded the corner with its lights flashing.

There was nothing Thembani could do. A worried Nkosinati would have heard the shooting. He returned to the shop's serving hatches, where business was back to normal. He placed his loaf of bread in his backpack along with a KitKat. Troubled thoughts dogged his steps all the way home. *How much more of this violence will we have? What about those stirred emotions from the past?* It was like a door he could not close.

A relieved Nkosinati fell into his arms when he opened the front door.

"I heard the shooting, so I was worried because it's the time you come home." She kissed him a few times. "I'm so relieved. What happened?"

"Let me first give our three-year-old a kiss. Where is Curtis-Thembani?"

"I really don't know,'" said Nkosinati. Her finger slyly pointed towards the couch.

"Well then, let us sit on the couch to have our chocolate without him."

The giggling youngster immediately emerged from hiding. 'I'm here. Where's my chocolate? Please."

"Well done, Curtis. I see you remembered the magic word."

Curtis-Thembani threw himself into Thembani's arms before they shared the KitKat, with Curtis-Thembani having two of the four strips. Thembani slipped a piece into Nkosinati's mouth. She kissed his fingers, sending a tremor of delight through his body. "It's those eyes of yours."

"You mean these?" She blinked a few times. They both laughed.

"So, what happened?" Nkosinati now had on her worried face.

"A kombi full of gunmen shot at a taxi dropping off passengers in front of Boys Town. I was in the taxi before the one they shot at."

"What? Oh my god! Thank heavens you're okay. So where were you during the shooting?"

Thembani held her close. "Like I'm holding you now, I held onto the tree in front of the Bull Brand shop while a Kombi full of men in balaclavas shot at the taxi then at the store. The attack lasted a minute or two, after which the taxi driver looked dead, with at least three bodies on the pavement. I could not do anything, so I left as the police arrived."

"It's the damned Balaclava Gang again," said Nkosinati. "How many people have they shot recently? Ten? Fifteen? It's like a war sometimes. Was the taxi driver a UDF man?"

"People said he was UDF."

"No doubt tomorrow's news will blame the attack on the Taxi Wars." Nkosinati's face was furrowed, her lips tight. "What kind of world awaits our son?" She wrung her hands, her beautiful face distorted with furrows.

He hated seeing her like this. Her hurt gnawed away at his insides, already raw from his earlier tension. Looking at his son only magnified his feeling of helplessness. He rubbed Nkosinati's shoulders. "Will things ever improve? I hate seeing you so sad. I have to succeed in my studies to bring about change in the country."

Thembani held Nkosinati close to him, kissing her cheek. She nestled in his arms as she did when she needed him close. In the meantime, Curtis-Thembani slid down his leg to roll onto the lounge mat with loud shrieks. Thembani smiled. His son had a way of evoking Thembani's feeling of pure love, though his inner turmoil did not ease while he sat there with his much-loved family. Instead, his thoughts kept returning to what he had done to try to bring about change. *What had his actions of 1986 really achieved? He still had not told Nkosinati about those events on Newlands station.*

CHAPTER 24: DEATH OF A LOVED ONE

November 1990

LEEU WAS SATISFIED as the day had started well with entertainment in his basement before sunrise. He was smug with anticipation of what promised to be a busy day with the planned attack on a UDF leader at his home, after which he and Koos had decided to look in on the night school after completing their official business.

By Leeu's own rough count at police HQ, their group had killed at least forty people since three months earlier. He suspected the number was higher, with a three-to-one ratio of wounded to those killed. He would prefer to double or triple their killing rate.

"They want a Defiance Campaign; we'll show them Defiance with a capital 'D' - Death!" Leeu laughed, handing the Klipdrift brandy to Koos before resting his arms on the steering wheel. The soothing warmth of the brandy made their cool autumn nights more tolerable. It also settled the tremors of his hands he had noticed in the past year.

They rolled up their balaclavas to expose their camouflage-painted faces, highlighting their pink eyelids with Leeu's blue eyes and Koos's grey-green eyes. The Kombi's interior flickered orange from the dancing flames of a burning council house. They heard a few gunshots.

"When will those people inside the house stop screaming? It's better if we shoot them first," said Koos.

"No. Those screams send messages to the whole neighbourhood - behave, or you're next," said Leeu.

A hand grenade explosion went off inside the house.

"Those *Kaffirs* (derogatory term directed at indigenous Africans) are having fun again," said Koos, who drew on his cigarette before he flicked the butt through the window.

"I'll bet Penny threw the grenade. That piece of Askari shit is a fucken law unto himself. His saving grace is he has the ruthlessness we need in the Gang. Like in SWA, he has more kills to his credit than anyone else in our group." Leeu took his last draw, then used the filled ashtray to stub out his cigarette.

A few more AK 47 shots rang out. "I wonder who they're shooting at. The neighbours? People trying to flee from the house? Or into the air? Those bastards all smoked pot with their brandy before the trip, so you can expect anything from them tonight."

"I prefer my *dagga* when I'm back at the Factory. I relax better after a smoke," said Leeu.

"Our Ovambo and Zulu askaris seem to compete to see who is the meanest," said Koos.

"They are more interested in the headcount to add to their bonus payments. How many did you think there were? I counted five. The UDF committee man, his wife with the three kids."

"We must watch those *kaffirs*. They'll always claim more."

Both lit a cigarette as Koos took off his balaclava. "This cheap wool always makes me itch. When I asked if he could get me a nylon hood, the commandant laughed, telling me to buy my own. There are times when I can shoot the stingy bastard."

"Me too," said Leeu, pulling at both ears. "He can work on my tits, though I respect the way he likes killing."

"Yes. Dupi's a killer, alright."

"Good, our men are returning, said Leeu. "They're laughing like they've been to a funny movie."

The men's silhouettes were prominent against the still fiercely burning house. One of them whooped as he let off a few AK 47 rounds towards the surrounding houses.

"There are no other people around," said Koos.

"People know to stay indoors when the Balaclava Gang strikes. At times like this, I feel like I've brought the SWA bush to the city."

Their noisy colleagues reached them to climb on board as many giggled or spoke simultaneously.

"It was an excellent outing."

"The UDF man cried."

"The woman was brave. She shed no tears, only held onto her children."

"The commandant will want to know who threw the grenade?" asked Leeu.

"Him!". With hilarity, five fingers pointed at Penny, whose booming laughter filled the van.

"Why am I not surprised. Did you have to?"

"Of course. I wanted them to shut up," said Penny.

"So, how many were there?"

"At least seven," said Penny immediately.

'Okay," said Leeu. "We'll credit you with six - that's one each." They all laughed. Leeu shook his head.

Already, the askaris had lit their home-rolled pot cigarettes while they handed around their Richelieu brandy.

With smug satisfaction, Leeu started the van and drove off along the poorly lit street. "Mission accomplished. Probably on page three, tomorrow's headlines will say, 'Family of five killed in yet another night of township violence.' In SWA, we had to bulldoze a trench to bury the dead. It's easier this way."

A WARM LEEU ROLLED his thick sweater sleeves to expose his tattooed forearms. He stopped before the twin containers where the adult classes were held.

"What do you think, Koos. Are we too late? The place looks all locked up."

"Their cars are all gone. Look, the Beetle's leaving, there, at the back. The VW belongs to the beautiful bitch. I'm more than ready to have a few minutes with her," said Koos, grabbing at his crotch.

"I'm going to cut them off," said Leeu. It's time to teach these two *Kaffirboetie* (nigger lovers) teachers a lesson." They slipped on their balaclavas. The rear van wheels spun as the Kombi took off. The tyres squealed around the first turn to the left.

An animated Leeu's blood boiled while his fingers clenched the steering wheel as the van bounced along the potholed road.

"Hey, slow down," said Koos. "Are you trying to kill us?" Leeu hardly heard him. He slammed on the brakes at the next corner; the van slid around the right-hand bend, close behind the Beetle. The askaris hooted with laughter as they were thrown around the back of the van. As was their custom, none of them wore seat belts.

"It feels like SWA days again, Leeu. Go, man." Penny said as he slapped Leeu on the shoulder from behind.

The van's lights were on full, so he could see the couple in the car. Leeu's accelerator foot was down hard onto the floorboard as he swung the Kombi across the middle of the unmarked road to overtake the Beetle. With Lydiah driving, Leeu recognised Miggie in the passenger seat. Lydiah had a fearful look when she glanced sideways with her eyes wide. *Good, she's afraid*. Willie turned his much-streaked face towards the overtaking vehicle.

Leeu's pulse raced. His dry tongue licked at his thin lips. He swung the van in front of the Beetle and then slammed on the brakes so that the van slithered to a sideways halt across the road in front of the Beetle, which managed to stop without hitting the Kombi.

"You men stay here," he ordered the askaris. He did not need *Kaffirs* for White man's business.

A smouldering Leeu jumped from the Kombi with his pistol in hand as he rushed towards the traitor. Koos had to go around the Kombi to Lydiah's door. The passenger car door was locked. An irritated Leeu, gritting his teeth smashed the window with his pistol.

"Why the fuck did you not open the window, you piece of shit?" Leeu screamed at Willie. He looked at the turncoat Miggie as if through a red mist.

"What the hell do you want with us?" Willie screamed at him. "And who are you?"

"I'm your worst nightmare!" Leeu replied as sweat rolled down his face inside the balaclava. He lowered his head to look across at Lydiah. Her beautiful, drawn face lined, her eyes wide.

"Switch off the engine bitch. You're going nowhere yet." Lydiah complied while Leeu, with his left forearm resting on the open window, extended his right arm till the gun was alongside Willie's head.

"Tell me, why are the two of you here in Crossroads teaching terrorists how to read? These people are our servants, our gardeners, our labourers. So why do they need to read? Huhh?"

"Leave us alone," said Willie. "We've done nothing wrong."

"You teach them to read. You teach the *Kaffirs* to think. Before you know it, we have a class full of fucken commie terrs who want to take over the country. What's with you people, Miggie?"

"Miggie? You called me Miggie! You must be ..."

A single shot rang out. Leeu's bullet passed clean through Willie's head. Blood poured from both wounds while Willie twitched a few times, then lay still, slumped sideways away from Leeu.

"Jesus, Leeu!" shouted Koos over the roof of the Beetle. "Your bullet went through her head too, while you nearly shot me as well - look at the bullet hole here on the driver's side window."

Leeu lowered his head to look at Lydia with her face towards him, where she lay slumped over the steering wheel. A wound at the back of her head oozed blood.

Leeu leaned into the car to remove Willie's wallet from his side jacket pocket. He retrieved Lydiah's handbag at Willie's feet, then removed their watches and rings, which he handed to Koos.

"The askaris can have those. They'll know where to sell them. Now it'll look like a robbery."

Leeu headed to the Kombi with an inner satisfaction suffusing his body. "Now people like Miggie will know not to betray the side of right. Ja, White is right! White is might! Look at how many terrs we knocked off tonight." He high-fived Koos. "Seven!"

"But why did you shoot him?"

"He's a traitor who knew me when I called him Miggie."

"What a pity; I was hard as a rock to play with the bitch. Now she's fucken dead. Though we better leave as there's a vehicle approaching us," Koos called out. The two stumbled into the van, where the askaris applauded them. The acclamation was louder when the men had the couple's possessions. Koos had already pocketed their wallets.

"You're a wonder," said Penny. "Two dead bodies with one shot! We did it in SWA one night. Put three to four guys against each other, then saw how many we could shoot with one bullet. Remember?"

"Of course." Leeu laughed. "It's one way to save on bullets! At least we've removed them from training more fucken terrorists".

The tyres screeched when they took off. Above the Beetle, a solitary flickering street light provided scant illumination on the grim scene below.

✻

Stanley finished the last of the evening's cases at the SACLA clinic. The nurse manager, Thulani, rushed in. "The clinic's ambulance has arrived. They found two injured people at the roadside."

Stanley slipped on a pair of gloves in anticipation of the first case. There was always a sense of uncertainty when waiting like this. How bad were their injuries? The gurney arrived with its bloodied load. Stanley was aghast when he recognised the patient with the bleeding head wound was Lydiah.

Thulani screamed. "Oh no! Not Lydiah!"

Stanley rushed over to the unconscious Lydiah. She was still breathing. A bit of blood covered her clothing, though her pulse was strong. Thulani soon had an intravenous infusion of saline set up while the staff helped place Lydiah on their operating table. With a portable theatre light directed onto the skull, a tremulous Stanley removed the dressing the ambulance staff had wrapped around the wound.

"Excuse me," said Thulani. "I'm going to the ambulance to check on the other person."

As much as Stanley worried the other person could be Willie, he had to focus on Lydiah. The bleeding had stopped; his superficial assessment was the bullet was not a skull-penetrating injury. He donned a pair of surgical gloves to inspect the wound. The shot had burrowed a tract under the scalp above and behind her ear, while a slightly depressed bone fracture had a few cracks radiating away from the point of contact. The impact of the bullet had knocked her out. After cleansing the wound, Stanley placed a sterile bandage over the area, leaving a nurse to finish the dressing. He heard loud crying from an approaching Thulani.

"What's wrong?" Stanley asked with a sense of alarm.

Her face was downcast, distraught. "It's Willie. I think he's dead!"

Stanley's heart hammered even faster as he ran to the ambulance parked outside the clinic entrance. Willie's head wounds were apparent where he lay on the ambulance gurney. Stanley confirmed there was no pulse. Willie's widely dilated pupils were a sure sign of irreversible brain death. Stanley hung his head in despair. *What happened here tonight? Who the hell did this?*

With a heavy heart, he covered Willie's head with the blanket. Stanley exited the ambulance so they could wheel in Lydiah's gurney. She was still unconscious. Thulani approached him.

"I'm sorry. I'll accompany Lydiah."

"Thank you, Thulani. Lydiah needs a CT scan to exclude any bleeding inside the skull before they suture the wound. I'll soon follow you. Fay will be devastated when I tell her. She'll come with me."

CHAPTER 25: THE FUNERAL

Early December 1990

LYDIAH RECOVERED FROM her head wound without needing any major surgery. However, her more significant hurt was deep inside.

She looked at the gathering of close friends and family who had come to fulfil Willie's wishes in the event of his death. 'Don't worry, love, I will outlive you by far. The Germishuys' die of old age or rot.' Her grief amplified as she recalled chastising Willie when he told them he was ready to die on the night of Mandela's release.

It was so like Willie not to want anything elaborate but different. Willie's cremated ashes were to be released in the area where he had caught his best crayfish at a spot they called the Old Aged Home. Stanley had parked their Jurgens caravan in the empty carpark near the crayfish factory at Kommetjie beach. The others had spread their blankets on the tarred ground before the van on a cool, windless, sunny day. Included in the gathering were Thembani, Ivan, a few other friends and Lydiah's family members. Nkosinati was at home with Curtis-Thembani, who had a severe cold.

Lydiah's older sister, Liz, prayed before Suzanne read a moving poem she had composed. She spoke of their deep love, their moments together, and her father's wicked sense of humour. She then recited a verse in Xhosa he had taught her about a father's love for his daughter. While she read, many were teary, including the five cousins who all loved their Uncle Willie.

The wet-suited Fay led Stanley to the sandy beach where washed-up kelp lay in untidy piles. The flat sea was silent as if in mourning, too. Lydiah placed the urn of ashes into Willie's catch bag attached to a bright orange buoy at the water's edge. The dive couple then headed to the spot about a hundred metres offshore where Willie had caught a much boasted-about crayfish, the best of the day.

With a heavy heart, Lydiah watched the pair return to the buoy after they had emptied the container. Fay and Stanley waved a fist on high to the mourners gathered on the beach before the divers towed the buoy well to the left, where they were to catch crayfish as Willie had requested. An hour later, they returned to shore with six decent-sized specimens in the catch bag.

Fay showed them the largest crayfish caught by her. "It's about the size of Willie's prize catch. Of course, he would have claimed his was twice the size." There was soft laughter from those gathered around them. "I'll let him have his way today."

In the caravan, Stanley steamed the crustaceans with seawater in a pot while the others enjoyed their drinks and nibbles outside, where they sat in the sun. Anecdotes about Willie were plentiful, often tinged with laughter when they regaled accounts of his impish humour.

Stanley appeared with the crayfish, now a tantalising orange red. "I have split the crayfish into these two bowls," said Stanley. "For those who like to crack, suck or slurp, I have the legs with jointed chest parts in the bowl. I know Willie would tackle the bowl first. The other bowl has the cut-up tail meat with a dipping sauce on the side." He placed the bowls on a camp table attached to the side of the caravan.

"This is the last of Willie's favourite dipping sauce," said Lydiah, who placed the container between the two bowls of crayfish. "He used a mixture of tomato sauce and mayonnaise. He would not tell me the recipe. 'The best chefs never divulge their ingredients,' he said whenever he made it. Willie added garlic, lemon juice and chilli to all his food so take care," said Lydiah.

"Dessert will follow later with Willie's favourite jelly made from the seaweed, agar-agar, he collected here on the beach. I can see some on the dried kelp stems over there," she pointed. "He cooked the seaweed with sugar, pineapple skins and Ideal evaporated milk. I used canned pineapples instead."

"Oh, good," said Thembani. "He shared some with me once at UWC."

Lydiah smiled. "Oh, Thembani, you and your food!"

Lydiah watched those strolling around the food table or along the beach, though she was elsewhere, her mind seeking pleasant memories of Willie rather than the constant flashbacks she had of their tragic last evening together. She knew a continuous hollowness inside her would take ages to settle, if ever. She went to the beach with Suzanne, where they held onto each other while their tears flowed freely.

When they returned to the carpark, many came over to hug them. Their kind efforts provided Lydiah with no comfort. The pain would remain, and the scars of losing Willie would never heal, especially considering the circumstances of his death. She was pleased she could not recall the actual shooting. Her last memory of the attack was the tattooed left forearm resting on the car door through the broken passenger side window.

They all had stories to tell about Willie while they shared the last of Willie's alcohol stocks.

"His favourite with crayfish was this Nederburg rosé," said Fay. "He said the red of the wine complemented the cooked crayfish. It's one of my favourites. Cheers, Willie." She raised her glass, as did the rest.

To gather people around her, Lydiah tapped on her empty wine glass with the handle of a fork. "Suzanne and I must thank all of you who've joined us today." She spread her hands towards them. "As special as Willie was to all of you, he was much more special to the two of us." Lydiah, with her mouth dry, struggled to contain herself.

"Some of you must wonder where his family members are. Liz invited them. Instead, they said he got what he deserved." Lydiah bit her lip. Many gasped. "It always amazed me how a man from his background could so embrace everyone like my Willie did. He taught at UWC when it was unfashionable to do so, yet he was committed to what he did. He died on his way after conducting his adult classes in Crossroads, where he taught with a passion. He regarded his work there as better than the work he did at UWC. That was my Willie, our Willie." She held Suzanne across the shoulder, drawing her closer. Suzanne returned her squeeze.

"The media claim he was the victim of 'township violence'. The police said they are investigating things." She snorted. "The killers were part of the shadowy Balaclava Gang. I know. I saw the shooter's pink eyelids with the blue eyes under the bloody balaclava. The one who shot my Willie had his sleeves rolled up to expose his non-camouflaged white skin. Willie's killer had a tattoo of the AWB flag on his left forearm - three black sevens in a white circle on a red square. There was a linear scar below the tattoo. The flag, like those eyes, is now tattooed in my brain. I hope he gets his comeuppance one day." Her fists were clenched as her heart pounded with the moment's intensity.

"Please forgive me." Her voice was strained. A number of the adults, Suzanne and her teenage cousins cried. "I had to share the story with you. I did not intend to spoil the day." She dried her eyes on her sleeve.

"Finally, we hope you can join in the game Suzanne has devised. Whenever we had the annual family get-together at my parents' graveside in Maitland Cemetery, Willie always joined in the children's games. He would hop over all the gravestones behind the kids." There were smiles on all the cousin's faces.

Suzanne then continued. "When I was younger, my favourite was how Dad would lift me high over the taller headstones so I could keep up with the rest of you, my older cousins. As the youngest, I was always last in line, so today, I will be in front as I lead the way over those knee-high posts around the car park. I know my Dad will be behind me, hopping, too. So, watch him, please, as he can sometimes be a bit slow." There were laughs and clapping from all. "Are you all ready?"

"Yesss!" the cousins all responded, then followed her as did all the adults. They returned after several minutes; older members sought a drink of water or juice. Led by Suzanne, the cousins screamed their way for more loops around the carpark.

"My Willie would've been there in the thick of things with them," said a smiling Lydiah.

Surrounded by so much laughter, Lydiah felt a comfort she had not known in the past dark fortnight. *Willie would have wanted a day like this.*

Ivan agonised over Lydiah's words, where he sat alongside Thembani on the blanket Stanley had placed in front of the caravan. Fay and Stanley sat on their camp chairs. The pair had a glass of wine in hand, while Ivan and Thembani had cans of Coke. Gone was Ivan's relaxed state of the past few weeks. His salvation had been his studies; they insulated him, allowing his nocturnal terrors to ease. Now, though, Ivan felt an inner chill familiar to him since his pretrial prison incarceration.

"You alright?" asked Thembani, who had been watching him closely.

Ivan remained silent before answering. "I know who shot them." His voice was hushed. "The tattoo belongs to Gerrie Kloppers, the security policeman who did this to me."

Fay gasped as Ivan showed his thumbs with their deformed, stained nails. "The man is a sadistic psychopath. His nickname is Leeu, named after the Lion matches he burns after driving them under the thumbnails. That's what he did to me during my pretrial detention. Hardly a day goes by when I do not think of what he did to many of us."

A tremulous Ivan lapsed into silence, rubbing at the nails. He was briefly taken back to when he signed the confession placed in front of him while he still had the charred matchstick remnants in his thumbs. He did not know what he had signed, but after that, he was soon charged with treasonous acts against the State.

"Years ago, I saw a patient with burnt nails like that," said Stanley. "The carbonised soot remnants in the scar tissue stain the area black. The patient also called the man Leeu."

"Leeu is Gerrie Kloppers; he Lionised my nails," said Ivan. "Nobody else would have a scar below an AWB tattoo like that. He always had his shirt sleeves rolled up whenever he interrogated me.

"The day he manicured me, as he called it, Leeu asked me, 'Do you know what my tattoo means? White is Right. Forget Black Power. Ja, White is Might. You will always think of it after today.'" Ivan's insides went all spastic. "I heard he eventually went to Namibia to join Koevoet. Now they've disbanded Koevoet, Leeu is here in the Balaclava Gang."

"It seems they've taken on the worst of the worst from Koevoet to join the Gang," snorted Fay.

"Along with turncoat askaris," added Thembani.

A smiling Lydiah came strolling over to the group with her arm over Suzanne's shoulder.

"You seem to be enjoying yourselves here, or have I interrupted a serious discussion," said a smiling Lydiah, who held Suzanne close to her. "We wanted to thank all of you."

"Well, I so enjoyed the crayfish," said Suzanne. "Dad taught me how to suck the bones to get at the crayfish fillet."

"I prefer the tails," said Lydiah. "So, Willie and I always swopped our tails and bodies whenever we had crayfish."

"I like both, though Stanley is a bones man." Fay smiled broadly.

"I'm like Fay," chuckled Thembani.

"What about you, Ivan?" asked Lydiah.

Ivan was caught off guard. He had been watching Lydiah all the time and had somewhat lost the thread of the conversation. "I take whatever comes my way," Ivan mumbled. He felt himself blushing, so he turned his head to the side until he felt more comfortable while his pulse returned to normal.

"Oh, good. Next time, I'll give you my bones while I'll have your tail." Lydiah threw her head back as she laughed. They all joined her, including Ivan, who felt an inner stirring that went well past the moment's humour. Here, again, was the arousal of suppressed emotions almost a year after he first met her.

"I enjoyed your poem, Suzanne. How long did it take to compose?" asked Thembani.

"Just one night," replied Suzanne.

"She's fluent in French and Afrikaans, as well as flying her way through Xhosa lessons," said Lydiah. "She's already better than me."

"But I'm useless at Maths!" Suzanne pulled a face.

"Maybe I could help you there," said Ivan. "I'm supposed to be okay at Maths."

"Supposed to be?" asked Thembani. "With two distinctions in Maths in his first year at uni, he's doing wonders with our adult classes in Crossroads."

"That sounds awesome. What do you think, Mum?"

"I'm okay with it."

"I could pop in on Tuesdays at seven-thirty."

"Tuesday will be fine," said Lydiah.

"Thank you ever so much!" said Suzanne, who kissed Ivan on the cheek.

"The pleasure's mine. It's not often I'm kissed by someone with such a posh English accent."

The group erupted with laughter. Ivan's eyes again drifted over towards Lydiah.

"Your Morrie still goes well," said Thembani on their way home from Kommetjie.

"Yes. I was pleased with how she handled the mountain coming up Ou Kaapse Weg (Old Cape Road)."

Before they descended the mountain, Stanley pulled into the Silvermine carpark. "It's been a while since I was here," he said.

They sat on a flat rock in front of the car. Ahead lay the Cape Flats with the Muizenberg Mountains and a waveless False Bay to the right. Straight ahead were the distant Helderberg Mountain peaks now cleared of the last of the winter snow. Table Bay glistened in the distance to the left from where the Constantiaberg range ran into Table Mountain, with a more angled appearance than the flat top when viewed from the front.

"These are the things you miss in prison. These views with warm people around one."

"People or person?" asked Thembani.

"Meaning?"

"Why Lydiah, of course!"

"What do you mean?" Ivan tried to suppress his discomfort.

"Well, whenever you are around her, you are like a love-sick puppy dog!" grinned Thembani, his perfect teeth all visible.

"You're mad! What do you know?"

"Ivan, I've been there with Nkosinati. I fell in love with her after her husband's death; in fact it was probably from the first time I saw her while he was still alive.

"I'd forgotten. It must have been awkward. I loved Lydiah from the time you introduced us on the night when they shot at the classes. As much as I tried to suppress the feeling, I can't take my eyes off her."

"I know. It's been clear to me over many months."

"Really? What do I do now, Thembani? How did you go about things?"

"My situation was different from yours. I saw Nkosinati every day at my parent's place. My Mamma was soon aware of my interest. She told me to be patient, give Nkosinati time to heal, and be there when she is ready. I made my move when she was due to return to her parents in the Transkei with a one-month-old Curtis-Thembani - I told you before."

"Yes, I remember."

"Let things develop naturally. If Lydiah's interested in you, it'll happen. She lost her soulmate - that's what she called Willie. I think of Nkosinati in the same way. In turn, she thought of her late husband in the same way. She changed with time. Lydiah will heal. You being there with Suzanne can become part of Lydiah's healing process. You will see her once a week at her place. Lunchtime with her at UCT will be another occasion."

"Thanks. Time will tell, so I'll have to be patient, but now it's time to head home."

Thembani high-fived Ivan, who felt a greater fervour within himself. *Maybe Lydiah could be the ultimate cure in my restoration. Can I be part of hers?*

CHAPTER 26: NECKLACING NIGHTMARES

Mid-December 1990

THEMBANI PULLED TOWARDS the fringes of the baying crowd. He had again supplied the tyre necklace for the punishment of a deemed traitor. A wave of nausea swept over him from his balled stomach. He was ready to vomit. Instead, he turned to leave as the next victim stumbled towards the middle of the soccer field where his fate awaited him. *What was the charge against the man?* Often Thembani did not know the answer.

The process of necklacing was gut-churning stuff. Thembani could not stand to see the stumbling human conflagration, the final shrieks turning to croaking before the slow collapse into the silent howling of death followed by the flaming, charred process. As quiet as the terminal, fatal scream was, it always cut through his brain. He had to leave before the blazing climax. As he turned, he glanced at the man whose facial features were clearly recognisable, especially the scarred forehead. He started to run away from the dreadful spectre of his own face.

Three gunshots woke him where he stood outside his home in his pyjamas with the police Glock in his hand. He had shot at shadows in the gloom of a cool, moonless night. His heart thumped madly in his chest as he stared at the gun that had killed Curtis on Newlands station four years ago. Sweat covered his face. His mouth was dry, bitter, salty.

Somewhere far away, he heard Nkosinati screaming at him to stop. Next, he felt her pull him towards her. He clung to her, sobbing on her shoulder. When he settled, she led him indoors. None of the neighbours had come outside. There were too many random shootings or deaths at night in Crossroads township; the curious had to wait until morning to seek clarification. Nkosinati closed the door behind them. Facial furrows like a freshly ploughed field distorted her features.

"What were you trying to do, Thembani. Have you gone mad? You jumped from our bed shouting at the top of your voice. Then you extract a gun from a hole in the floor I did not even know about. Next, you rushed outside to shoot at what? What? Where did the gun come from? At least our son Curtis-Thembani slept through the shooting. Imagine if he had seen you!"

He could see her distended facial veins with her tear-stained cheeks. His heart went out to the woman he had come to love so much over the last four years. She had asked so many questions; he did not know where to begin.

"I had another nightmare."

"They've become more frequent over the past year. What's bothering you? Is there something you've not told me?" Tense facial lines distorted her beauty.

Thembani struggled. *What do I tell Nkosinati? The truth? All of it? Will she understand how the allure is my exorcism from my experience on the station?*

"It's the necklacing," he whispered. "I see these people dying. Tonight, I thought I saw my burning head." He pointed to his forehead. "I saw my scar! The next thing I know, I'm awoken by the noise of the gun shooting. I'm so sorry. Please forgive me."

"You mentioned these dreams to me before." Her voice was earnest; she held his hand while she rubbed the back of his hand with the other hand. "Why do you have them? You must tell me if you know!"

He noticed how wide her eyes were. He did not want to lie to Nkosinati who was such an honest, caring person. *Should I at least tell her part of the story?* He turned to look her in the eye. He stroked her cheek. When he held her hands, Nkosinati's body stiffened.

Thembani coughed, then took a few deep breaths. His pulse raced before he continued, his mouth much dryer than before. The conversation was one of the worst moments of his life.

He spoke quietly while he held both her hands in his. "Before a necklacing, you know there's a trial. Witnesses are called. The accused may or may not be in court. An appointed judge decides on guilt as well as the sentence. Necklacing is inevitable if they have collaborated with police or Witdoeke." He paused as Nkosinati looked at him with an unaccustomed fierce intensity.

He stammered as he continued. "The sentence is enacted by informal officers of the court who will take the prisoner from the court to the local soccer field a few blocks away from our place." Thembani pointed in the direction of the field then wiped at the sweat on his forehead with his sleeve.

"Other informal officers supply the petrol." With difficulty, Thembani finally whispered. "I sometimes supply the tyre."

"Excuse me. Did you say you supply the tyre? *You?*"

Thembani heard her tone of disbelief. She dropped his hands to turn her back on him. Her sobbing sliced through him. The only time he had felt such pain was in 1986 when Curtis had died on the station.

She pushed his hands away when he tried to place his hands on her shoulders, stepping forwards to avoid him.

"You abhor killing. Yet you do this? Is this what you want to teach Curtis-Thembani?" Her strident voice pierced through his head. "I love you; our son admires you. How can you do this to us? Why? Tell me *now!*"

"I love you so much, Nkosinati. The most wonderful moment in my life was when I married you. Having our son added to my joy. The past four years with the two of you have been ... sublime, magical. I worship both of you. To hurt you as I have is unforgivable."

She brushed away his hands as he again tried to hold her. She expected to hear more. *How much more? How do I tell her my dreams about necklacing are not as bad as my earlier terrors involving Curtis, Pat, and Ebrahim on Newlands station?*

"When I told you before I disapproved of necklacing, I meant it. I cannot stand the sight of the stumbling, flaming body of a screaming person about to die. The worst part is the way they continue to stagger around when they cannot scream any longer. It's like a silent horror movie in real-time slow motion."

Thembani broke off. He had to gather his thoughts. "Necklacing has a repulsive magnetism. It's like wanting to stroke a hungry lion, yet when they lift the tyre, I have to leave before the flames, or the screaming begin. Despite this, I often return after a few weeks with the next tyre."

"How long have you been involved in this ... necklacing?"

"For two years now."

"And how many times? Ten? Twenty? Huhh?" Nkosinati's body trembled while she stared at him.

"No. Seven." His insides were raw with shame. His pulse hammered in his ears. "Please forgive me. I hate concealing anything from you. I promise you my necklacing days are over. I love you too much to lose you. Please forgive me."

Nkosinati turned to face him. Her hands were on her hips. *Oh no, she wants to know more!*

"So, what about the gun? Tell me now!"

Thembani squirmed under Nkosinati's gaze while her harsh tone grated on his ears. He had never before seen her so angry. This was their first real blow-up. *Do I tell her of the circumstances of how the gun killed Curtis?* His mind raced with the four-year-old disastrous events, which were still as fresh in his mind as if they were yesterday.

"The gun is not mine. Tonight was the first time I fired the weapon." He lapsed into silence.

"As you know, Thembani, I'm aware of how you took two lives when you and Curtis saved me in Crossroads. Have you used the gun to kill anyone else?"

Thembani wiped at his sweaty brow. "No. I have no heart to shoot anyone."

'There's more, isn't there?" Nkosinati's eyebrows arched steeply.

'Sadly, yes." He rubbed at his nose. "I have never used the gun until tonight. It's part of a story I cannot tell you yet. Please, bear with me. One day I'll be able to tell you about the gun."

"Does the story have to do with Curtis' death? You said you would tell me his secret too, one day. What went on with the two of you?"

Thembani again dabbed at his forehead with his handkerchief. He sensed a softening in Nkosinati's voice. "Yes. When possible, I'll tell you everything about the gun and Curtis; I promise you; give me time. I'm not ready yet."

Thembani sighed. Nkosinati's rigid back from behind was a sign she had not yet forgiven him. He turned from her to sit on the sofa. His head, buried in his hands, was dizzy with a jumble of blurred images he would prefer to confine to oblivion. As always, Curtis' last words echoed in his brain - 'I'm done for'. Tears filled Thembani's eyes.

CHAPTER 27: MATHS LESSON

July 1991

LYDIAH WAS ON HER WAY to the students' Union for her weekly lunchtime date with Thembani and Ivan. She had an extra spring in her step today as she wanted to share her news with them. She had not felt so good since Willie's death seven months ago; she could barely contain herself.

The midday autumn sun felt pleasant on her face. She had applied fresh lipstick before she left to meet them. Her light facial makeup included a hint of purple and pink on the upper eyelid with a thin strip of black on the eyelids, complementing her green eyes. She wore a red cashmere jumper reaching to her neck. A full-length intense black skirt extended to her black shoes with heels of a sensible height suited to a day on her feet.

Ahead she saw Ivan, so she walked faster towards him. She pushed back the soft curls of her light brown hair from around her face. She started to smile as she approached him from behind.

"Ivan!" she called. Her heart rate increased when he turned with his face all smiles as she approached him. She felt a strange need to throw herself into his arms. Instead, she gave him a firm hug, followed by a kiss on the lips, rather than her normal peck on the cheek. Lydiah sensed Ivan's surprise. There was a bit of tension in his body, while she experienced a pleasant stirring, way within herself.

"Lydiah. It's always wonderful to see you, though there's something more about you today."

"Yes? What?" she asked.

"Where do I start," Ivan looked quizzically at her while he held her at arms' length. "Everything! I suppose, starting with your hair. I'm not sure I ever noticed the blond streaks before."

"It must be the sun, as well as the English genes, of course. Anything else?" she asked almost mischievously.

"Well, the jumper really suits you. Ahh! the face, especially the eyes."

Lydiah flickered her eyes in an exaggerated fashion. "It's a new mascara, rather expensive too." She threw back her head as she laughed. Ivan joined her; his smile was broader than she had seen before. "But I'm on a bit of borrowed time. Let's find Thembani. I have important news to share with the two of you."

She slipped her arm into his then briefly rested her head against his shoulder before they strolled towards the Union. She felt an unexpected inner tingling; it felt right to walk with Ivan in this fashion. She hoped he did not mind.

Thembani rose to greet them. "You two look so ... energised."

"Well, blame Lydiah. She's bubbling away here next to me. I can't stop her," Ivan laughed.

"Really. What's up, Lydiah?" asked Thembani.

"Excuse me, please. All students, including the two of you, must now call me Professor when you address me."

The two men whooped with delight.

"That's wonderful news," said Thembani.

"Amazing! Well done, Lydiah." Ivan shook her hand then kissed her on the cheek, as did Thembani.

The joyous trio tucked into their fare. The two men regarded Lydiah's salad as rabbit food, while she always teased how their cheddar cheese sandwiches were eaten by seamen rather than university students with distinctions.

Thembani looked at her beaming. "I always knew you would be professor one day. So, when did they inform you?"

"This past weekend, eight months to the day since Willie's death. You can imagine me having those mixed emotions, then Suzanne set me straight. She said the professorship was part of me moving on. I suppose she's right. Willie always said I would do it one day. After my PhD, he often called me Prof. You two know what a tease he was."

Thembani laughed. "He was wicked sometimes."

"Well, that's wonderful news," said Ivan. "She's raised the bar for us, Thembani."

"If neither of you does a PhD, I will shoot you!" Lydiah admonished the two. "There's no doubt you both have the potential, so I will nag you to death until you do it."

"Of course, Professor," said Thembani as they all laughed.

Lydiah glanced at her watch. "Oops! I have to spoil the fun, because I have to lecture to the third-year students."

She kissed Thembani on the cheek then strolled around the table to Ivan to kiss him too. "I'll see you tonight. I never thought I'd see Suzanne so excited about Maths classes. You've done well with her. Thank you."

Lydiah turned to leave. Again, there was a lightness in her being she had not felt since Willie's death.

Ivan finished off the last of his sandwiches. Thembani had been watching him closely. "What's up? You look amused."

"No. I'm perplexed, even curious," said Thembani.

"Really. Why?"

"It's Lydiah. I've never seen more love on your face than at lunchtime today. I can't say I blame you. She was at her stunning best today."

"If that's the way I looked, then I'd have to confess it's the way I felt. My heart was palpitating, while my head was in a spin. I thought everyone would have seen it. She looked exquisite, so radiant, captivating. She made all my nerves tingle when she met me, kissed me on the mouth, then hooked me in the arm to rest her head on my shoulder. It felt like she belongs there, Thembani." Talking about Lydiah had increased his pulse rate. "Everything she does or says, every facial twitch registers with me. I relive them all until we meet again. No woman has ever made me feel like this."

"I have only one word, Ivan. L-O-V-E!" Thembani emphasised each letter when he spelt the word, smiling broadly.

"But it's all unexplored territory; where do I go from here?"

"I can't believe it's eight months since we chatted at the top of Ou Kaapse Weg. I sense a chemistry has developed between you two. Maybe you've not noticed a change in Lydiah until today, yet lately I've noticed a softening of her demeanour whenever you speak. Is she ready to let you in? I don't know, though I've seen those eyes before." Thembani stopped; his eyes teared up.

"When we finished our bus ride to her parents in the Transkei, Nkosinati had the same look in her eyes. She had a touch of something at the beginning; towards the end of the magical trip, I saw deep love there." He stopped to gather himself. "Maybe you two need a similar bus ride. That's the one to Umthatha which takes forever." Thembani chuckled in his infectious fashion in which Ivan had to join.

IVAN SAT OPPOSITE SUZANNE at the dining room table where they conducted her lessons. He used a pad of A4 sheets as a blackboard. They always started with the previous week's homework.

"Well done yet again, young lady,"

"'I always like the way you say that.'"

"What part?"

"All three, though I like 'young lady' the best."

"What's so special about that?"

"It always sounds so ... respectful. I like that. So does Mummy."

"That's nice to hear. Now, what about your homework?"

"I see there's hardly any red there except 'WELL DONE!' in capitals. I did not think I would ever enjoy Maths, yet I am now with the best in my class."

They continued their way through the evening's programme he had prepared.

At the end of their session, Suzanne put down her pencil. "It's so nice how the thick fog of letters or symbols has become much clearer with Algebra." Suzanne paused. "Now, may I ask you a personal question?"

"Of course." Ivan narrowed his eyes expectantly.

Suzanne took a deep breath. "Do you like my Mum?"

Ivan looked at Suzanne with wide eyes. There was a fierce intensity in her blue eyes. She had a soft lisp, and he adored the thin front tooth gap of hers. "Of course. She's a lovely lady."

"But do you *really* like her?"

"I suppose I do. Why do you ask?"

Suzanne looked at him, her face now furrowed. "Well, she's always talking about you."

"I'm sure she must talk about other people too," said Ivan, defensive yet probing at the same time. He noticed a quickening of his pulse.

"True. Though it's different the way she talks about you."

"Really. How?" Ivan's heart rate was now much faster.

"I don't know how, it's definitely different. Trust me." They both laughed.

Ivan heard Lydiah coming downstairs. His heart skipped a beat when she entered the room. He averted his eyes to gather the papers he placed in his backpack.

"By the sounds of it, you two are having fun."

"Mum, I'll turn in early tonight as tomorrow's museum school trip starts early."

"Then don't take a book to bed with you." Lydiah laughed.

"No, I won't." She hugged Ivan then kissed her mother before she went upstairs.

❋

Lydiah went to the lounge. "Would you like to have a drink with me? I'm still in a celebratory mood. I have half a bottle of champagne in the fridge from when the family were here on Sunday."

"I would not mind staying, but could I have a cup of Milo instead. I know it's Suzanne's favourite."

"By all means," said Lydiah. "Come, join me in the kitchen where there are a few leftover nibbles. Do you not drink alcohol?"

"I used to drink a beer or a bit of wine occasionally before prison. I have not touched a drop since my release. Milo is different, like chocolate. When you've been thirteen years without those, you can't have enough of either."

"Cheers! Here's to us." Lydiah clinked her full glass on his mug of Milo. "Take care; it's steaming hot. Let's go to the lounge."

Lydiah watched Ivan with a feeling of inner contentment as the constant gnawing away at her insides had dissipated over the past few hours. There was a sense of relief feeling the way she now did, as if there was a pleasant rousing within her.

She placed the plate on the coffee table before she removed her shoes to sit on the sofa with her legs stretched out. Ivan sat at the other end of the couch, with her feet against his thighs. She raised her glass to him before sipping at it. She watched the way Ivan held his mug of Milo with two hands, sniffed at the drink with his eyes closed, then sampled it. Everything he did seemed so fine, so delicate. She had not previously noticed how slender his long fingers were.

"I've never before seen someone drink Milo so ... sensuously," she smiled.

"I like the way you drink your champagne. You are halfway through the glass, yet there's no lipstick on the rim. Then there's the lovely red of your top shining through the glass. With the wall lamp light overhead, the effect is stunning, to say the least." Ivan raised his cup towards her.

"And I like the way the light catches the swishing curl in the middle of your forehead. It's cute. I won't say sexy," she giggled.

"The curl is one of those things I wanted after I was released. I went in there with it. It's part of what I needed after prison."

"So, how far are you in the process of coming back?" She drank from her nearly empty glass. Until the weekend, she had not drunk since Willie's funeral. She savoured the slow mental release with an inner body comfort she now felt.

Ivan was slow to reply. "The eighteen months since my release has been a drawn-out process. Prison was often about ... survival of the fittest. I was constantly on the alert. The hardcore types would take you out, so you constantly looked over your shoulder. Life in there is cheap; it's worth nothing. When I try to relax now, it's still difficult. My studies are my escapist salvation. My weekend work at Mr G's helps the body and the mind. Who would think mixing concrete, then pushing a barrowload of the stuff could be therapeutic." He laughed.

Lydiah took pleasure in these moments when his chin cleft was deepest, now partly shadowed by the lamplight, highlighting his angular features with his prominent cheekbones. *Is there more in what I'm feeling?*

"I'm about to pour the final bit of bubbly. Would you like another Milo?"

"No thanks."

Lydiah went to the kitchen then returned to the lounge to place her nearly full glass on the coffee table.

"I need to pop upstairs to get your surprise present."

"For me? I hate surprises! I can't stand the suspense. Please tell me." His face was a mask of false pleading.

"Liar!" she snorted. "If I told you, then there'd be no surprise," she said as she darted upstairs to retrieve the parcel she had wrapped earlier. There were hearts on the wrapper. She had hardly noticed them earlier. On her way back, she peeped into Suzanne's bedroom, where she was fast asleep. Lydiah closed the door to her bedroom. On the way downstairs, she had to steady herself by holding onto the staircase rails.

Seated alongside Ivan, her heart was stirring in an almost forgotten fashion as she looked into his enquiring hazel-coloured eyes. On his furrowed brow the curl had pushed sideways. She held the parcel behind her back. Her heart drummed away in her chest, with the beats reaching to her neck. *Oh no!*

"Are you going to hide my gift from me all evening?" His expression was one of urgent entreaty.

"No. If you guess correctly, I'll let you have one."

"That can only be chocolates," Ivan's face beamed when Lydiah held the box behind her head.

"I said one only."

He leaned over to wrap his arms around her in an attempt to get at the box. A giggling Lydiah caught her breath. Her heart now raced; she bit her lips before she lifted her head to kiss him with a fervour she had consigned to oblivion. She dropped the box onto the floor to run her fingers through his soft curls as she drew him closer. The kiss seemed to last forever. She felt his strong arms around her. He then traced his fingers along her spine to her lower back. She ached inside, choking with a raw visceral emotion, tingling with his every touch.

The full-length total body warmth they shared on the couch was a delight she wished to savour more of as she snuggled further into him. Neither of them said a word. She buried her head into the side of his neck, holding him close as her tears started to flow. She could not stop them. Her soft sobbing came from deep inside like a mixture of pain and joy. Ivan held her close; one hand stroked her hair while the other rubbed her shoulder. He still said nothing. He kissed her forehead, while both hands rubbed at her shoulders.

Silence enveloped them where they lay on the sofa. She gave him a lingering kiss before she bent over to retrieve the box of chocolates from the floor.

"Thank you," she said, giving him the box.

"Why, thank me? I'm the blessed one with your kiss, and the chocolates. Want one?'" Ivan started to unwrap the box.

"That's two questions to answer. First, the thanks. You did not grope me."

"I respect you too much to do that."

"Second. Yes. I'll have a chocolate." She lunged at the opened box, now held high, beyond her reach.

"That's one only," Ivan said as he lowered the box, while they enjoyed the fare in amongst their giggles.

"I like the hearts on the wrapper," Ivan said as he looked at the box. "Lindt, I've not eaten those before. The almond nut pieces in the dark chocolate are excellent.?" Ivan popped another ball into his mouth.

"It's my favourite chocolate. We may have to fight over them."

'I don't know about that. You gave them to me, remember?"

She sat back, and finished off the last of her bubbly while she watched Ivan slowly unwrap the chocolates before he bit into them.

Lydia wriggled her feet under his legs, enjoying the way his warmth seemed to pass through to her body.

"There are two chocolates left." He popped one into his mouth. "Would you like the last?"

"If you take the wrapping off, then yes."

Ivan obliged with his knee on the ground as he handed the chocolate ball to her. With the Lindt ball in a bulging cheek, she crunched away at her treat before she swallowed the creamy delight. Like the chocolate, she felt herself melting. Her inner wetness pleased her as Ivan's soft eyes fixed on her. She was taken aback at what she saw in his eyes. *It is love!*

She drew his hands to her throbbing breasts, her inner craving sought satisfaction. Her hands started to wander everywhere, as did his. He felt as ready as she was. Every touch of Ivan's was like a flame to the dormant needs she thought were extinguished forever.

"I want you," she whispered in his neck. "Right now. Never mind the clothes." She removed her panty to have him between her thighs, where he soon buried himself in her. They both eclipsed simultaneously. Lydiah dug her nails into his back. She felt his firm pressure on her breasts. Lydiah's feelings came from much deeper than any of her previous experiences. Maybe the ultimate high came from those extraordinary depths. She felt spent. Ivan withdrew from her as Lydiah started to cry.

With his arms around her, Ivan kissed any part of her close to his lips before he lay back. His was a powerful comforting presence.

Once settled, she again ran her fingers through his hair, then traced her fingers around his lips. His eyes were closed as if taking it all in. His spicy aftershave with floral overtones made her head spin.

"That was wonderful. It's been a while."

"Speak for yourself," said Ivan, with a broad grin.

"This is so unexpected. I thought my love-making days were all over."

"Let's not rush anything. From different perspectives, it's new to both of us. But, whatever you decide, you must know I have loved you ever since I first set eyes on you from the day we first met."

"Oh Ivan, I'm so touched. I suspected nothing. It must be your forehead curl."

"So now cute becomes sexy?"

"Oh yes," Lydiah drew him close; Ivan had rekindled a lost part of her.

"So, was there a message in the hearts' wrapper around my chocolates?"

"Yes, there is a message - I love you, Ivan Pettersen," she said as she held him tight with his head on her chest. Lydiah could hardly believe she had said it, but she knew it was real; she needed it probably as much as he did. She lay there, in no hurry to leave the warmth and comfort of his presence.

CHAPTER 28: BOYS' NIGHT OUT

August 1991

LEEU WAS IMPRESSED with the exploits of the Balaclava Gang. After twenty months with them, the initial whispering campaign about them had snowballed to a level of much community concern in Crossroads and in Khayelitsha. These two townships were ANC or UDF viper's nests where the feared Gang did most of their work. Other gangs did similar work around the country.

The State's enemies, Communists or terrorists were their primary targets. However, there was a blurring around the edges with their efforts to stop any compromise between Whites and Blacks. He was part of an ultra-right-wing drive by many police personnel who wanted to maintain their preferred discriminatory State by all means possible. White is Right! White is Might! spurred them on.

He and Koos drove from central police headquarters after one of their regular briefings. The Kombi sped along the motorway towards the Truth Factory before their next mission of malice.

"Know what I like the most about our work, Leeu? We can drop the *Kaffirs* to do the dirty work while we wait in the Kombi slugging our Klipdrift."

"True. Though I must keep my juices flowing by joining in the action whenever I can," laughed Koos. "We are the creators of destruction, chaos and death."

"But those forty sacked kitskonstabels (instant constables) you took on last month are something else. Even I'm cautious around those murderous bastards."

"Fear not; they're as loyal as they come," said Leeu. "We pay them well enough. All HQ is interested in is the body count at the end of a job." To Leeu's amazement the new recruits were able to walk from their original jobs without surrendering their weapons although many had been fired because of armed robbery, murder, hijackings, car theft and rape.

"I'm concerned the way many of them arrive at work already pissed," said Koos.

"How often are we not pissed too?" Leeu laughed. "Truth be told, there are times when I don't know what day of the week it is." Leeu laughed louder. "I live in a world suspended between reality, and a constant state of boozing. A touch of cannabis helps me a few times a week too." He did not add how his basement games added more spice to his secret life.

"I'd have to agree with you there," said Koos.

"I think of us a gang with its own rules. I admired the Nazi death camps. I suppose in our fashion, we have the same here without the gas ovens." Leeu patted his gun.

They drove through the gates at the Factory. Leeu tooted the Kombi's horn, with the roller door opening soon. There were already enough of them if they needed to go out. First, though, they had to deal with a stubborn MK commander who would not talk despite all their treatment.

"The only useful thing about the terr so far is the overtime we can claim," grumbled Leeu. "Once he tells us where the arms cache is, we can finish him off. So today we'll try ice therapy."

"What's that, Leeu?" asked Koos.

"'Watch me, dear colleague." Leeu cracked the fingers of his hands.

They strolled over to where a bloodied naked man hung suspended from the overhead beam. They had secured his cuffed hands over the wooden joist with his feet off the ground. A group of the askaris hovered around close by. Penny strolled over with his casual swagger.

"He won't talk. Do you want me to finish him off?"

"He's supposed to be a commander," said Leeu. "He should know more about arms caches than anyone else. What treatment have you tried?"

"Everything except the kitchen sink. Punching bag on a rope, rib and cheekbone fractures, waterboarding with the hood, electrocutions. We already lionised his thumbnails. He screamed loudest when we manicured him. Now the tough bastard needs a bullet between the ears," Penny snorted. The askaris liked to bet whether the bullet exited the opposite ear or at 15-minute clock-face points around the ear.

'Before you have your wish let's ice him.' Leeu rubbed his hands. "I've not done one before, though the visiting security officer I spoke to last week said it's effective."

"You know me," said Penny. "I'm always willing to learn."

"You have to suspend him by the ankles with his legs apart. His head must be off the ground. I'll fetch the ice from the freezer."

Leeu soon returned with a bag of ice blocks. He slipped on a pair of rubber garden gloves then forced the square blocks into the shrieking man's anus. Penny struggled to keep the ice in place with his gloved hands. Once Leeu had emptied the bag, he held the buttocks together with duct tape wound a few times around the top of the man's legs in a figure of eight fashion. Throughout it all, the rest of the men had the hysterics.

Leeu stepped back, covered in sweat. "Well, I'm not sure I'll do the ice trick again. It's too much hard work; at least he's in serious pain. The Security guy said it's like having a red-hot poker stuck in your arse. Once the ice melts, there's no evidence of what's been done."

Penny came over. His belly wobbled with his laughter. "Now that's something else. It's the loudest he's screamed since we started to work on him."

Leeu excused himself to go to the toilet where the smell of urine assailed his nostrils. He did not wash his hands in the suspect-looking hand basin. Instead, he lit another cigarette then inhaled deeply. The smoke rose to dance in the narrow beam of sunlight shining through a high cracked window.

The prisoner's shrieking stopped after Leeu heard a shot ring out. *Bloody hell, that fucken black bastard has shot the terr!* He hoped Penny had waited long enough.

When he returned, the terrorist's body, wrapped in a tarpaulin sheet, lay on the Kombi floor. A puddle of clotted blood pooled in the drain below the overhead beam.

"What the fuck's going on here," Leeu shouted.

"Relax, boss," said Penny. "We have an address, though I'm not sure I would ever ice anyone again. What do you think?"

"Ja, maybe. What's the address?"

"It's at 168A Ntlazane Road, Khayelitsha."

"You bloody dimwit. He's duped you. That's the address of councillor Mbatha, one of our men."

"No way. Bloody hell!" said Penny as his askari mates erupted with laughter while a few came over to commiserate with him.

"But I would have shot him too had he told me that." He patted an embarrassed Penny on the back.

"Well, there's nothing else to do so we may as well go to Khayelitsha. There's a UDF rally against increased housing levies at the senior school. Let's load up. Koos will drive as I want to do the shooting tonight." UDF protest meetings were prime targets of the Gang's drive-by shootings.

Eight of them piled into the van after he and Koos had applied their black camouflage paste. The balaclavas were already on board. Leeu brought along his AK 47, his preferred tool on these trips. Leeu flicked away his finished cigarette before the two policemen slugged more brandy from their bottle. The six ascaris passed their own fuel around amongst themselves. The two groups never shared their bottles which were often empty by the time they reached their destination.

It was their normal noisy, boisterous ride with his colleagues teasing Penny all the way. From the N2 Highway, they took the Mew Way exit. High streetlights cast dim light onto the street below, where there was a mishmash of housing and stores. A mix of rusted corrugated iron or wooden fences, higgledy-piggledy wire, or precast concrete walls, lined the busy road's narrow pavement. Building material filled a long length of the pavement, forcing pedestrians to walk on the busy street instead. Beyond Pama Road, they pulled over onto a dark sandy strip on the right where there was a tract of low bush where they dumped the terrorist's body. After a final swig from their bottles, they put on their balaclavas. Koos pulled one from his pocket.

"It's acrylic, bought on special at Ackermans. Now I won't itch."

Leeu laughed. "I thought only the poor *Kaffirs* and *Hotnots* shopped there. Did you go shopping with your camouflage paste on?" Leeu laughed.

"Fuck you!" Koos was not amused.

They bounced back onto Mew Way before taking a left turn into Spine Road.

Leeu sweated under his balaclava; he hated the damned thing. He opened his window, as did the rest of them, all facing towards the left.

"Okay, men. It's a left turn ahead followed by another left turn, then we can let rip from the road through the gates or the wire fence as we drive past the school." Leeu's gun rested on the open window's edge. "I'll fire first."

"I'll slow down a bit now," said Koos.

As soon as they reached the school's front driveway, a rapid burst of gunfire erupted from the rear seat. *It's that fucken Penny!* A fuming Leeu joined in the shooting while Koos drove slowly in first gear along the street.

People outside the school building tried to run away; others threw themselves onto the ground. The noise in the car was deafening. The ammoniacal smell of cordite from seven AK 47s firing away was intense. Leeu could taste it. He coughed along with a few others.

"Sorry, men!" said Koos as he swung the Kombi toward the middle of the road to avoid the parked cars outside. He accelerated while the men continued to shoot at or through the parked cars. Hoots of laughter followed when one of the vehicles erupted into flames. At the corner, they turned left to reach Spine Road where Koos drove towards the N2 Highway over a kilometre away.

There was hilarity all round. Leeu pulled off his balaclava with the sound of gunfire still ringing in his ears. He was mindful of how hot the AK 47-gun barrel was. They left the windows open to clear the van of the acrid cordite smell. Already, more brandy added to the evening's sport.

"I hope the shooting puts the shits into them!" Leeu said to Koos. "White is right! White is might!" He punched Koos on the shoulder. He felt a smug satisfaction at another job well done. He no longer worried about a headcount. Whatever the media reported would be different to HQ's figures come payday.

Their route took them past the two school containers; Koos took a potshot with his fingers at the classes.

"It's now nine months since we killed Miggie," said Leeu.

"Ja, the lucky bitch survived. If I'd known she was still alive, I could've had her as planned," said Koos.

"The trouble now is the *Kaffir* and *Hotnot* smart arses from UCT have replaced them. The *Hotnot* is a known terrorist who has done prison time after blowing up electrical power substations. I manicured his nails in '76. We have to keep an eye on the two of them," said Leeu, lighting a fresh cigarette as they drifted into an unaccustomed silence.

Leeu looked forward to the day's end. He wanted to try something new at home where he constantly reinvented the games played in the basement bedroom. After almost two years, Leeu could not believe how life in Cape Town felt even better than it had in SWA.

CHAPTER 29: FIRST RECRUITER

September 1991

Ivan sat in his car in the late afternoon warmth in the highest university car park, facing the side-on view of Table Mountain with the imposing Devil's Peak to the right. Now, almost two years since his release from prison, he never tired of seeing the mountains in their different moods, even today when an ominous black cloud covered both mountain tops. The obscured sun had less than an hour to go before sunset.

In the past four months, his relationship with Lydiah had more than filled the void in his life. Their moments together were special, treasured by Ivan who now rarely had troublesome nights. His sleeping hours were instead filled with images of his time with Lydiah. He had told her about his prison experiences, including his episodes with Leeu as well as his more devastating gang rite membership experience.

Lydiah related his experience to her own near-death moments at the funeral of a schoolgirl in 1976, and at the time of Willie's death. However, she seemed more concerned about his tattoos, especially the gun on his forearm. Her distaste must have stemmed from her two close brushes with death, both involving guns. He had considered laser tattoo removal though residual scarring could be a problem as well as needing multiple sessions of therapy. An alternative was to tattoo Table Mountain to cover the gun.

As much as Ivan wanted to tell her everything about himself, he kept to himself the experience of how he ended his gang membership, despite the occasional nocturnal revisiting of those interminable minutes in the burning Chevrolet. Always central to the unsettling visions was the cigar stuck in the bloodied head on the rear seat with two jets of blood from Ses' headless corpse on the front seat. The bodyguard's ripped-open chest frequently completed his trifecta of tormenting recalls. There were occasions when he would sweat profusely during the day when flashback images of those moments broke through.

NOW, WITH THE MORRIS' window open, a refreshing breeze fanned his face while he worked his way through the notes he had made during the lectures of the day. Thembani would be along later. A late-model silver-grey Mercedes Benz sports car pulled up alongside his Morrie. He had seen the driver before on campus. The driver kissed a beautiful woman before exiting the car, and waved to Ivan who returned the greeting by nodding his head. He was somewhat surprised when the silver-suited driver came over to extend a hand towards him.

"Hi there. I'm John Johnston, from Elsies River, like you. I've seen you around."

Ivan shook the hand. He liked the firm handshake. "I'm Ivan Pettersen. How'd you know I'm from Elsies?"

"Oh, word gets around. Can we chat?"

"Why sure. Come around. The door is unlocked." He packed his notes into his backpack before placing them on the back seat.

"A Morris Minor. Not many of these left on the roads these days. What year?" He sat partly sideways on the passenger seat facing Ivan. His aftershave smelled expensive.

"1965. The 1000 model was the final in the series in '71."

John laughed. "I learnt to drive on my father's Beetle of about the same vintage. However, I must say I prefer my present German model these days." He flashed a finger towards his car. His girlfriend waved at him. "Huh! She thinks I waved at her."

"Your girlfriend?"

"Kinda. They come, and they go." He chuckled. "You probably know I'm a law student with another year to go. But, let me get down to business," He paused, looking steadily at Ivan. "Our organisation needs you."

"What organisation? Why?"

"Before we go any further, I need you to promise me our conversation will be in the strictest confidence and must never leave the Morris." His dark eyes projected his earnestness.

"That will be difficult to do without me having an inkling of what the subject matter is." Ivan spoke guardedly.

John frowned, drumming his fingers on his legs. "Partly it's about upgrading your Morris to a vehicle like mine, maybe even a girl. She has an amazing sister."

His smile looked forced. Where's he heading? Ivan breathed more deeply.

"It's a business proposition from the Achar-Americans. They sponsor my studies, among other things."

Ivan's eyes narrowed, his pulse raced, and his stomach muscles quivered. Curiosity now drove his reply. "Well, I'm surprised, of course. Curious too. Yes, I can hold my tongue. What's your interest in me?"

"I suppose it's about the brave new world we are in after Mandela's release. Things are moving fast. Around 1979 Prime Minister Botha used the expression 'adapt or die' to outline his distorted vision of a modified South Africa. In a different context, the Achar-Americans must now do the same thing." Throughout his talk, his piercing eyes stayed on Ivan's.

"Few people drive a Morris these days. The world has moved on. Look around you. Cars used to be manuals; now they're all automatics. Black and white TV sets, now massive colour sets with video. From LPs to CDs, and transistors to iPods. Computers didn't exist when you went to prison. The world has changed so much." He paused as he scanned Ivan's expressionless face.

"Some of my colleagues know about you. They are ex-26 members. They tell me you were a senior officer at the time of your release in December. I know how prison gang membership entails blood. We need this kind of steel in our leaders, though more important to me are the distinctions you achieved in your exams. We need your intellect."

Ivan was somewhat aghast at the direction of the conversation. *Maybe tell him to shut up, leave me alone? I'm committed to where I'm at.*

Ivan sniffed. "How? Why?" He regretted how curiosity had again won the mental tussle.

"We are looking towards tomorrow's world. I'm the head of the Achar-American steering committee looking to the future of our organisation. I need you. We need you. Come with us or be left behind as we prepare to join the New World. Like the prison gangs, the township gangs are evolving. Gang restructuring is taking place." The penetrating eyes now seemed to beseech Ivan.

"The late Ses was a liability - old school, too violent, also out of touch with global politics, trade, and drug links. New supply lines have opened with African countries previously closed to us. Our country is the world 's leading producer of Mandrax and cannabis, our mainstay over many years. Yet they will soon be small bikkies once we have the supply lines to bring in cocaine, crack, amphetamines, opium, heroin, LSD ... Excluded from the world before, the international cartels are keen to supply us. Drugs and guns will be our business." His eyes now sparkled with animation. "What do you think?"

"Did Yster ask you to approach me?"

"No. He sent word you were to be left alone, though I had to approach you. Please don't tell him about us meeting. You know he expects obedience, but I need you, Ivan. I don't need the action side of you. I need what you have up here." John pointed at his head. "The two of us can be the future kingpins of the A-As, the entrepreneurs of tomorrow. Adapt or die is the mantra of any modern business. Essentially, that's what we are. A local business poised to go global." An animated John shuffled in his seat as his arms opened wide.

"Let me mention another potential benefit. I live in my own Sea Point apartment where they're selling a similar penthouse suite on the top floor next to mine. Of course, there's a mountain view on one side with the sea view on the other. Did I mention the private lift? You can move in next door to me. I've asked them to hold the property till tomorrow! It's why I had to meet you today."

Somewhat taken aback Ivan rubbed at his thumbnails. Sea Point had the most expensive real estate in the country. During more than a decade in Pollsmoor, Ivan had paid the price. He thought of the prisoner he'd stabbed, of Ses and the bodyguard. Is it my time to cash in?

He glanced at the Mercedes Benz. The girl blew him a naughty kiss, winked, then laughed, with her head thrown back. He slowly tapped his lips with an index finger. Then, in his mind's eye, he saw his tearful mother break down when he was led from the dock after his sentencing. Ivan recalled the stirring of warmth he felt with her first hug when he reached home; the more profound emotion he had from the first time he saw Lydiah, more so now since their relationship had moved on to one of shared intimacy. Ivan smiled at these thoughts as he turned to face John. In the distance he could see Thembani approaching the car.

"Thanks, John, but the answer is no. And, yes, I'm comfortable with my Morrie."

Disappointed, John pouted his lips. "That's a pity. I sense the resolve in your voice. We'd have made a superb team. If you change your mind, let me know - here's my card. Go well with your studies."

"You too, John."

The two shook hands as Thembani arrived at the car.

"Fancy car," said Thembani, strapping on his seat belt. "Fancy suit. Fancy woman." He whistled. "You know him?"

"Now I do. He's a law student, ex-Elsies River."

"I've seen him around. Sometimes he comes with a BMW, the 750-model."

"He came over to say hello."

"He must have a bit of money to his name."

"Too true. How was your day?"

"Brilliant, like all other days'" said Thembani. I can hardly believe our second lot of finals are due next month."

"If we do as well as we did last year, then we should be okay, though always my attitude is one day at a time, one exam at a time. The most important test is always the next one."

"Now there's a bit of prison-driven philosophy from you. I like it!" Thembani cracked up.

Ivan loved the way his friend erupted with his infectious laughter. Ivan nodded his head slowly as he turned off Settler's way onto Duinefontein Road. John Johnson had surprised Ivan with his openness, though John also knew quite a bit about Stanley's time with 26. Ivan fingered John's gold-edged card he had placed in his shirt pocket. *Should I accept his offer?* After a few minutes, his thoughts turned to Lydiah, and he flicked the card through the car window.

CHAPTER 30: GRADUATION

November 1992

THEMBANI HAD TO PINCH himself to prove he was not dreaming. Three years after joining UCT, he was about to graduate with distinctions in English and History. Becoming Thembani Dlamini, BA(UCT) had been a tortuous journey.

The road taken by the bookworm from caddying at the King David Country Club had not been easy, with many speed bumps along the way. His 1980s near-death experiences during the Release Mandela March, the Fires of Crossroads, and the Newlands station attack with the deaths of his three Comrades were a far cry from where he now stood on the steps to Jameson Hall awaiting his capping.

The family had hired a mini taxi van to bring them through. Filled with pride at their home, Thembani strode to the taxi with Nkosinati on his arm while a cheering Curtis-Thembani ran around them. When they collected his parents at the family home, he felt sublime when he walked hand-in-hand with them ahead of his siblings. Outside, the immediate neighbours applauded his rare achievement. Their taxi ride was a noisy trip, with everyone speaking or laughing at the same time.

The famous Jameson Hall steps were crowded as the graduates gathered with their supporters. Thembani wore his black suit with a blue stipple in it. He insisted on wearing the same suit he wore on the day of his marriage. Both occasions represented pinnacles in his life. The hired black gown and cape with a blue hood matched his suit and royal blue tie. Nkosinati had applauded when he presented himself to her at home.

She looked resplendent in her rose-pink dress, complemented by a cute hat placed at a jocular angle on top of her delicate curls. Her floral perfume, part of the magical bus ride, still made his head spin.

"This is how I imagined you when you agreed to go to UWC. The next time, you will be in purple. Yes, then you will be Dr Dlamini!" she teased.

"Well, Mamma, Pappa. It's my graduation day." Thembani beamed. "I kept my promise."

"Yes, you did, son," said his mother, resplendent in royal blue, her favourite colour. Like Nkosinati, she sported a hat for the first time.

"I always believed you would, Thembani. You were too bright to be a caddy all your life." His father laughed. He sported a new dark suit with a white shirt and a red tie.

"I have all of you to thank. In different ways, all of you contributed to me standing here today, gowned, caped and hooded. Nkosinati encouraged me to apply. Being the compliant husband I am, I did." Thembani could not suppress a chuckle.

Nkosinati snorted. "If only he was always like this."

He hugged Nkosinati before he called a passing photographer. They were all giggles while the photographer organised them on the steps with Jameson Hall behind them. Thembani insisted the photos had to include Devil's Peak to the left of Jameson Hall. Woodstock Cave on the Peak reminded him of where he had introduced their revolutionary group of four to the toyi-toyi in 1985.

"I have to go and be seated now," said Thembani, looking at the Casio G-Shock watch Nkosinati had bought him. "It's such a pity each graduate only gets two tickets. Thank you, Pappa. It's wonderful to have the two women of my life share the occasion with me."

He hugged his family, ending the greetings with his son. "I love you, Curtis-Thembani, as much as my friend you are named after." Even today, the mention of Curtis Fouche's name troubled Thembani. *When do I tell Nkosinati the full story?*

"I love you too, Daddy." Thembani handed his son over to his uncle; the two soon hopped their way down the steps.

"We may be away about two hours, so you guys look after Pappa. It's probably best to go over there to the right, where there will be food and seating in the Students' Union. We'll meet there when we're done."

They waved at each other as Thembani, swollen with pride, mounted the stairs toward the Hall's entrance with the joyful women in hand. At the top of the stairs, he turned to look across the Cape Flats towards the distant Helderberg Mountains, partly obscured by the early summer haze.

"Amandla, ngawethu!" he called out loud, fisting the air. Several people around him responded with fisted salutes. Life had never felt so good.

Ivan was overwhelmed when he heard his name. "Ivan Petterson, with distinctions in his first, second, third and fourth years." He was the only person to graduate with honours in every year. As he presented himself to the Chancellor, his applause seemed longer than it had been with the other students. Maybe it's my perception or my conceit! He smiled broadly. He had been grinning all day.

So much had preceded his delayed moment, a pinnacle in his life, besides Lydiah, with whom he had moved in six months earlier. At least his horror night-time moments had stopped because Lydiah nudged him awake to find solace in her arms. She believed he was re-living the terrors of his time in prison. Guilt-stricken, Ivan still withheld from her the gut-wrenching moments of the flashbacks to Ses' fiery death.

Lydiah had reintroduced him to the movies, theatre, music, and her trove of books. He savoured their long seaside walks at various sites along False Bay or Table Bay with occasional forays to his favourite, the more distant Hout Bay, where lunch was the popular batter-fried snoek with slap (barracuda with long soft) chips at the harbour-side eatery. The three locales allowed him to rediscover Cape Town's most scenic spots, where they often had braais (barbe-ques) at roadside facilities, surprisingly free of apartheid's separatist graffiti signs.

Ivan and Lydiah loved fires, as did Suzanne, who often accompa-nied them, contributing to the pleasure of their trips as a family. A highlight had been their recent hike to the top of Lion's Head, with the 90-minute brisk walk providing the most spectacular views of the Mother City. A Table Mountain hike still awaited them.

On Ivan's way to his seat, he raised his hand to a madly waving Lydiah seated a few rows behind the students. She looked stunning in her eye-catching red dress. His seated mother waved at him with both hands. In her colourful blue outfit, his mother looked radiant. Both women returned the kiss he blew at them.

"Ohh! He's my son," he heard his mother's voice.

He would have loved to see his father there as well. The way he insisted Lydiah take the second ticket was magnanimous. He re-called with warmth how his father had persisted until Lydiah accept-ed when he said he was claustrophobic. The liar!

The next hour was interminable as Ivan rested the tight-fitting cap on his knee. The green hood had clashed with his dark blue suit and sky-blue shirt, though Lydiah had found him a matching striped tie.

More than anything else, he wanted his parents in his arms to hold onto their graduate son. Their journey had been torturous; to ultimately qualify had been the cornerstone of his survival in Pollsmoor prison. The only person he had shared those harsh experi-

ences with was resplendent in dazzling red close to where he sat. He
felt fortunate to have Lydiah in his life.

Now 1993 beckoned. Ivan would do his PhD at UCT, where he
had a post as a part-time lecturer. Delivering a couple of lectures daily
to students would not be too much of a burden or a distraction from
his doctoral work. These developments were far more than his original plans to qualify and find a job. He had already refused mouth-wa-
tering offers from several multinational companies who always head-
hunted the top graduates.

Thembani had the same offer as Ivan of doing his PhD with a
spell of daily lecturing. It would help both of them because staff
members had discounted fees on any studies they enrolled in at the
university. While the subsidy was to his benefit, Ivan could not ig-
nore how here was yet another decades-old, Whites-only entitle-
ment.

On his way from the Hall, he had the two women of his life
hooked on each arm again. Outside, they made their way to the students' Union. A loud shriek indicated Colleen's location; she was
soon all over him.

"Whoa, sis! Give the others a chance, too," said Ivan, hugging her
firmly.

His father clung to him. As Ivan felt his father's tears wetting
both their cheeks, Ivan finally let go, too. Never before had he sobbed
the way he did while he clung to his parents. Ivan finally broke
through the years of suppressed emotional shackles in their huddle of
conjoined love and joy. He unashamedly allowed himself the luxury
of uncontrolled weeping; the overdue emotional catharsis felt like a
rebirth of the self.

All the family laughed or cried. Lance, now a taller version at five
years old, pushed his way through to Ivan. "Now it's my turn." Ivan
obliged the outstretched arms and whirled the youngster around in

his arms. Lance planted a wet kiss on Ivan's cheek, who reciprocated with a kiss on each of Lance's dimples.

"But why are you all crying, Ivan? Are you happy again?"

"Definitely, my boy."

"Then I'll be happy too." Lance buried his dimpled face into Ivan's chest. Ivan's heart filled with joy like never before.

With Lance still on his arm, he hugged Suzanne with the other. "Thank you, Suzanne; you helped to make my day a whole family day."

Suzanne kissed him on his tear-stained cheek. "You're welcome, Ivan. I'm glad to be family, your family." She gave him a thumbs up.

A strolling professional photographer came by. "Do you people want a group shot?"

"Oh, yes, please!" said Colleen. "My Kodak Instamatic will not do the occasion justice."

"We'll have a few," said a radiant Lydiah. "I'll treat."

"Let's choose a spot over there," said Ivan. "We'll need the Peak with the Hall."

"A graduate called Themba requested the same spot earlier today. His hood was blue."

"You must mean Thembani," said Lydiah. "See Ivan, great minds think alike!" She laughed, as did the rest of them.

Her euphoria thrilled Ivan, who held her tight during the first shot, followed by similar stances alongside each family member.

"Take a few great shots, please," said Ivan. "I don't want Thembani having the better photo."

"With his smile, he'll be difficult to beat," said Lydiah.

While they had their photographs taken, the warmth of family love engulfed Ivan. To finish the dream, he had to hand over his graduation certificate to his parents. Then, the photographer would record the moment when he expected his former self to re-emerge.

CHAPTER 31: CLINIC DRAMAS

November 1992

STANLEY GENERALLY FELT relaxed whenever Fay drove. He enjoyed watching her, particularly when the emotions bubbled to the surface as they often did. Tonight's drive to the SACLA clinic was no exception.

"The country has certainly had five days of high drama since Chris Hani's assassination last Saturday," said Fay.

The leader of MK died after a shooting in front of his fifteen-year-old daughter outside his home. A White Afrikaner woman dobbed in the assassin, Janusz Walus, detained with Derby-Lewis, the shadow Minister of Economic Affairs.

"How far does the complicity extend?" asked Fay as she stopped at the clinic.

"Tomorrow's stay-away to commemorate Hani's death is likely to be massive. Now reality intervenes, and we have work to do," said Stanley.

STANLEY COULD NOT BELIEVE his eyes. An ashen-faced man had walked through the waiting room to sit on a chair outside the doctor's consulting rooms. With a plastic Pick' n Pay shopping bag in his hand, he looked like he had returned from the supermarket, except his shirt front, like the bag, was a bloodied mess.

Stanley ran over towards him with the ever-present charge nurse manager, Thulani. Stanley caught the man when he toppled forward, and his shopping bag slipped from his hands. Stanley recoiled at the sight of the fresh loops of intestine spilling from the bag onto the floor.

Thulani shrieked. "Oh my god! What do we have here?" With her face a distorted mask of hard lines, she put her hands to her mouth.

Stanley called out. "Quick, bring him a trolley."

By then, Thulani had regained her composure to start an intra-venous infusion of saline. "O-negative blood!" she called to no one in particular, but a fresh pack of blood was soon running, by which time the pale patient was in their operating room.

"What happened to you," Stanley asked the barely conscious pa-tient, who turned his eyes towards Stanley. There was pain there, with impending death already shrouding his face. Stanley shivered at the gruesomeness of the case while he inspected the abdominal wound; there was no active bleeding to be seen.

The man placed a weak hand on Stanley's forearm. "It was the Witdoeke. Four of them held me down while one of them slit me open. A stranger put my stuff in the shopping bag, then helped me come here. Save me, doctor. My two children need me."

"I'll try my best, though you must be in a major hospital."

"Do we have any Morphine or Pethidine left, Thulani? He needs an IV shot to relieve his pain." All Stanley could do was cover the wound with an abdominal pack and then send him off. "Someone must collect those intestines in a clean basin and cover them with a sterile drape soaked with saline. Is the ambulance here?" Stanley rattled off these requests with a sense of despair, knowing a long life was impossible with such an extended length of his bowel missing.

The clinic sent their worst trauma cases to Groote Schuur Hospital, where the surgeons would make the final decision.

"Will I live, doctor?"

"I don't know," said Stanley. His voice was low. The troublesome question was always easier to answer when someone had advanced cancer. *But how do I bluntly tell a father of two kids he has no hope of surviving in the long term?*

When he had done what he could, Stanley stripped off his sterile gear while the staff wheeled the man to the ambulance with his bowel loops wrapped in a moist, sterile parcel. As Stanley watched, his sense of hopelessness was at an all-time low. In the distance, he could see Table Mountain and Devil's Peak silhouetted by the lit-up western sky after sunset. As with his patient, Stanley saw no silver lining in the few clouds over the mountains.

THE TEA BREAK FROM work with Fay was muted. Fay knew of the case. "So, what will happen to him?"

"If he's unlucky, he'll survive his surgery only to await death by insidious starvation."

"That's awful," said Fay. "What a way to go."

"Maybe he'll survive long enough to see his family in the Transkei."

Both lapsed into silence. Fay kissed him on the cheek before she returned to the pharmacy, while a down-hearted Stanley returned to the doctor's consultation room.

STANLEY HAD FINISHED the last patient when Thulani opened the door to his consultation room. "We urgently need you here. Our returning ambulance found him at the roadside." She looked shattered, so Stanley knew to expect something out of the ordinary. Besides Thulani, all he had to do was follow his nose to the operating theatre, where a still-alive person groaned pitiably on a trolley.

The man's body was burnt black from head to foot with islands of exposed pink subcutaneous tissue oozing precious body serum with dilute blood. Inexplicably, the fire had spared the lower left calf region. The smell of burnt flesh mixed with petrol revolted the experienced doctor. Pitiable groans emanated from where the man's lips used to be. The nose was not recognisable, while his carbonised, bloodied eyelids looked like they had melted and stuck together.

Stanley had a strong constitution, but even the gruesome sights, smells and sounds of patients in distress over the years could not soften the impact of this patient on all his senses. His stomach churned with the familiar tight band across his midriff. Close to vomiting, waterbrash filled his mouth.

"I presume they necklaced him," said," said Stanley.

"Yes. His attackers must have had insufficient fuel to finish him off," said Thulani, her eyes brimful with tears. Over many years, Stanley had never seen her look so drained.

"What do you want to do. I doubt I can find a vein to insert an IV line." There was a distinct lack of enthusiasm in Thulani, who would always attend to the worst cases. Stanley looked at one of the most experienced nurses he had ever known, sharing her despair.

Stanley swallowed hard to control his emotions while trying to find a vein in the tiny bit of unburnt flesh on the man's left leg. All the while, the charred body whined away. The almost inhuman sound gave Stanley the chills.

"Here's one here." He tapped at a vein on the inside of the calf. Have the Morphine ready."

"It's our last ampoule," said Thulani.

Stanley soon had saline dripping in via a thin intravenous cannula. The man's woeful moans ceased soon after Thulani administered the Morphine, while his breathing assumed a more peaceful rhythm. Stanley drummed his gloved fingers on the trolley. He could do no more.

As he was about to remove his gloves, Thulani held a fifty-millilitre ampoule of potassium chloride towards Stanley, whose eyes opened wide. On looking at her, she raised her hands, then looked at the charred mess in front of them. Thulani looked shattered as she glanced at Stanley. Her eyes questioned and beseeched him at the same time.

"He's done for, Stanley." Her hushed voice sounded troubled.

He closed his eyes, then took a deep breath. "Draw up the vial, please, Thulani."

Thulani handed him the filled syringe. Drip-infused potassium over a few hours was a lifesaver in the appropriate circumstances. Stanley completed the intravenous injection in less than a minute. Thulani crossed herself. Stanley felt the pulse stop within a few faint beats, followed by cessation of the man's breathing.

A hollowness hit Stanley while he removed his gear. "At least the Morphine spared him the pain of the potassium shot. I hope we never have to do that again."

"Me too, Stanley. At least now he is at peace. Thank you."

Stanley went over to hold Thulani, who broke down in his arms; he was close to breakpoint, too.

FAY'S EFFERVESCENCE could not cure the lows he felt when they drove home. Two such violent cases in one evening would always dent his armour. "I'm glad you're driving. I would have driven too fast with the way I feel." His fists were tightly clenched.

"Apartheid generated the mess here in our Cape Flats slums," said Fay. "Will the atrocities ever end? Are we over-optimistic about the future as we live through a period of hope since Mandela's release?"

"Sometimes the worst thing in life is to achieve one's goals," said Stanley. He felt Fay rub his hand. "My main fear is the worst legacy of apartheid in a new South Africa will be an increase in crime and violence."

They drove on mired in silence, providing a cover of sorts where Stanley could hide. Feelings of post-traumatic stress sometimes still reared its ugly head to torment him at moments like this. *Will my mental shield be shattered by the night's events?*

CHAPTER 32: THE SULTANS OF CHAOS

December 1992

LEEU RELISHED THE THREE-year spiral of conflict in the townships since his time in Cape Town. His domestic setup worked well, unlike his time in SWA, where he had had difficulty satisfying his most secret fantasies.

His favourite Dire Straits music blared away on their way to deliver a parcel to the gang leader of the Elsies River chapter of the Achar-Americans. Axe, the leader since Ses' death, had reorganised the gang's operational dynamics. His name resulted from his weapon of choice.

'You guys did well last week,' said Leeu. He shook hands with Axe in the yard where he stood with his men. Well-constructed shacks surrounded the central paved area. The men had closed the high corrugated iron gates after the Kombi entered.

"It wasn't easy," said Axe. "You probably know we killed your ANC man; his two MK bodyguards were well-armed. I lost one of my men during the shootout when we burnt the place down. Now, do you have my stuff?"

Leeu nodded, signalling to Koos to open the rear Kombi door. Tonight's drop-off was boxes of hard drugs. The last time they delivered Parabellum 9 handguns to Axe.

Axe signalled to two of his men to check the boxes. When satisfied all was in order, Axe grunted, "Good. Is there anything else you need?"

Leeu cracked his fingers. "Not today. How about you?"

"What about the AK 47s I asked you about last month?"

"I'm still trying. Police HQ is not too keen, so I'm pushing them to approve it. I've requested a dozen guns with enough ammunition."

"To stay number one in the township, my men must have them. Are you dealing with the fucking HighLifers too?"

"No. Only with you." Leeu lied. "We're satisfied with your work. You deliver on time. Now we must go to another meeting."

"That man always gives me the creeps," said Koos as they drove off.

"Axe is okay in a pit bull fashion, as long as we are the ones holding his chain!" Leeu handed a lit cigarette to Koos as he inhaled deeply on his cigarette, held his breath, then exhaled in a thin stream through pursed lips. "I wonder what Councillor Mbatha wants today."

"He always wants us to knock off his opposition councillors in Khayelitsha," said Koos. Many councillors competed over the new housing programmes, with much State money available to the contractors.

"Well, he who pays the piper calls the tune," said Leeu. "And that's us."

They turned right at the southern end of Mew Way, then left, in amongst the scrub-covered low dunes fringing the undeveloped part of the False Bay coast. The sea air smell was sharp from the choppy white-capped waves nearby. The Helderberg Mountains to the east were clear, whereas a hazy Table Mountain was much farther away to the west. Finally, they turned onto a sand track leading to a clear, flat area.

"I hate the way the black bastard is always late." Leeu looked at his watch.

"May as well enjoy our time at the beach," said Koos, who pulled the Klipdrift from the car door pocket. He handed the open bottle to Leeu, who swallowed several mouthfuls. With the driver's seat down low, Koos lit up before downing a mouthful of brandy from the bottle.

"Sometimes I think I could do this forever, though life would be too boring. Ahh, there they are. He's in the Beamer SUV. Last month, he had the Benz. I'll go over to chat as he prefers to keep things confidential."

"We must stop meeting like this, Mr Kloppers," said Mbatha, whose two bodyguards stood away from them.

"Well, it's about as private as one can find here," said Leeu, who drew deeply on his cigarette. "How's life treating you these days, Mr Mbatha?" *How I resent calling the Kaffir councillor 'Mister'.* He ground his teeth.

"In one word, hectic! A lot is happening in Khayelitsha, where the ANC cadres are everywhere. As if that's not enough, I can't trust my councillors, who all want in on the new building projects. No one trusts no one. Today's friend can be today's enemy." Mbatha dabbed away at the sweat on his face with a handkerchief.

"So, how can we help you today?"

"Last year, you organised quite a bit of chaos to destroy over two hundred pondoks. We need something similar to force people to move from their shacks into the upgraded developments we are constructing."

"It will take time to arrange," said Leeu. "We have enough Witdoeke with kitskonstabels to help us the way we did in '91. Of course, HQ would have to confirm it, though I'm certain I can convince them."

"That's good," said Mbatha. "Within the next three months or so would be great. Thank you."

The two men shook hands before returning to their vehicles.

Once seated in the vehicle, he and Koos had more brandy. He enjoyed the cool sea breeze through the open car window. Koos still lounged in his seat where he had slept during Leeu's conversation with Mbatha.

"What did he want?" asked Koos, stretching himself.

"He wants more of '91 to push some pondok dwellers into the housing project he is building," replied Leeu. "It should not be an issue as long as HQ approves; I'm sure they will."

"These councillors are amazing, said Koos. "They are ready to kill each other, while the UDF or ANC fighters want to kill them."

"From what I've heard, the ANC Special Defence Units want in on the action too," said Leeu. The SDUs patrolled the parts of Crossroads and Khayelitsha controlled by the ANC under President de Klerk's new dispensation. "Some SDU's actions are more criminal than political."

"Look on the bright side," said Koos. "Stirring the pot is easier." Both men laughed.

"Ja,'" said Leeu. "My father used to say they lack brainpower."

"Mine too," laughed Leeu. "Now these fucken *Kaffirs* want to take over the country, look at the mess they're already in."

"Ja. We have councillor infighting and SDU conflicts with gangsters trying to expand their territories. What more do you need?"

"What more? Why, us, of course," Leeu laughed. "And don't forget the Taxi Wars. No wonder I love Cape Town."

Koos started their Kombi. "It's been a quiet day, so we may as well swap some stories over a braai at the Factory."

"If they're not lying again," muttered Leeu while lighting a cigarette.

They drove past the SACLA clinic opposite the containerised night school. "It's over a year since we wanted to teach those two a lesson at the night school. The uppity *Kaffir* and *Hotnot* swine have recently graduated. Maybe we can organise an attack as an add-on after one of our other missions. DuPi hates the place, though HQ may not be keen if we attacked them without provocation. Of course, we can always invent one," he laughed, coughing simultaneously.

THERE WAS A COMFORTABLE smugness permeating Leeu's whole being. Life was meant to be a mad frenzy as long as they were the organisers. With Dire Strait's music blaring forth, Leeu felt like they were the sultans of chaos.

CHAPTER 33: CELEBRATIONS

December 1992

LYDIAH HUMMED WHILE she checked the nibbles the caterers had prepared. She smiled inwardly. After two years of widowhood, she was at peace with herself, apart from her concerns about Ivan's weekly nightmares. She drew comfort from the way he would settle in her arms whenever she woke him when he groaned in his sleep. It was a sure indicator of revisiting his past prison demons, including his time with 26. She accepted his explanation, though he always seemed uncomfortable when they spoke about his dreams. Despite her trust in Ivan, she had the nagging doubt there was more to his nightmares than he had told her. *Should I approach him about my concerns?*

Suzanne sniffed at the air as she entered the kitchen. "It smells yummy in here. Do you know what I've liked in the past year? It's seeing my happy Mum return from wherever she had disappeared." Suzanne came over to kiss her on the cheek.

Lydiah held back a tear. "Thank you, Suzanne. You helped me greatly during those tough months after Willie's death."

"I'd like to take all the credit, Mum. In truth, though, I'd have to share the credit with Ivan. More of the old you reappeared when he moved in with us last year. See, I told you things would work out fine."

"Sometimes I think you know too much, though Ivan is special. He's so different to our Willie in a positive fashion. You know what I mean."

"Uh-huh. At the end of one of our maths sessions one day, he approached me to ask if I minded him moving in to live with you. He was so nervous till I told him I was delighted because I had already noticed a change in you long before that. He looked so sheepish when I teased him about the way he always looked at you." Suzanne tittered.

"Oh? You didn't tell me about that."

"I couldn't. In fact, I shouldn't have told you now. Ivan swore me to secrecy, so please don't tell him I told you."

"My lips are sealed, though you gave Ivan excellent advice. It's about the same you gave me. Did you plan these events?" She leaned forward to kiss Suzanne, who shrugged her shoulders with a broad, innocent smile on her face.

LYDIA TAPPED HER BUBBLY glass with the handle of a fork. The noise of the gathered friends settled as they all turned to face her where she stood on the elevated pathway leading from the lawn to the fruit trees. The south-westerly wind wafted her hair around her face.

"I must thank all of you who are here to celebrate our two new graduates. I'll try to keep my chatting brief, though Ivan will have to watch Thembani as we all know what a talker he can be." A ripple of laughter went through the group gathered around her.

"Without further ado, I will call on our new graduates to say a few words to us."

"'Okay," said Thembani. "I'll kick off; I'll be brief, if I can," he tittered. "On occasions like this, one always puts parents first. Mamma, Pappa, how you two fretted over me in the '70s and '80s. 'Education will set you free' was a constant mantra from the two of you. As much as I could, I followed your advice. Thank you. My BA degree, I lay at your feet. In a better world, both of you would have had one too."

Lydiah led the round of applause as the Dlaminis raised their glasses of Coke on high to their son, their faces aglow with pride. Thembani went over to hug them both before he continued.

"Nkosinati would have to be next. She taught me the meaning of deep and true love and blessed me with a wonderful son, Curtis-Thembani. She is the one who turned me around from the despair of the '80s to where I am now, starting with her encouragement to join UWC." He struggled to maintain his composure. He held on to Nkosinati at his side. She, too, was all tears, along with a few others, including Lydiah, who knew what life was like to rediscover oneself and find true love again.

"Lydiah and the late Willie pushed me further - all the way from UWC up the hill to UCT," Thembani grinned. "Would I have chosen the path on my own? Who knows. They saw something in me, now here I am, with BA (UCT), after my name. They were my main mentors at UWC; what an honour to now have Lydiah as a colleague and friend." He gave Lydiah a thumbs-up, and she blew him a kiss in return.

"Of course, I would have to include my full-time mentor, Mr G, too. On day one on the job, I had the fastest promotion in history from labourer to quantity surveyor." Thembani laughed along with the rest, then raised his glass as did his benefactor. With twinkling eyes, Mr G raised a fist on high. Thembani returned the gesture.

"Absent today is another of my sponsors, Mr Goldberg. Now bed-bound with illness, he was my main book provider in the days when I was his caddy; he looked after a few of us with his informal scholarships. His humanity has always astounded me, even in the way he addressed me as 'Mister Dlamini' whenever we were on the golf course. He gave me hope in White South Africans." Thembani had tears in his eyes as he paused.

"It's wonderful to see Dr Gershon and Fay here today." They raised a glass towards him. "Years ago, Dr Gershon saved my life. Despite you telling me to do so, I still can't call you Stanley." He laughed.

"Finally, to my son Curtis-Thembani, come here, my boy. We need a family photo. Amandla ngawethu." With a laughing Curtis-Thembani on his arm, the two of them raised their fists. All responded while many went over to slap Thembani on the back.

Lydiah banged her glass with her fork. "Thank you, Thembani. You and Nkosinati have touched us in so many ways. Your intelligence stunned Willie and me when we first met you as a student at UWC. To see you here today with your BA with so many distinctions is no surprise." Lydiah led the round of applause.

"Now, it's Ivan's turn. All of you know the story of our relationship." Lydiah stopped to bite her lip as her emotions welled up. Ivan squeezed her hand. "So, here he is, Ivan Pettersen, B. Eng (UCT) who, like Thembani, had distinctions every year." She started a soft round of clapping.

"Thanks, Lydiah. Yes, our relationship, our romance, our love is special. Like Thembani, though, my parents come first. 'Education will set you free' - I see the Pettersons read the same book as the Dlaminis!" A wave of laughter followed, especially from his parents and Colleen. He pointed at his sister while he put a finger to his lips with the kind of grin which always gave Lydiah goosebumps to watch. She smiled; maybe the cleft chin with the forehead curl moved her the most.

"At the graduation ceremony, I reflected on how my B. Eng was like a tiny distant flame keeping me alive during my darkest hours inside Pollsmoor prison. Now, I have a raging fire within me.

"Mr G over there," he showed two-thumbs-up towards his smiley-faced employer. "He's the ultimate example of a decent human being. Years ago, he would have been awarded a top citizen's honour award in a fairer society. Maybe that day is not too far off in a new South Africa." He raised his glass of Coke towards a blushing Mr G. Many applauded.

"Besides running his business while financially supporting many students, he still managed a double degree himself - Law two years ago, and now, he also has a Commerce degree. There's an inspirational example set by a sixty-plus-year-old. May I ask all of you to toast the third graduate in our midst."

A call of "Hip, hip, hooray" filled the air from everyone around while Mr G went a beetroot red, wagging a finger towards a broadly smiling Ivan. Lydiah was amused to see Mr G blush so much; known to her late father, she was fond of him.

"The main group here today are the nee-Adams'. I have been impressed by how Lydiah's sisters, Liz and Hope, and your spouses have accepted my relationship with your Lydiah. Rest assured, guys, I would give my life to look after Lydiah and Suzanne." Ivan waved two hands on high as the close family members applauded.

"Naturally, Lydiah and her daughter Suzanne deserve special mention." Lydiah enjoyed the way Ivan now held her around the shoulder. She leaned her head against him while he squeezed her arm. His other arm was around Suzanne, tucked in by his side. "Even while they dealt with the trauma they had to go through with Willie's death, both have helped me in my recovery. My time in prison was a potentially life-destroying experience. They helped me to heal; they helped me to rebuild myself. At the time of my graduation ceremony, when we walked from the Hall, hand in hand like a family, I felt my former self reappear; it was the first time since my imprisonment. You two have my eternal gratitude."

Lydiah, close to tears while Ivan spoke, turned into his chest to weep. He joined her with his head buried in her hair. Others had their tissues in hand to control their flowing emotions. Suzanne, her face wet with tears, joined them in a family huddle.

"Okay, folks," Thembani's voice boomed forth. "There's been a lot of emotion around here today. I'm pleased to say it's been mostly positive. Curtis-Thembani is distributing copies of Nkosi sikelel iAfrika for those who need it. I beseech you all to join me in singing the ANC anthem." He cleared his throat. Everyone awaited his cue. He swallowed hard while he bit his lips to control himself. His eyes welled up.

Lydiah watched him struggle. *Oh no, he's losing it!* When Lydiah eventually heard a more controlled Thembani sing, his rich baritone voice sent shivers along her spine. People joined him; many sang from their sheets. Lydiah and Suzanne sang without a sheet; Willie had taught them well. She hugged Suzanne with one hand, her heart swollen with emotions of memories past and present. Suzanne sniffed away at the hymn's end. Beside her, Ivan sang with closed eyes as if he were with his fellow political prisoners in Pollsmoor prison again.

"My apologies; I lost the plot a bit at the beginning when my emotions got the better of me. It's been many years since I last sang Nkosi sikelel iAfrika." Thembani paused, blinking his eyes, momentarily back in the Cortina when he listened to his dead Comrades finish the hymn he could not sing at the time. Nkosinati held his hand while Curtis-Thembani leaned against his leg. When Thembani looked up, a smiling Dr Gershon gave him a thumbs-up; a knowing smile passed between them. He returned the signal with a solemn nod of his head.

"As we head into the troubled months ahead of us where uncertainty clouds so many issues, on behalf of my fellow graduates, may I wish you all safe times ahead. If you have goals to pursue, don't give up. Amandla!"

In the expected fashion, everyone returned Thembani's fist pump and the call. "Ngawethu!"

Lydiah and Ivan stayed in the garden when the rest went inside, where the caterers served cupcakes with tea. With his arms around her from behind, Ivan kissed her in the neck, where they sat on a bench. "You okay?"

Ivan was unique in his ability to pop the timely question. She drew his arms closer to herself. "With arms like this to hold me, how can I not be?" She felt safe there, enveloped in his bear grip.

Suzanne returned with Curtis-Thembani and Lance in hand. "Mum, people are leaving."

"Thanks, Suzanne. I'll be there now."

"It's been a lovely celebration, thanks. Seeing you in my favourite red dress made the day extra special," said Ivan.

"Yes. I felt extraordinary. Now, if you can release me, I'll greet the guests."

Ivan held onto a hand. "Better yet, we'll farewell them together, as I need one of those cupcakes," he chuckled.

Lydiah had placed a special order with the caterers to provide their most decadent chocolate cupcakes. The couple swung their hands while they walked indoors; Lydiah did so with a hop in her step.

The final pair they escorted to their car was Fay and Stanley. "We're glad you came," said Lydiah, hooked into Fay.

"It was our pleasure," said Fay. "It's lovely to see you and Ivan look so happy whenever we see you two. I suspected Ivan was interested in you since we first met him at the time of Mandela's 1990 release."

"There's much truth in your observation, though I knew nothing of his interest then." Lydiah laughed.

The Dlaminis lingered on after the rest had gone. The children had disappeared upstairs. Suzanne's room was a child's wonderland of toys, and Curtis-Thembani's squeals of near hysteria were audible downstairs.

"What I love is how we have four UCT people here tonight," said Ivan. "We are Black South Africans. There's Nkosinati from the Transkei, Thembani from Gugulethu, and Lydiah and I are from Elsies River. We are a handful of the marginalised majority who now tread the country's best university hallways. Barely five years ago, we could only dare to dream."

"Now we live the dream," said Nkosinati. "Those were my thoughts on my first day at UCT towards my Master's."

"I presume you have the family members' staff rebate on your fees," said Lydiah.

"Yes, she does. It's why there's a Peugeot 504 station wagon parked outside today. The difference in fees meant we could afford one," said Thembani. "There's enough room at the back so Mamma and Pappa can sleep alongside Curtis."

"Has Ivan told you about the lecture programme he conducts in the local schools?" asked Lydiah.

"I'm in awe of his work," said Thembani.

"Thembani told me a bit about his project," said Nkosinati. "Now I can hear it straight from the horse's mouth."

Ivan looked a bit embarrassed before he spoke. "I try to steer the youth away from gang life with fortnightly visits to Elsies River schools. I start by asking how many would not mind going to prison. About a quarter will raise their hands.

"They already know about the major prison gangs, so I start with how five to six inmates would rape them before the end of the first week before one of the prisoners would claim them as a girlfriend. Within a month, they would see a couple of violent attacks or deaths from crude handmade weapons. I strip away at prison life to the harsh daily realities of them being part of the walking dead." Ivan rubbed his chin cleft.

"They must learn to respect people, hard work, and themselves. 'Say no to drugs; say no to gangs' are my constant themes. I tell them how Yster, my prison gang boss, did not smoke or touch drugs and how he obtained his Junior Certificate (tenth grade) while doing prison classes. The last thing he said to me when I left Pollsmoor was,' Knowledge is the true power'. When done, I again ask them who would like to go to prison. It's rare to see any hands go up."

Lydiah and Nkosinati applauded him. "Well done, Ivan. We probably need more people to deliver similar lectures at our marginalised schools," said Nkosinati.

While they spoke, Thembani's parents came in from the garden where they had been sitting.

"I enjoy your garden, Lydiah," said Mrs Dlamini. "Maybe we'll have our own one day."

"You and Pappa will, Mamma. Yes, one day you will."

"That would be good," said Mr Dlamini. "It's part of every Black person's dream to have a solid house in a safe neighbourhood."

"It was my parents' house after they had to sell the Newlands family home to the Group Areas Board when I was young," said Lydiah.

"I must confess," said Nkosinati. "When de Klerk repealed the Act in 1990, Thembani and I immediately started looking at places within walking distance of UCT."

"Since my appointment, the State pays as much as forty per cent of the mortgage I needed to renovate the house recently," said Lydiah. "Only White civil servants used to receive the subsidy. Seventy per cent of them are civil servants, so it's no wonder the National Party won elections with such handsome majorities for so many years."

"Now, as much as I would like to stay, it's way past Curtis-Thembani's bedtime, so we have to take our leave," said Nkosinati.

The two families hugged before they left.

"They're such a special couple," said Lydiah,

"Thembani gave me hope when I thought there was no chance with you. 'Give Lydiah time to heal', he said. Now, here you are, deep in my heart." They shared a passionate kiss outside the front door.

"Thembani was right. I'm glad you waited." Lydiah clung to his arm as they entered the empty house. Suzanne had gone with her aunt Hope to join her cousins over the weekend. Once in the lounge, Lydiah leaned over to kiss him, drawing his hands to her breasts. His face changed from surprise to pleasure as his eyes scanned her face, followed by his kisses to her neck. His aftershave wafted around her nose, spurring her on. "I want you here on the couch again, but without clothes this time."

Both of them were soon locked into each other. Lydiah's head spun during their frenzied moment of unbridled passion. In the depths of Ivan's passionate hazel brown eyes, she sensed how he had joined in releasing their inner selves.

Their body heat mingled with the summer warmth where they lay in each other's arms on the couch covered by a thin duvet generally draped over the seat. On the same couch, Ivan had been candid about his time in prison, including how he had joined the prison gang. As comforted as she felt, she needed to resolve the doubts she had about Ivan's nightmares.

"I often think of how brave you were when you told me about your time in prison, though your nightmares bother me. Are they entirely about your prison time?" Lydiah's heart beat faster with each word as she sensed a tensioning of his body alongside hers.

Ivan rolled onto his side to look at Lydiah with his eyebrows bunched and his forehead creased. "As much as I wanted to tell you the rest of my story, I haven't been able to."

Ivan paused, looking past Lydiah towards the lounge window before his restless eyes settled on hers again. Over many long minutes, she shared his roller-coaster wild car ride with Ses, ending in Ivan sobbing on her shoulder as he declared how afraid he was of losing her over such a shameful episode in his life.

Somewhat aghast, a breathless Lydiah stroked the shoulders of the man she had come to love so much. As appalled as she was to hear about Ses, she recognised how his incarceration had driven him to undertake such extreme action to put his life on track again. His sister, Colleen's involvement in the tragic episode, added to Lydiah's understanding of how a freshly released prisoner undertook what Ivan did to be freed of his gang ties, as well as avenging the attack on a much-loved sister.

She was touched by his tears after he had told her about Ses' death, attributed by the police to a high-speed accident. How could she refuse a man with such courage to tell her of those experiences? Would the revelation relieve his nightmares?

She held him tight; she was not going to let him go. "Ivan, you know of my near-death experiences. With the barrel of a policeman's gun in my face, the gun jammed when one of them tried to kill me in '76; worse yet, when shot in the head with the same bullet that killed Willie. I've had my murderous, vengeful thoughts, especially towards the swine who shot Willie and me. Given a chance, I'd kill the tattooed monster myself." Lydiah's hands were tightly fisted when she finished. "I love you so much, Ivan. We can see this through together."

"I'd like to think I'm done with killing," said Ivan.

"I see you take your gun with you to your night school classes. I shudder whenever you do it."

"For a sense of security, I started carrying the weapon after Willie's death. I'd prefer to be rid of the damned thing."

They lay in each other's arms in the failing light after sunset. Lydiah sensed a comfort in both of them. She hoped Ivan's worst moments could finally be put to rest the way she had managed with hers.

CHAPTER 34: SECOND RECRUITER February 1993

February 1993

IVAN STILL FELT RELIEVED after his revelations to Lydiah two months earlier. His nights of uninterrupted sleep pleased Lydiah, who was always alarmed at how he used to groan or sit bolt upright in bed when his dreams were at their worst. His main aim now was to acquire his Ph.D. to again hand over his certificate to his parents outside Jagger Hall.

After dropping off Thembani outside Heideveldt station, Ivan was about to pull off when he saw a bearded man pointing an index finger at him with one hand while waving wildly at Ivan with the other. The man walked at pace towards the Morris. There was something familiar about the balding man.

When he recognised the man, Ivan stepped out of the car to greet him.

"Abdul Majiet? I hardly recognised you."

They hugged before Ivan held him at arm's length. He was shocked to see how wasted Abdul was.

"Can I get a lift with you to Elsies River? I suppose you still live there." Abdul's eyes scanned all directions, including over both shoulders.

"Of course."

"Maybe we can drive away from the people here."

Abdul frequently glanced around as if on the lookout. *Is he on the run?* Ivan was astonished to see his former Comrade. In early 1976, Abdul, two others, and Ivan formed an activist cell; Abdul was the linkman with the ANC's MK. Ivan drove north towards Settlers Way.

"Where to?"

"Maybe to Epping Industrial Area. Cruise around the streets there. I don't know of any quiet spots."

"Yes, there's been a lot of building there while I was inside. So, what have you been doing? You look like shit. I thought you were in Zambia or Zimbabwe."

"I was. Also in Botswana; Tanzania too, in different MK camps."

"You look like a man on the run. How long have you been back? Are you on a mission?"

"I've been in Cape Town a while. I stay all over the show. Always on the move. Mission? What do I say? Anyone who returns is on one, I suppose. That's why I wanted to chat with you. I first saw you dropping someone off at the station two days ago. I hoped I'd see you tonight."

"What do you want of me," Ivan asked with a sense of alarm as memories past assailed him, none more so than the doubts he had about Abdul.

"We need you to join us. Would you be interested?"

Ivan pulled over sharply into an empty car park in front of a closed factory with a rusted heavy chain wrapped around the barred gates. He switched off the car, drumming his fingers lightly on the steering wheel, then turned his attention to Abdul. "Look, I've done my time. I'd like to think that I helped set in motion where we are today, including Mandela's release with whatever follows."

"Yes. Like others, you have a rightful claim to be proud of. Now we are after much more." Abdul tugged at his unkempt beard.

"How much more?" Ivan asked.

"Is Koeberg nuclear power station big enough for you?"

Ivan nearly flipped.

"We need a major event to push President de Klerk across the line. We have ways to access the place, though we need the right oomph to set things off, the kind of stuff you can do. It would be greater than anything ever done against these bastards." Abdul's face was flushed, his eyes glistened, still looking everywhere. A bit of spittle clung to his lower lip, as had always been the irritating case in the past.

"I'm not sure I want to bomb anything again." Ivan's heart drummed away. *Can I trust Abdul?*

"But tell me first, what did you do after I was arrested in '76 when Peter and Jakes disappeared off the face of the earth."

"We all went to Yugoslavia. I became a munitions supplies person after my training. We returned to Tanzania after a year."

"Where are the other two now?"

"Ja. It was a lifetime ago. A lifetime." He looked thoughtful. Abdul looked toward the distant mountains, way past the factories around them. "Peter and Jakes died somewhere on the SA border with SWA."

"Shot? When? By whom?"

Silence followed. "This was over ten years ago now." Abdul swallowed hard.

Something's bothering him. "By whom? You didn't answer me!" Abdul always had a way of annoying him, none more so than right then.

"SADF (South African Defence Force). Maybe Koevoet ..."

Abdul was sweating, yet the weather was cool. "Are you hiding something from me, Abdul? Were you there at the time?" Abdul seemed to squirm in his seat. Ivan was discomfited by those shifty eyes which never looked one in the eye. The damned smooth talker aroused suppressed suspicions about himself.

Ivan's pulse beat faster. "Well," his neck muscles corded as Ivan's eyes narrowed.

'Yes, though I was lucky to survive the experience."

"What experience? Damn you! You are dodging the question. I could always tell when you lied. You sound like the Abdul of old. I grew up with Jakes and Peter, schooled with them, screwed with them. They were my closest friends. Now talk! What bloody experience? I want to know." With his balled fists, he was ready to punch Abdul, who sat there like a buck caught in a car's headlamps. *The bastard is hiding something.* "I want the bloody truth!"

"The troops shot them."

Ivan lunged forward to grab Abdul by the front of his anorak. "Were they ANC troops? You can tell me, man. I have been in a high-security prison with many MK fighters. I know the ANC were ruthless at times. Did Jakes and Peter face an MK firing squad? I want the truth; I'll know from your eyes. Talk!"

"Yes." He whispered.

Ivan pulled him close enough to smell the familiar stink of Abdul's breath. "Were you part of the firing squad who shot Jakes and Peter, you swine?" By now, he held the anorak tighter around Abdul's neck with both hands. "How did you feel when you shot them, Abdul? Tell me! How many times did you shoot them?"

This time, Abdul held his gaze. In his eyes, Ivan saw fear, eyes in search of mercy. Then he saw tears as Abdul moaned, like a sound from a bottomless pit of remorse. Maybe they came from the same suppressed emotions which Ivan knew so well.

When he let go of the anorak. Abdul collapsed in his seat. The tears still flowed while the moaning continued. Ivan sat with his hands fisted while he rubbed at a thumbnail with the other thumb. He could understand the pain, with the dilemma of whether to shoot or be shot.

"Right. You've answered my first question. The next one has been on my mind for seventeen years." He stared hard at his nails, then rubbed them when he turned his eyes to impale Abdul. He felt his heart rate thump away with his jaw muscles tense. His fists were now balled tight with his knuckles white.

"Did you betray me to the security police?" Abdul's eyes widened. They held Ivan's stare before they withered away while the awful moan again escaped from his lips. Tears flowed and disappeared into his beard. His nose was snotty as he sniffed to clear it.

"Is your silence a yes, Abdul?" Ivan asked with his neck veins distended, his face all lined. The volume of his voice had doubled.

Abdul took his handkerchief from his pocket, wiped his eyes, then blew his nose before dropping his head to sniff away.

"The police asked me a few things known only to you, Peter, and Jakes. About the things we had done, sites bombed. Those two were my closest buddies. I think they knew what was coming the night they disappeared. They arrested me the next day.

"And you? You were never arrested. I know you only left a few weeks later. Months later, I was charged. I ask you again, did you betray me?"

It was the heaviest silence Ivan had ever experienced, broken only by Abdul, who was now more controlled with less sniffling than before.

"Why was it not Peter and Jakes? Maybe they were allowed to leave after telling the police. What makes you think I turned you in?"

Ivan again grabbed him by the anorak. "Because I believe you were capable of it. I always felt uneasy about you, so did the other two, and you were the only one who actually knew where the explosives were hidden. Only you could have told *that* to the police, you swine!"

He shook Abdul like a limp doll, banging his head against the side window. Ivan felt as if the painful years of suspension of self, wanted to hear Abdul confess, listen to him cry, see his pain, let him suffer.

"You bastard Ivan. You're still Mr Arrogant, Mr Know-all. You haven't fucking changed!"

"So, you betrayed me then. Are you doing the same now? Have you turned? Are you now a bloody askari? After all, you'd then be the ultimate traitor? Are you trying to set me up?" he shouted at Abdul.

"Bugger you, Ivan!" Abdul pushed Ivan's hands away. "I should never have bothered to contact you. Prison has fucked your brains!" He exited the car, slamming the door behind him. "Piss off!" He raised a middle finger at Ivan before stomping off in the direction of Elsies River.

Ivan's breathing was fast as he dropped his head onto the steering wheel with his eyes closed. The images assailing him were part of the disturbing vortex of the act of stabbing in the prison yard superimposed by Leeu's forearm tattoo and his comrades facing a firing squad. After several minutes, a sense of calm returned to Ivan.

He started the car and drove off. There was no sign of Abdul on Ivan's way to Halt Road.

To have Abdul Majiet trying to recruit him within six months of John Johnson was another weird experience, though John was correct about planning for the future. He and Thembani were already doing so. Ivan also had Lydiah and Suzanne to consider. He knew how life had a way of making bad things even worse. *I hope it will not be my fate again.*

CHAPTER 35: SHACK ATTACK

July 1993

A DISAPPOINTED LEEU had seen the second quarter statistics. After their two attacks in Khayelitsha, he expected them to have more than thirty killed. The way July was going, there was no doubt the present quarter's figures would be higher. Tonight's work would ensure that. The plan was to incinerate a block of shanties in Khayelitsha's Site B. More important to him was the overdue attack he and Koos had planned on the containerised classes. Ivan, the *Hotnot* terrorist, with his smart-arse *Kaffir* buddy from UCT, would be there tonight.

"The night needs to be memorable." Commander du Plessis was more austere than usual. "We need to avenge the barbarous APLA (Azanian People's Liberation Army) terrorist attack on St James Church in Kenilworth last week." Eleven White churchgoers died, with 58 wounded in the worst assault on Whites in Cape Town.

Du Plessis spat on the ground. His trimmed moustache bristled. Light sweat coated his bald frontal patch. He paced the floor in his customary fashion in front of the seven sombre-faced White officers who would lead the night's attack.

Four Kombis were ready to leave once their Black colleagues arrived. "The area we have selected is an APLA viper's nest. Councillor Mbatha needs them to move out. But, more importantly, we need to avenge our Kenilworth dead."

"We'll depart in half an hour to meet on Lansdowne Road past the burnt-out church at seven-thirty. Do you all know the church?"

"We should," Leeu laughed. "We burnt the damned thing down last year." They all laughed.

"With the new moon tonight, the dark will suit us."

Leeu cracked his fingers, keen to be on the road. After they were done with Khayelitsha, he wanted to Lionise the container class-rooms.

Leeu stopped in front of a tangled mess of blackened timber posts with rusted, twisted, corrugated iron sheets where the burnt-out church used to stand. He was about to switch off the engine when the rest of the troops arrived. He responded to du Plessis' thumbs-up with one of his own, then followed after they drove by him in a northward direction. "OK, men, balaclavas on, including you, Penny. You did not wear yours in the last fucken attack." There was a loud burst of laughter from the back. *One day, I swear I will shoot the bloody Kaffir.*

A swift heartbeat replaced his calm with a mouth as dry as saw-dust while his fingers clamped around the steering wheel. He thrived on these moments before battle. There was no anxiety or concern re-garding himself or those around him. Instead, the prospect of vio-lence inspired him more than anything else in his life.

"Look at the mess, Koos." Leeu lifted his hands from the steering wheel towards the ramshackle pondoks, some of the most derelict structures in the township. "These people are primitive. They live like animals."

"Look on the bright side, Leeu. Tonight's attack will be easier when the flames hop, skip, or jump their way from one closely packed shack to another," laughed Koos. "I can't wait."

The road was dark. About four hundred metres apart, ultra-high streetlights shed dim light on the derelict structures below. They were after a block two hundred metres long with four to six pondoks in forty rows lining the narrow alleyways; each shack had an average of five occupants.

One kilometre on with no lights close by du Plessis pulled over to the side of the road. Rain was unlikely and the stiff breeze behind them was perfect. With his pistol in hand, Du Plessis waved his men into position ahead of him. The men spread across the road of firm-packed sand. Penny carried the flame thrower, his favourite device during these attacks.

Leeu was now most tense, primed to go on the offensive against the APLA terrorists. He licked his lips; his mouth was dry, his pulse well up. The hip-high AK 47 was ready. Seconds before du Plessis' first shot to signal the start of the attack, a tarpaulin-covered hovel started burning fiercely. *Oh fuck! It's Penny again. DuPi will be furious.*

Pandemonium erupted, with everyone shooting away at the surrounding structures along the narrow sandy street. They worked their way along the length of the row of shanties, and all of them were soon ablaze. Entering the labyrinth of narrow pathways between the structures would be too dangerous. People with children ran in all directions, often cut off by the spreading inferno. Screams reverberated around them while the tall flames extended in all directions, driven by the wind in search of combustible material. Tarpaulins flared instantly, their supporting structures following within minutes. Barking dogs added to the noise of fleeing people as parents clutched their children close. Everyone was desperate to escape from the fires and the hail of AK 47 bullets fired by the troops. The smell of burning was everywhere.

Leeu was exultant. Bodies lay on the ground, a few burnt fiercely alongside the firestorm of their homes. These were the apocalyptic moments he thrived on. He fitted a fresh clip to his hot weapon to shoot at houses on both sides of the broad track they were on.

The heat intensity now drove back the police unit at the end of the housing block.

"Fall back!" Du Plessis' voice cut repeatedly through the screaming, the shouting, the dogs barking, and the raging flames as they leapt from one flimsy home to another. The strong wind generated horizontal tongues of fire as they sought more sustenance away from the road.

The troops piled into their vans as APLA fighters started shooting at them. Bullets flashed in the dark where they ricocheted off the shanties' metal sheets. The vans sped off, bouncing their way onto Lansdowne Road. Penny roared with laughter. The kitskonstabels had jumped into the other vans. Radio contact confirmed they were all on board.

Leeu was furious. "It's just like those fucken *Kaffirs* to jump into the first three vehicles they came across," he muttered to Koos.

"Wow!" Penny declared. "I look forward to using the flame thrower again. On our return, I could have torched the opposite pondoks with a bigger fuel tank."

"I'm glad we finished when we did," said Koos. "The terrs would have really cut loose with their weapons if we'd stayed longer."

They had been there for less than five minutes from start to finish.

"We started a serious fire there," said Penny who patted the equipment lying on the floor at his feet. "So where to now, Leeu? The Factory?"

"Koos and I have another job to do first. You could join us if you wish or wait in the Kombi."

"What's the plan?"

"We have to teach a couple of teachers in Crossroads a lesson."

"Has du Plessis OK'd it?" Koos asked.

"No. DuPi doesn't know, though he hates the school. To him, it's a place where they train communist terrorists. We can have a bit of serious sport with them tonight; we'll tell him later how we acted on a hot tip-off."

"Ahh! Teachers! Count me in. A few of them caused me much grief during my time at school," Penny beamed. He now had his AK 47 in hand. "What's the plan? Set the classrooms alight? The flame thrower fuel tank is empty."

"Not sure yet. Maybe we'll just open the doors and then shoot them from the outside, followed by grenades. We'll play it by ear," said Leeu, drooling at the prospect.

CHAPTER 36: NIGHT SCHOOL ATTACK

July 1993

THEMBANI LOCKED THE first classroom container before he strolled over to the second in the dark of a moonless night. The limited street lighting was a fair distance away. Behind the containers across an empty strip of land, faint lights came from the dense pack of nearly invisible pondoks, partly obscured by a dense cluster of tall Eucalyptus trees silhouetted by the starry night sky.

He entered the second container where two of their students at the back of the class pored over the evening's maths lesson with an absorbed Ivan. The rest of the students were already gone. Thembani bolted the partly opened door to allow in a bit of the winter cold through the narrow gap. He sat at one of the desks to correct a student's homework. Lulled into drowsiness, Thembani's head nodded intermittently while he struggled to stay awake. Finally, he put his head on the desk to doze off.

He had no sooner done so than the rattling of the door returned him to reality. From outside, someone cursed. Thembani ran to flick off the light switch alongside the door. All was silent outside. He stood inside the closed half of the door. There was a gap of less than ten centimetres between the two doors. There seemed to be more than one person outside. At least two of them spoke in Afrikaans.

"Afrikaners," he whispered to Ivan, who had reached him. They could not see each other in the dark. The two students stayed at the back of the classroom.

"What do you think we should do?" Ivan asked, his voice hushed. "Maybe it's the Balaclava Gang."

"It could be. Let's wait. If need be, we have our escape hatch; also, I have my Glock. "

"And I have a Parabellum."

They lapsed into silence. Thembani could hear his heart beating. *A Parabellum? The gun of gangsters?*

There was a loud banging at the door. "Open up!" The accent was unmistakably the voice of an Afrikaner.

"What do you want?" Thembani called out. He pressed himself firmly against the closed half of the door.

"We're after a fucken *Hotnot* and a fucken *Kaffir*! Open the door or else."

"Or else what?" Thembani stepped back with his Glock held firmly in his hand. His pulse beat frantically as he licked at his dry lips with a dry tongue; the bitter-salt taste of his mouth was intense while his insides seemed to flip around inside his belly.

"Let's go to the escape hatch," he whispered to Ivan.

There was a rattling of metal at the door, followed by the clatter of metal on the steel container floor. Next, Thembani heard the unmistakable hissing of gas from a tear gas canister. In the dark, the two friends stumbled their way along the sides towards the rear of the classroom. Ivan removed the holding bolts of a metal flap; he had organised the fitting of the 'just-in-case hatches' to both containers after Willie's death. Thembani pushed the students through the low opening.

"Run straight ahead to the houses across the road," Thembani instructed Ivan as the tear gas reached them. While holding his breath, he pushed Ivan ahead of himself, then closed his stinging eyes until

Ivan pulled at his arm. He crawled through the hole to inhale deep breaths of fresh air.

"What now?" asked a breathless Ivan.

"Head towards the trees in front of the houses over there! Keep in line with the container so they can't see us."

Ivan took off with Thembani hot on his heels. Running across the open, irregular ground in the dark was not easy. Thembani found himself struggling in places with knee-high weeds with hidden obstacles to trip him up. Ahead of him, Ivan stumbled over something. Thembani stopped to pull him up.

"You OK."

"I think so."

They reached the tarred road where the Kombi screeched around the corner in a half-slide.

"Head towards the Eucalyptus trees in front of the houses," said Thembani.

They crossed the road as the van's headlights hit them. The sound of automatic gunfire shattered the evening's silence. Bullets cut a swathe through the bushes around them, where they sheltered behind the thick tree trunks. The bark spray from his tree reached Thembani, where he sat on his haunches. Ivan stood behind his tree. Both had their guns in hand.

"Shooting at them would give away our positions," said Thembani.

"We have to go to the shanties over there, about forty metres away."

"The main problem is the bare sand to reach those shacks," said Thembani.

As they made their way through the trees, the shooting stopped as they were now being stalked by the men on foot. They did not know how many men there were. Two of them carried torches.

"I found their tracks," a deep voice boomed forth.

"An askari tracker," whispered Thembani. "He may be an ex-Koevoet Ovambo."

"Those trackers are the best in the world," said Ivan as they reached the edge of the stand of trees.

"They are closing in on us," said a breathless Thembani. There seem to be three of them."

They broke cover to charge towards a gap they had spotted between the closely packed shanties. Halfway across the sand patch, Thembani's heart thumped away like never before, his mouth a familiar dry hole.

With a few paces to go, bursts of gunfire shattered the silence of the night. Thembani heard the bullets passing through the air around them before ricocheting off the metal shanties. Sweat poured from his face, and his throat burned with the effort of running. Both of them dived forwards, then slid on their bellies into a sheltered gap between the pondoks.

The two huddled close to each other, where they lay in the dark of the narrow alley while the staccato barks of semiautomatic gunfire erupted around them. After a few minutes, an eerie silence replaced the loudest shooting Thembani had ever heard. His ears rang with the sound. His pulse settled somewhat, his breathing now not as fast.

"You alright," asked Thembani.

"I've taken a flesh wound to the left shoulder. What about you?"

"I'm good."

"I thought we were done for."

"Me too, until I realised most of the shots came from the pondoks, not the bush."

Even as they spoke, gunmen with AK-47s in hand appeared from the surrounding gloom to search for the aggressors along the edge of the trees.

"What's going on here?" asked Ivan.

"They must be our MK brothers. Khayelitsha is full of them. We chose the right spot to run to," Thembani's laughter was unrestrained as he hugged Ivan.

In amongst the hubbub, they heard the two men from the evening's classes calling them by name. They came over to Ivan and Thembani; one of them had an AK 47 in hand.

"Well, I'm glad to see you two here," said Thembani.

"We knew your only chance was to find as many Comrades as we could, sir," said the one with a gun. "I knew there was a meeting in progress over there," he pointed. "They had their weapons with them. There they are!" He pointed both hands at six of them, dragging two bodies from the bush.

Ivan and Thembani went over to the corpses. One was a big Ovambo, while the other was a skinny White fellow.

One of the Comrades swaggered over to them. The commander of the group introduced himself. "Hi. I'm Thula. We know there's one more. We hope it's the red-haired fellow, Leeu Kloppers. A few of us have a score to settle with him. They're lionised like yours, Ivan." He held up his thumbs with deformed thumb nails.

He had no sooner finished speaking than a loud cheer erupted from the bush. The freedom fighters soon appeared, dragging Leeu along the ground between them.

"We've got him; he's alive!" said one of his captors.

One of the fighters shone a torchlight onto Leeu. They had removed his balaclava. There was no mistaking the red-haired man, even with his blackened face. He bled from bullet wounds to his right shoulder and both legs. They dropped him alongside the bodies of his two colleagues where he sat on the ground. Many came over to spit on him or to kick him. All cursed or swore at him.

With a broad smile on his face, Ivan strolled towards Leeu. On his haunches, Ivan exposed the underlined forearm tattoo where the camouflage grease ended. Ivan spat on the tattoo.

"That's for you and your fucking racist AWB!" Ivan stood as all the fighters applauded him. He returned their applause with a fisted salute.

Thembani was beside himself as he fisted the air. "Amandla ngawethu!" to which they all responded. The intensity of their collective joy was palpable.

CHAPTER 37: DEATH BY FIRE

July 1993

IVAN FLEXED THE FINGERS of the injured left arm. The bleeding had stopped. One of the fighters retrieved the Kombi keys from Leeu's pocket before collecting the van. They loaded the two bodies at the back before placing Leeu on the floor in line with the sliding door on the side. An armed Comrade placed a can of petrol between Leeu's legs before he sat on the seat behind Leeu.

"Let's inspect your wound," said Thula, who flicked a finger at the Comrade holding the torch.

Ivan removed his sweatshirt and tee shirt. A trickle of blood flowed from the injured muscle tissue above his collarbone.

"You're lucky," said Thembani. "Any lower would've been a mess."

"There's only a bit of pain now."

Thembani fashioned a dressing from Ivan's tee shirt with his Okapi knife.

"Now we have to deal with our white trash," said Thula, pointing towards a scowling Leeu who had not said a word.

"Maybe we Lionise him or something like that," said Ivan.

Thembani laughed. "What do you think, Leeu?"

"I should have killed youse two long ago, fucken *Kaffir* and *Hotnot*." He spat at them.

"Ohh! Temper, temper, Leeu. You could burst a blood vessel, you know. Now, we don't want that, do we? Not yet anyway." Thula laughed. "You guys coming?"

"Count me in," Ivan scrambled into the van. "You coming, Thembani?"

Ivan sensed an inward tussle within Thembani, who had a pained look on his face. He turned away from Ivan.

"No. I'll wait here till you return."

"OK then, let's dump him," Thula laughed.

THE KOMBI BOUNCED ALONG the sandy track close to the Kuils River to stop amongst a few low dunes in a flat scrub area with occasional clusters of wattle bushes. The Comrades all dismounted. A *bakkie* (pick-up) parked close by to take them back. They left Leeu on the Kombi floor, where he sat in a puddle of his congealed blood with his legs around the petrol can.

"So, Leeu, how do you feel?" asked Thula. "Maybe it's time to pray? What do you think?"

Ivan watched as the man's eyes darted from Ivan to Thula. The narrowed eyes projected intense hatred while an emptiness about him seemed resigned to the ultimate. "Fuck all youse terrorists!" He screamed loudly. "What have I done, Lord? How could you do this to me? I'm going to be killed by a fucken *Hotnot* and a fucken *Kaffir*!" Tears now added to the black-stained cheeks of a man seemingly without emotion till then.

An incensed Ivan at the open side door of the van pulled his Parabellum from his pocket. He saw red with rage. "*Hotnot? Kaffir?* You killed Willie and nearly killed his wife, too. You have no fucking decency at all, you vark! (pig!)"

He fired his gun at the petrol can between Leeu's legs even as Thula pulled Ivan backwards; the pair rolled on the sand as a fireball erupted from the van's side door.

Leeu's agonising screams lasted many minutes. To Ivan, it felt like hours. Scream after scream seemed to come from Hell in the form of a lamentation of painful wailing, changing to a howling dread, to end with a croaking sound followed by the silence of death as the sound of the raging fire took over. Leeu's flaming limbs still thrashed around. The smell of the petrol-fuelled burning flesh nauseated Ivan, who retched a thin stream of vomit onto the sand. Thula drew him away from what was soon a fiercely burning Kombi.

Ivan retreated with his gun hand at his side. He felt no elation. No satisfaction. Only an emptiness. The killing was more than that of a White man. He was Leeu Kloppers, the ultimate security policeman from Hell.

"I'm sorry I pulled you the way I did," said Thula. "I lost my eyebrows a while ago when I did the same thing to an askari we punished."

"Thanks," said Ivan. "I was pretty close, so I may have lost more than eyebrows."

They all clambered aboard the open-backed pick-up. A comforted Ivan enjoyed the cold winter air on his cheeks and through his hair. He closed his eyes as he took a few deep breaths.

"Our community appreciates the work you guys do here at the school," said Thula. "We felt awful when the Balaclava Gang shot Mr Germishuys and Ms Adams."

"It was Leeu who shot both of them," said Ivan. "Tonight was payback. Thank you, Thula."

"The pleasure is ours, Comrade. Amandla ngawethu."

"Amandla ngawethu." Ivan joined Thula with a fisted Black Power salute as the pick-up stopped at his car.

After alighting from the bakkie, Ivan hugged Thembani.

"Thula, here's my gun. I'm done with killing," said Ivan.

"Have mine, too," said Thulani. "I've never had the heart to use it."

"We always need weapons like this," said Thula, who looked at the guns, pursing his lips before he slipped them under his belt. "The Parabellum is popular with the gangs, whereas the Glock is a police special. I won't ask you how you came by them," he laughed. "Now, keep safe. We need you teaching here again." He hugged them before they shook hands with all the men.

"You OK to drive?" asked Thembani.

"Yes. I'll be fine."

Once in the car, Ivan started the engine. With their fists extending through the window, the two friends simultaneously called, "Amanda, ngawethu!".

All the fighters returned the call and the salute; they waved their AK 47s in the air, hand-slapping the car as Ivan wondered whether Leeu's fiery death would add to his other disturbing experiences.

CHAPTER 38: RECONCILIATIONS

July 1993

THEMBANI SAT SIDEWAYS, facing Ivan as they drove off. "The Comrades told me this area is under ANC control, a bit like we had with the Bonteheuwel Military Wing." The BMW was one of the best-organised of the township guerrilla groups in Cape Town. For several months Bonteheuwel was a no-go zone until the police killed the twenty-one-year-old BMW guerrilla leader, Ashley Kriel, in 1987.

Thembani looked at his colleague. "You alright?"

Ivan seemed far away, his facial lines deeply etched while his hands gripped the steering wheel in an unaccustomed firm grip. "I'm tired of the killing. Is death the only answer? Thula told me they dealt with Abdul Majiet when he tried to recruit people to attack the Koeberg power station. Abdul did not know he was on MK's hit list. I believe he was the one who ratted on me to the police."

Ivan turned away, looking into the distance at nothing in particular. "I will tell Lydiah about Leeu when I reach home. She already knows what I did to join the prison gang. My non-fatal stabbing haunted me throughout my time in prison. Membership with the prison gangs is forever, though I received a special dispensation to be free."

"Was yours a life to leave?"

Ivan stroked his chin cleft. "Yes. Six months ago, I told Lydiah how a gang leader and his bodyguard died in a fiery car crash I engineered while driving. Police regarded his death as a high-speed accident. I escaped unscathed." Ivan drummed his fingers on the steering wheel as he drove.

"How did Lydiah take the news?" asked a curious Thembani.

"She was ... sympathetic, I suppose. Her near-death experience as a student in '76 and then again in '90 left her with a kernel of deep understanding." Ivan paused again, deep in thought. Then, turning his head towards Thembani, he asked, "What about you? Is Curtis Fouche part of the Glock story?"

An intense spasm hit Thembani's belly. How did Ivan know Curtis' surname? Thembani drummed his fingers on his knees. "You knew him?" He breathed deeply to control the bubbling within.

"I knew of him when Curtis, Pat de Bruin and Ebrahiem Khan died during their grenade attack on Newlands station in '86. In Pollsmoor, the prisoners held an annual informal memorial service in the prison yard to commemorate all our fallen Comrades." Ivan braked behind a lumbering truck. "I presume your son is named after Curtis Fouche and yourself?"

Thembani held onto his gelled knees. Ivan had effectively worked out much of Thembani's guarded past. *How much should I tell him?* He licked at his dry lips, with his heart beating much faster.

"Yes. His parents, Dumisa and Nkosinati, decided on the name after Curtis and I saved them in an attack in which three Witdoeke lost their lives. We were in a kill-or-be-killed situation. I met Curtis when he saved my life by stabbing a White policeman who had shot me in the arm during the Release Mandela march in 1985. At the Gugulethu 7 funeral, he again saved me from a police dog trying to rip my leg off. Those are a few reasons he was more to me than a Comrade."

The images of the Newlands station attack threatened to overwhelm his senses. He sweated profusely with his hands tightly fisted in his lap. "My killing of two Witdoeke in a stick-fight was a grisly experience."

"It must be painful to recall.'

"Only Nkosinati knows the story."

Ivan gave him a squeeze of the thigh. Thembani placed his hand over Ivan's, returning the squeeze.

"It's nice to hear how the deaths of my three friends were commemorated in Pollsmoor." Thembani turned from Ivan to wipe at his tears with a handkerchief.

"Were you on Newlands station with the three of them, Thembani?" Ivan asked softly.

It was as if a hole had opened under Thembani, who seemed to be in free fall with the horrid memories of those condensed minutes on the station. He often had painful recollections of their attack, always culminating in the jumble of his Comrades' bodies on the Newlands station platform after their hand grenade attack on White train passengers. Many a dream had ended there with Curtis' last words in his ears: 'Go, man. Save yourself. I love you, brother. Leave now. I'm done for!'

"Yes. I was." Thembani whispered.

While driving, Ivan glanced at him briefly, then placed his hand on Thembani's before squeezing it. "Does Nkosinati know?"

"No, not yet, though I promised to tell her one day."

"Your torment is much like mine. Maybe now is the time to tell Nkosinati after relating the evening's events to her." A prolonged silence followed his comment.

"You're probably right."

"Part of our struggle is sometimes about taking lives, especially the likes of Leeu," said Ivan. "This brutal regime only responds to violence. It's why I took to destroying substations and pylons. I would like to think I'm done with violence in my life." He rubbed his chin cleft.

"The two of us have positive things to focus on in the years ahead." Ivan glanced at his friend. "For generations our women have shared the load of our oppression in different ways. They are our pillars of strength, our ultimate refuges."

Thembani turned his head from Ivan. "From the news at the time, the police claimed that they killed all the attackers on the station," said Thembani. "I have agonised over the Newlands station saga. The police Glock killed Curtis." Thembani stopped abruptly. Curtis' final words, 'I'm done for!' echoed in his head again.

Thembani shook his head. "You're right. It's time I told Nkosinati the full story." He remained silent while reflecting on how Dr Gershon was probably the only other person who knew of his involvement in the Newlands station attack.

"It helped me a great deal when I told Lydiah of my experiences," said Ivan. "Just do it. Now, we better make tracks, or our women will be worried about us. It's already late. We have fresh dressings at home, so Lydiah can clean and dress my shoulder."

"So, what happened at the river?" asked Thembani.

Ivan spoke after a brief silence. "Leeu was a bloodthirsty psychopath. Who knows how many he killed. Look at Willie, nearly Lydiah, too. To have him at my mercy like tonight was good. About his death? No feelings, really. No joy. No sorrow. Though I wish I knew the origin of his hatred - nature or nurture?"

"I chose nurture!" said Thembani. "From the time of breastfeeding."

"Why did you not come along to watch the fireworks?"

"I've had my issues with necklacing. I put them to rest tonight. Nkosinati will be pleased. Where did you get your Parabellum?"

"That? From an associate of sorts. He's gone now," Ivan smiled.

Thembani appreciated Ivan's silence. Thembani kept to himself his knowledge of Curtis as Bishop Lavis' Armpit Assassin. His main concern was how Nkosinati would react to the news of his role in the Newlands station attack.

CHAPTER 39: ELECTION DAY

26 April 1994

IVAN WAS AWAKE EARLY on election day. Beside him, Lydiah dozed on her side. Ivan looked at the face that had bewitched him from when he first saw her four years ago. He still marvelled at how their love had developed. Even more was the way she had reacted to his involvement in Ses' death. Lydiah's deep understanding stemmed from having long canvassed women's rights since her university student days when oral contraception was part of women's liberation resisted by many men. She abhorred violence against women.

The nine months since Leeu's death had passed quickly. The media reported how three police had died during a routine police patrol in Crossroads on the same day when "political infighting" in Khayelitsha resulted in twelve deaths with dozens of shanties burned down. Ivan suspected the fire was the work of the Balaclava Gang.

Lydiah had responded well to the news of Leeu's death, especially later when they heard how his family members had found two Black women handcuffed to a bed in Leeu's soundproof basement. A few weeks later, the police recovered the superficially buried skeletons of two women and an infant from the property.

IVAN AND LYDIAH WERE excited at the prospect of South Africa's first genuinely democratic election in its entire history since Jan van Riebeeck landed to form a Dutch Colony in 1652. Majority rule day followed a hectic few weeks of electioneering with the couple door-knocking their neighbourhood to support the ANC; people's responses were mostly positive.

"It's time to bury apartheid," said a much-wrinkled woman.

"Finally, power to the people," proclaimed a group of young soccer players whose fisted Black power salutes preceded a loud "Amandla ngawethu!".

"How I've lived to see this day, which I thought would never be," came from a grey-haired man with tears in his eyes.

BREAKFAST WAS A HURRIED affair. Suzanne had decided to go along with them, though they warned her the voting could take quite a while. They were all casually dressed in khaki shorts with ANC tee shirts. Ivan's exposed forearm now sported a healing month-old tattoo of Table Mountain obscuring the Parabellum. Above the mountain, the rising smoke from the gun was now a dove of peace with a green olive branch in its mouth. The other tattoos had also been transformed into doves. His mother preferred his new body art.

"I hope it'll go well around the country today," said Lydiah.

"It should be fine as long as the Balaclava Gang behave themselves." Ivan blew at his cup to cool his coffee.

Around the country, more than 10,000 deaths had marred the four years since Mandela's release. Most of the deaths were in the country's north, a result of police shootings, including those killed during the previous year's sham elections.

"Let's keep our fingers crossed," said Lydiah as she finished her coffee.

Ivan strode around the table to kiss Lydiah on her neck.

"OK, love birds, smile!" Suzanne, camera in hand, snapped them. With her ANC cap askew on her head, she was ready to photograph all day.

"You better bring a spare spool or two," said Ivan.

"Just don't take any of me when I'm crying," smiled Lydiah.

"We better be off you two. My parents are expecting us at eight," said Ivan.

They drove to Ivan's parents' home in the specially spruced-up Morris. ANC stickers adorned the car's windows,

Ivan's father was suited for the occasion, while his mother wore a new rose-pink outfit with a hat to match.

"You two look special," said Ivan.

"I had to dress up," said his Mom. "It's in case Mandela appears today. He dresses so well. I'd drop your father in a flash if Mandela winked an eye at me."

As expected, Colleen laughed the loudest. "Please don't do that, Mom," said Colleen, "Then I'll have to look after Dad."

"Don't worry, Mr Petterson. I'll take you in." Lydiah leaned over to hold the smiling man by the hand.

"Do you know a Black National Party canvasser dared to come to my door yesterday," said his mother. "I told him he was a damned traitor before I told him to go to Hell along with his party. After what the Whites did to us, I can only vote ANC until I die." Ivan kissed his mother before he gave her a hug.

"So, I'm ready to cast my first vote ever at seventy-two years old," said his father.

"Mine too, at seventy," said his mother. Her eyes teared up. "When they released Mandela, I prayed I would live to see today."

Ivan had tears in his eyes, too. Hidden in his mother's voice was their collective grief. Life could not be better than to walk to the car with his mother hooked into one arm with Lydiah on the other, where she held onto his father's hand. Colleen stayed behind to mind Lance. She would vote later. Cape Town's emblematic mountains were as clear as they were on the day of Ivan's release from Pollsmoor. *Will the new South Africa be better? Surely, nothing could be worse than the last few centuries.*

Thembani's heart had not stopped thumping since he woke up. Today was the culmination of over 30 years of turbulence in which paroxysms of political violence had threatened the build-up towards the country's first democratic elections.

He had had to deal with his own tribulations, especially the tense discussion with Nkosinati after Leeu's death regarding his involvement with his three Comrades in the Newlands station hand grenade attack in which seven Whites had died. She was further horrified to hear Thembani's Glock was the weapon used to kill Curtis.

As he had hoped, Nkosinati related how she had had similar thoughts to Thembani of violent retribution when police had killed her brother during a University of Durban students' demonstration in 1976. Their emotion-filled conversation went through till the early hours. They realised how youthful revolutionary zeal could only find a solution in extreme violence to remove their brutal oppression. Like Thembani's three Comrades, many committed people lost their lives in the process.

Their discussion was a relief to Thembani. Over the ensuing months, there was a relaxation of his tormented dreams. With the dawn of a new day, the couple prayed their energies would be directed towards more positive goals under majority rule in a country where their son, Curtis-Thembani, could live without the barriers his forebears had had to endure for centuries.

THEIR VOTING BOOTHS were at a school within walking distance from home. To be in a queue of thousands of Black voters inching forward to vote was indeed a dream come true. People's constant murmuring was often interrupted with laughter in keeping with the occasion. People greeted each other; many stopped to exchange personal news. The young, the old, the well-heeled and the down-and-out were all there. People hugged or kissed each other. A man carrying his father on his back headed towards a special booth for the disabled.

There were fisted salutes all around them. The apartheid yoke had been lifted. Many had contributed in different ways to breaking the shackles of forty-six years of National Party rule. He regretted how his fallen Comrades Pat, Ebrahim and Curtis would not have their day, too. He could see Ebrahim chew at his gum while Pat drew on his cigarette, and Curtis blinked his eyes. *My vote today is also your vote, my brothers.* "Amandla!" *He heard their reply in unison -* Ngawethu! Thembani smiled.

Nkosinati looked stunning in her emerald-green dress. An ANC cap sat at a mischievous angle on her head. The rest of them all wore one, including his parents. Thembani had on his suit as befitted the occasion. Ahead of him, his parents had on the same outfits they had worn on his graduation day.

"Your father and I have not worn these clothes since your wonderful day," said his mother. "But today is as important as will be your next graduation. I will not say it is more special." His mother laughed. "But I did buy a new eye patch."

"Yes, I noticed, Mamma. The most painful moments of my life were when the police shot you and Pappa in '76."

"As you see, son, even our shootings could not stop us." His mother grinned from ear to ear. "I'm so proud of you, my boy. May you continue to do well in the new South Africa."

Despite his limp, his father had coped with their walk in the early morning heat. His father had hardly stopped smiling since their arrival two hours earlier. They had rounded the final turn to head towards the tables where their ID checks would precede the voting.

"Are you alright, Pappa?"

"All week, the happiness I feel has replaced all other feelings. It's been good to know that, today, on 26 April 1994, we bury apartheid; my 1960 Langa march ends here today." His father gesticulated forcefully as he stopped with his eyes in the distant past, maybe reflecting on how the police beat him during the march after he had first arrived in Cape Town from the Transkei seeking work.

"When you were born a few days before the march, on the day of the 1960 Sharpeville mass killings, I named you Thembani as a beacon of hope." His father looked at him. "May your light shine even brighter in the new South Africa, son." His tearful father hugged him.

"1976 was the worst time of my life when the police shot the two of you. Now, here we are on the best day of our lives!" On the verge of crying, it was Thembani's turn to give his father a prolonged hug.

"But now we have just a few metres to go. Please excuse me while I walk the final steps to the election booth with your mother."

Nkosinati hooked into Thembani. "I like your suit."

"Thank you. Emerald green suits you, like most things." He enjoyed how Nkosinati pulled on his shoulder to rest her head there.

The hubbub around them increased in volume. Those who had finished voting milled around, joining others in singing liberation songs. Thembani soon heard the rhythm of the toyi-toyi. His baritone voice added to the harmony of the thousands who could not resist the popular song.

Nelson Mandela

He says freedom now

Mandela says away with slavery

In our land of Africa
Nelson Mandela says fight for freedom.
Mandela says freedom now.
Mandela says away with slavery
In our land of Africa
Rholihlahla Mandela
Freedom is in your hands
Show us now the way to freedom

In our land of Africa[13]

He high stepped his way alongside the rest and sweat soon covered his face. He sensed his three fallen Comrades stepping in his wake with their shields held high and spears ready. When done, Thembani returned to the queue smiling broadly before his final processing.

He held Nkosinati's hand until they separated to enter the privacy of their voting booths. He closed his eyes. His heart palpitated as it had when he proposed to Nkosinati, the other momentous occasion in his life. He looked at the black dye stain marker on his thumb. Now, finally, he would have a say in running his country.

After voting, Thembani went into a huddle of joy with the family. They joined the crowd in singing Nkosi sikelel iAfrika - the initially banned hymn was now the prospective national anthem. The harmony of all those voices thrilled Thembani, who struggled to voice the lyrics. Above the many voices, he heard Curtis' crooning voice with the softer accompanying voices of Pat and Ebrahim. Now, Thembani could not hold back the flood of tears. It was the first time he could shed tears of joy in honour of his three departed Comrades-in-arms.

Stanley finished his phone call with Jayantilal, who was on duty, then joined Fay in the kitchen.

"JT says he'll vote tomorrow. He ordered our first mobile phone - the Nokia 2110." He had ordered a smaller Motorola flip phone to fit into Fay's handbag.

He sat beside Fay at the rounded kitchen nook table. Both had a glass of red wine in hand while they watched the final minutes of an orange-red sunset underlined with a thin sliver of an equally red cloud. The sun slipped behind Table Mountain, now silhouetted against the sunset-stained western sky. The kitchen window picture-framed the last of the day's light to bathe the kitchen in the comforting glow of the sun's departure.

"What a historical day it's been," said Fay.

"It still is. Even nature is celebrating." His hands waved at the fading light.

"I liked those ANC poster headshots of 'Mandela for President, The people's choice.'"

"For me, the unbridled joy around us was the best part, truly a celebration of freedom."

Stanley sipped at his wine. He and Fay had shed a tear when they saw the Mandelas casting their votes on television. What they experienced in Elsies River township was duplicated in every television clip they showed from major city centres to dusty villages.

"My favourite was the son pushing his elderly father in a wheelbarrow," said Fay.

"The highlight for me was those kilometre-long snakes of people queuing in an orderly fashion, especially in Natal." He recalled how alarmed he was months ago when he saw one of the Natal township signs saying, 'You are now entering a war zone.' ANC clashes with the IFP in Natal had caused thousands of deaths over three years; police death squads with their proxies were suspected of most of the killings.

"Today, we reclaimed our country!" Fay punched one hand into the other.

"After living every day of our lives under apartheid, it's satisfying to see it on the trash heap of history alongside fascist Nazism," said Stanley.

"Yeah, flushed forever into the sewers of South African history." Fay looked at him, her face all radiant. "Another enjoyable TV clip was from New Zealand, where an expatriate White woman came over to hug a Black couple because they were the first happy faces she had seen outside the booths. She said most people looked like they had come from a funeral."

"Many Whites would have thought so, too. Let's toast again to the future."

"This one is to Fah. My beloved brother died seeking this day of freedom. Amandla, ngawethu!" Fay power-fisted the call.

Stanley followed her lead. "Amandla, ngawethu! Mayibuye, iAfrica!" He had never seen Fay smiling so much when mentioning her late freedom-fighting twin brother.

The couple watched the last of the thin ribbon of red-and-orange-lined cloud through the kitchen window above the Mother City's mountains. Stanley felt an inner peace not felt before. *Is this the future bright lining we hope for here on the Cape Flats, where we live in the shadow of Table Mountain?*

A SPECIAL REQUEST FROM SHADLEY

IF YOU ENJOYED READING *Cape Town's Necklaces of Fire*, then a short review on your Facebook or other social media sites would be much appreciated – a simple "What a read"; "Most enjoyable"; "Riveting and informative"; ... or more would suffice. An emoticon would also be suitable. An online review posted on Goodreads, Better Reading or equivalent sites for readers would also help.

Such is the world we live in nowadays, with authors having to promote themselves with a bit of help from readers and friends! For this, ngiyabonga, I thank you all. Keep well.

GLOSSARY

ABBREVIATIONS

ANC African National Congress
AWB Afrikaner Weerstandsbeweging - Afrikaner
Resistance Movement
LTA Lagunya Taxi Association
MDM Mass Democratic Movement
MK Umkhonto we Sizwe, military wing
of the ANC
UCT University of Cape Town
UDF United Democratic Front
UWC University of the Western Cape
WEBTA Western Cape Black Taxi Association

TRANSLATIONS

Amandla, ngawethu! Power to the people!
amaboona Afrikaner Boers

bakkie light pick-up
dagga cannabis
dongas water-eroded gullies
Hotnot derogatory term directed at a person classified as Coloured
Kaffir derogatory term directed at an indigenous African person

Kaffirboetie nigger-lover, lit.
kitskonstabels instant constables
Mayibuye, iAfrica! Come back, Africa!
pondok shanty
snoek and slap chips barracuda and long soft chips
vark! pig!
Witdoeke White cloth forces

ADDENDUM

WHILE THE BOOK IS A sociopolitical thriller set in a historically relevant period in South Africa's history, all the characters are fictitious, as are the details related to the thriller. For accuracy, there are many historical references to the country from 1960-1986.

There are references to real people like Nelson Mandela, Oliver Tambo, Prime Minister Botha, Dr Ivan Toms with Revs David Russell and John Freeth, Father Laughton, Archbishop Tutu, Mayor Gordon Oliver, Reverend Frank Chikane, Moulana Farid Esack, Nazeem Mohammed and Alan Boesak, Ashley Kriel, Chris Hani, Janusz Walus, with Derby-Lewis, the shadow Minister of Economic Affairs.

Any similarities with other people would be coincidental.

OTHER BOOKS BY SHADLEY FATAAR

1. *Fury and Revenge in Cape Town* – published 7.7.2023.

1. *Toyi-toyi, Cape Town's War Dance* – published 23.10.23.

These are the first two books of the trilogy: *In the Shadow of Table Mountain, Cape Town.*

E-BOOKS AND PAPERBACKS can be obtained by visiting the author's new website at:

https://www.shadleyfataar.com/[1]

For direct paperback sails or to join updating e-mails, drop the author a line at:

zonshad@gmail.com

Appended footnotes follow overleaf.

---

1. http://shadleyfataar.com/

[1] *Witdoeke*. White cloth forces were a State-supported, contra-group who wore white cloths or scarves around their arms or necks during periods of township battles against the ANC or UDF [United Democratic Front] supporters.

[2] AWB The Afrikaner Weerstandsbeweging (Afrikaner Resistance Movement) was a neo-Nazi, White supremacist political party-cum-paramilitary organisation.

[3] The white pipe uses a cannabis-Mandrax-tobacco mixture to obtain an added high.

[4] The worst such funeral episode was in 1985, with 35 mourners killed in Uitenhage in the Eastern Cape.

[5] Dr Ivan Toms established the free South African Christian Leadership Assembly Clinic with Revs David Russell and John Freeth. The activist Toms supported gay rights and led the End Conscription campaign.He spent nine months in prison after defying his military call-up.

[6] The mine-resistant Casspirs were 4-wheel-drive troop transporters used extensively in the South African border war and later in the township disturbances.

[8] 21 March is now celebrated in the country as Human Rights Day. The United Nations proclaimed it the International Day for the Elimination of Racial Discrimination.

[9] In 1994, Colonel de Kock was given two life sentences and 212 years in prison. Known as 'Prime Evil' by the press, he was directly or indirectly implicated in hundreds of killings.

[10] "One settler, One bullet" was the slogan of the Azanian People's Liberation Army (APLA), the armed wing of the Pan Africanist Congress (PAC).

[11] The man, John Battersby, was a reporter.

[12] Constantia is a premier residential area on the slopes of Constantia Mountain, south of Table Mountain.

[13] From: *South African Freedom Songs,* [2001] - translated from the original in Xhosa.

Don't miss out!

Visit the website below and you can sign up to receive emails whenever SHADLEY FATAAR publishes a new book. There's no charge and no obligation.

https://books2read.com/r/B-A-LELY-OKGQC

BOOKS 2 READ

Connecting independent readers to independent writers.

www.ingramcontent.com/pod-product-compliance
Lightning Source LLC
Chambersburg PA
CBHW031926060726
47496CB00007BA/2145

* 9 7 8 0 6 4 5 8 2 4 6 5 0 *